"I want us to be blood sisters."

"Um . . ." *NO!* my mind screams. Every cell in my body rebels against the thought. Mixing our blood is just gross. And weird. There's nothing in me that wants any part of this. I rack my brain, searching for a reason, any reason at all that won't offend her.

"Look, I know we only met a couple weeks ago," Shelly says in a small voice, "but I feel this connection with you. Like we were always meant to be friends. This ceremony represents that. You're my sister, through and through."

I take a deep breath. This idea she's suggesting is more than a little creepy. But Shelly's been through such a rough time lately. It's not going to kill me to drop a little blood on a cutting board. If it makes her happy, I should just say yes. It's not that big a deal . . . even if it makes all the hair stand up on my neck.

"Okay, fine," I say, before I can change my mind. "Let's do it."

GIRL
ON THE
VERGE

Also by Pintip Dunn

The Darkest Lie

Published by Kensington Publishing Corporation

GIRL
ON THE
VERGE

PINTIP DUNN

KENSINGTON BOOKS
www.kensingtonbooks.com

KENSINGTON BOOKS are published by

Kensington Publishing Corp.
119 West 40th Street
New York, NY 10018

Copyright © 2017 by Pintip Dunn

All Kensington titles, imprints, and distributed lines are available at special quantity discounts for bulk purchases for sales promotion, premiums, fund-raising, educational, or institutional use.

Special book excerpts or customized printings can also be created to fit specific needs. For details, write or phone the office of the Kensington Sales Manager: Kensington Publishing Corp., 119 West 40th Street, New York, NY 10018. Attn. Sales Department. Phone: 1-800-221-2647.

Kensington and the K logo Reg. U.S. Pat. & TM Off.

eISBN-13: 978-1-4967-0361-3
eISBN-10: 1-4967-0361-8
First Kensington Electronic Edition: July 2017

ISBN-13: 978-1-4967-0360-6
ISBN-10: 1-4967-0360-X
First Kensington Trade Paperback Printing: July 2017

10 9 8 7 6 5 4 3 2 1

Printed in the United States of America

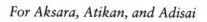

For Aksara, Atikan, and Adisai

Prologue

A fish swims beneath the open staircase in my *Khun Yai*'s house. A real live fish, with its translucent fins fluttering in the water, its belly gold-scaled and bloated from regular feedings. If I part my knees, I can catch long glimpses of its lazy swimming through the gap in the stairs.

Of course, I'm not supposed to part my knees. It's not lady-like for a twelve-year-old girl, not here, not in Thailand. The land where my parents grew up; the place that's supposed to be my home, too. That's what the banner said, when my relatives came to pick us up at the airport. "Welcome home, Kanchana."

Never mind that I only come to Thailand every couple years. Never mind that I don't look like anyone else here, with my American build and my frizzy, out-of-control hair. Never mind that I don't look like anyone in my hometown, either, since I'm the only Asian girl in school. Never mind that the only reason we're here now is because my father's dead and my mom can't keep it together.

For a moment, pain lances through me, so sharp and severe that it might as well slice my heart in half, like in one of those video games my friends like to play. I squeeze my eyes shut, but that doesn't keep the tears from spilling out. Neither do the glasses sliding down my nose. And so the tears drip down, down, down, past my unladylike knees, through the gap in the stairs, into the fish basin below.

The drops scare the fish, who swims away with its tail swishing in the water, no longer languid, no longer lazy. So, even this creature wants to get away from me—from my grief, from my strangeness—as quickly as possible.

"There you are, *luk lak,*" Khun Yai says in Thai, coming down the stairs. She is my mother's mother, and since we arrived, she's used the endearment—*child that I love*—more often than my name.

"You're up early." She pats her forehead with a handkerchief. It's only seven a.m., and already sweat drenches my skin like I've taken a dip in the basin. No wonder they take two or three showers a day here.

"Couldn't sleep. Jet lag."

"I've been up for a couple hours myself." She eases onto the step next to me, her knees pressed together, her legs folded demurely to one side.

Immediately, I try to rearrange my body to look like hers and then give up. My legs just don't go that way.

"What do you want to do today?" Khun Yai asks. "More shopping?"

"Um, no thanks." I make a face. "Didn't you hear those salesgirls at Siam Square yesterday? They rushed up as soon as we entered and said they didn't have anything in my size." My cheeks still burn when I think about their haughty expressions.

She sighs. "The clothes there are just ridiculously small. We'll go to the mall today. They should have something that will fit you."

I stare at her diminutive frame and her chopstick legs. "One of the salesgirls asked how much I weighed. Another grabbed my arm and said I felt like a side pillow."

"They didn't mean any harm. It is just the Thai way to be blunt." She catches my chin and tilts up my face. "You are so beautiful. I wish you could see that."

I could say so many things. I could tell her that I'm ugly not only in Thailand but also in the United States. Even though I'm not big by American standards—far from it—I could confess how the boys call me Squinty. How those Thai salesgirls snick-

ered at my poodle-fuzz hair. I could explain how I'm from two
worlds but fit in neither.

But I don't. Because my words will only make her sad, and
there have been enough tears in our family.

She stands and holds out her hand. "Come. I want to show
you something."

I rise dutifully and take her hand because that's what good
Thai girls do. They act as they're told and don't ask questions.
They show respect by bending down when they walk past an
adult, and they never, ever touch the head of an elder.

I may not look like the typical Thai girl, but darn it, I'm
going to try my best to be one.

We walk through the house, across the shiny marble floors
and past the intricate teakwood cabinets, and enter Khun Yai's
private wing. She shuts the door and switches on the air condi-
tioner. The stream of cold cuts through the heavy air, and I feel
like I can breathe again.

She crouches in front of a safe, spins the dial, and takes out a
jewelry pouch. It is made of bloodred velvet and decorated with
gold lettering.

I bite my lip. "What is it?"

"A family heirloom. Open it."

With trembling in my fingers that I don't understand, I loosen
the drawstring of the pouch and pour the contents into my
hand.

It is a necklace. But that might be the understatement of the
year. If what I'm holding is just a necklace, then the plane ride to
Thailand is just a hop. The stinky durian is just a fruit. My
yearning to shove my awkward, bumbling self into a graceful
and confident skin is just a feeling.

Sapphires and rubies are set in a delicate gold filigree, alter-
nating blue and red along a raised spiral. The intricate pattern is
distinctive, yet unfamiliar, and the gems flash like fire.

My chest aches. I've never seen anything like it. Most of the
time, beauty is in the familiar. A song that's been listened to a

thousand times. A face that matches your society's standards of perfection.

But sometimes, you see an object and you feel it in your heart. And it doesn't matter if you've just seen it for the first time or the hundredth.

"Would you like to try it on?" Khun Yai asks.

I whip my eyes up to meet hers. "Can . . . can I? I don't want to break it."

"Nonsense. Necklaces are meant to be worn." She guides me to a rectangular mirror on top of a dressing table.

I don't normally like to look at myself. I can't stand to see my thick, unruly hair. The lenses of my glasses are always smudged, no matter how many times I clean them against my shirt.

But right now, the only thing I'm focused on is my neck, long, thin—and bare.

"This necklace has belonged in our family for six generations," she says, bending the malleable hook at the end of the chain. "My own grandmother gave it to me, with the stipulation that it be passed to my eldest granddaughter."

My mouth dries. My mother—or as I call her, Mae—has an older brother, but he never had children. And her two younger siblings all had kids after her.

"You mean to say . . ." I trail off, unable to speak such a presumptuous wish out loud.

"Yes, *luk lak*," she says gently. "This heirloom will belong to you someday."

She drapes the necklace around my neck. The gold settles against my collarbone. The color makes my skin gleam, so that it no longer seems yellow and wan, but radiant and warm. The sapphires and rubies contrast with my black hair and eyes, and I know in an instant that these are the hues I should be sporting—should've always been sporting. I think of Khun Yai wearing this necklace before me, and her grandmother, who wore it before her. And I'm no longer floating around between worlds, lost. Unanchored. This piece of jewelry connects me to all the women in my family's history.

"Lovely," Khun Yai pronounces.

For a fleeting, infinitesimal moment, I feel something I've never felt before. Certainly not at the school dances, where the boys' eyes skim right over me. And certainly not here, in Thailand, where they look at my average build like I'm a linebacker.

For once in my life, I look in the mirror and I feel beautiful.

Chapter 1

Four years later . . .

I brush my newly straightened hair off my shoulders. Eight hours at the hair salon, and the skin around my hairline is singed with chemical burns. But it was worth every minute. I never dreamed I could have hair like this. Straight, straight, straight as a board. A waterfall of silk from my scalp to my shoulder.

I love how the hair skims along my cheeks. I love how all I have to do is run a comb through the silky strands. I love how I no longer have to wear a ponytail. Every. Single. Day.

I love how I now look like all the girls in Thailand, even if I'm at school in America.

"Oooohhh, Kan, check you out!" Lanie calls from across the hallway. "Looking good, girlfriend. Very exotic."

Just like that, I wilt. I slam my locker door closed, my good mood evaporating.

God, I hate that word. *Exotic* means different. Unfamiliar. Originating from a distant and foreign land. And I'm none of those things. I'm just me.

"Kan always looks good," my best friend, Ash, says loyally. She's standing next to Lanie and, as always, is dressed as though she's walked off a modeling runway. "And I don't think she's exotic at all. I think she's about as normal as someone as gorgeous as her can be."

"Of course," Lanie says, flushing. "That's what I meant."

I shoot Ash a grateful look and smile at Lanie to let her know I'm not offended. And I'm not. Not really. Lanie's been my friend since we were kids, and I know she means well. She was just trying to pay me a compliment. I'm being too sensitive. But damn it. I wish she'd just left off that last word. She never would've said it to Ash or Izzy or any of our other friends.

Exotic, however, is a step up from *ugly.* And if I've graduated to that, I suppose I should take it.

I'm about to join my friends when Ethan Thorne turns down the locker corridor. I freeze. Fellow junior and ballroom dancer extraordinaire, he's blond and blue-eyed and so handsome you can't believe he belongs to a small town like Foxville, Kansas.

He glances up. Oops. I'm staring like I'm totally crushing on him. And maybe I am. But no one else has to know. I'm about to avert my eyes when he nods—a slight, almost imperceptible movement of the head. But a nod nonetheless.

Say hello, you fool. At least smile at the guy.

Before my stupefied muscles can obey, however, he's halfway down the hall, his signature black pants and T-shirt jumping out at me in the mass of students.

I drift to the cluster of girls standing across the hall. The pungent scent of tangerine perfumes the air. Probably somebody's lip gloss, since they're all freshening their makeup now that the school day's over. Ash is telling the others how Brad Summers asked her out, but Izzy bumps her shoulder against mine. "Setting your sights a little high, Kan? The best of us have tried and failed to get Ethan Thorne's attention."

She should know. She waged a full-out campaign to date him last fall, with no success.

"Oh." I fidget with the strap of my backpack. Is it so obvious I'm interested? "It's not that. He works at Miss Patsy's dance studio, like me, and, um, I was thinking I should say hi. Since we work at the same place and all."

She raises a freshly waxed eyebrow. I can still see the red marks on her eyelid. "Are you friends? Did he say hello to you?"

"Well, no," I admit. "We've never even talked. But he always smiles at me when he sees me. And sometimes, he holds the door for me if we're leaving at the same time. . . ."

His actions had seemed so significant in my head. But now that I say them out loud, I sound pathetic. Like I've built up this grand friendship over a few smiles and a couple of head nods. Clearly, Izzy agrees.

"Don't worry, Kan." She might as well pat me on the head. "I'm sure you'll meet the man of your dreams before we graduate. Maybe a new guy will transfer in midsemester. And you know what the best part is? Maybe he'll be Asian, just like you!"

My lips feel like rubbery chicken. *Izzy doesn't mean it like that,* I try to tell myself. *She's not saying the only way a guy would be interested in you is if he were Asian. She doesn't mean that you have no shot with blond, blue-eyed Ethan.*

But as I look at her narrowed eyes and her mean little smirk, I get the feeling she knows exactly what she's saying. And exactly how it's making me feel.

Like the sixth-grade girl I used to be, with poofy hair and glasses. Like the time the school photographer yelled, "Open your eyes!" when they were already open. Like when Walt Peterson snuck a gong into school—and rang it every time I entered the room.

I feel like the girl who will never, ever belong.

Later that afternoon, Ash and I are at Miss Patsy's dance studio.

"Me first! Me first!" yells a little girl with tiny braids and the most adorable button nose.

"No, me!" Another girl, equally adorable, but with blond hair instead of black, shoves the first girl out of the way. "I want to be first!"

My lips tug. I can't help it. At four years old, even bad behavior is kinda cute.

Ash claps her hands over her head. I could see her as a schoolteacher in a few years' time. "Girls! Everyone will have a turn. Please form a line!"

They form a crooked, meandering line, and I mouth *thank*

you to my best friend over the girls' heads. As always, Ash is saving my butt. She doesn't have to be at Miss Patsy's, but she's hanging out with me for the company—and so she doesn't have to go home.

Her parents have been fighting lately, the tension between them so thick it saturates the air. Ash is certain that a separation between them is imminent, and she's been so down, even if she won't show it to anyone but me. Her characteristic glow is missing, and her eyes pull down at the corners. I wish there were more I could do for her.

The first girl hops onto the wooden block, and I take her measurements for the costumes I'm making for the upcoming dance recital. There are places in this country, I'm sure, where parents have no problem shelling out a hundred bucks for their preschoolers' dance recitals. Foxville, Kansas, isn't one of them.

That's where I come in. Miss Patsy provides the materials, and I get invaluable experience, another entry on my résumé, and the feel-good glow of hearing these little angels squeal.

If I can keep said angels from combusting while they wait their turn.

"How about a song?" Ash suggests desperately. "Or a game. Maybe you could draw on these coloring pages Kan brought? They have ballerinas, just like you! Here are a bunch of crayons. . . ."

She might as well not have spoken. They turn up their super cute button noses and continue to wreck havoc. (God! All their noses are cute! How is that possible? I never had a nose like that. Mine is flat and flares at the bottom.) One girl tosses my scraps of fabric in the air, while another attempts to climb the musty curtains.

Ash rushes over, pulling the girl down before she can fall on her head, and I glance at the clock. I only have fifteen more minutes to get them measured before class, and I've only finished one girl. What am I going to do?

And then the door opens, and Ethan walks into the dance studio. The girls run to him like he's a rock star. I don't blame them. He looks kinda like a musical sensation with his tight black shirt and pants. Most of the guys at school wouldn't be caught dead wearing clothes like that, but they suit him. Involuntarily, my eyes travel over his six-pack and the long, lean muscles of his thighs. Oh, yeah. They suit him, all right.

He glances around the room, taking in Ash, who's picking up the scraps of fabric, and me, with the measuring tape around my neck.

"Want to play duck, duck, goose?" he asks the girls.

Like magic, they shriek and arrange themselves in a circle on the floor.

My mouth drops open, and I exchange a look with Ash. Are you kidding me? How on earth did he do that?

He looks up to catch me watching and winks.

I duck my head. My fingers shake as I measure the next girl. It was a wink, for god's sake. Just a wink.

"No wonder you like working here." Ash drifts over to me. "He's enough to convince me to give ballroom dancing a try."

"Shhh!" I say furiously. "He'll hear you."

But he's completely immersed in the game, his movements exaggerated as he taps a girl's head and then tries valiantly to avoid being tagged. His arms pump the air, and his legs fly all over the place. And yet, the girls catch him every time, to gales of giggles.

Once, the girl with the tiny braids slips and falls. Her hopes of tagging Ethan seem to evaporate, but when he reaches the open spot, he performs a victory dance, which involves a lot of butt shaking and fingers pointing in the air. As the other ducks roar with laughter, the girl picks herself off the floor and tags him out.

The smile spreads across my face like dye seeping through fabric, and even Ash's nudges can't erase it. Ethan. Ethan Thorne. I've always known who he is, of course, although we've never been friends. You don't go to a school like mine, in a town like Foxville, and not know all 120 kids in the graduating class. Hell, I was in the same kindergarten classroom with almost a quarter of my classmates.

The next girl gets on the block, and I wrap the measuring tape around her waist, making sure it's not twisted. All the while, I run through everything I know about Ethan. He's a ball-room dancer. There's no high school circuit in our state, so he's a member of the community college dance team and travels to competitions nearly every weekend. He's not part of the in-crowd—he's a little too different for that—but he's a cool and well-liked guy. I've heard some of the boys ribbing him about his dancing, but he just shrugs like the jokes roll right off his well-muscled back.

I finish measuring the last girl, and Miss Patsy, the dance teacher and head of the studio, strides down the stairs. Ethan ushers his ducks into the empty classroom.

Ash gives me a hug. "I have to go. I can't avoid my house for-ever." She rolls her eyes. "Thanks for letting me hang out."

"Thank *you*. I never would've gotten those girls measured without you."

"Nah. You've got your knight in black knit swooping down for the rescue." She waggles her eyebrows, and I give her a shove. We both erupt into giggles.

I promise to call her later and then retreat into a quiet class-room. All thoughts of Ethan fly out of my head. I sketch two different designs, one in ice blue and the other in hot pink, with lots of ruffles and flounces. And, of course, stiff tutus. Both de-signs are gorgeous. As I sketch, I wish I were a little girl again, so that I could wear these creations, too.

When I finish, I realize the dance studio is deserted. Crap. I check my watch. It's only seven, but these days, it gets dark early. I hadn't realized it was so late. But no matter. This is a small town. Nothing ever happens in small towns. Right?

Wrong. Nothing *interesting* ever happens in small towns, but crimes? Murders? Rapes? We're no more immune than the urban areas. Just last week, a woman was assaulted as she jogged through the park at sunrise.

Goose bumps erupt on my arms, and my heart crashes against my ribs. Ridiculous. I'm only nervous because it's so quiet that you could hear a ballerina rise to *en pointe*.

Still, I take out my car key and hold it with the sharp, metallic edge poking through my fist. Taking a deep breath, I cross the darkened studio. I am almost at the exit when Ethan emerges from the gloom.

I jump. The key slides from my fingers and clanks against the floor. "Ethan! You're still here?"

Instead of responding, he picks up my key, hands it to me, and holds open the door. Not only is it dark outside, but the wind's picked up, swirling bits of litter round and round the parking lot. The trees are shadowy skeletons, reaching their long, thin fingers toward me.

I shiver. *Small town. Nothing ever happens in a small town.* I repeat the words to myself firmly and then turn to Ethan, who is locking the door.

"Were you waiting for me?" I blurt out. "You didn't have to do that. Miss Patsy gave me a key; I could've locked up."

"Not a problem." He flashes a smile, one that seems as natural to him as breathing, and without another word walks to his car.

I let out a breath I didn't realize I was holding. Maybe he wasn't waiting for me. Maybe he was busy with work, too, and it's only a coincidence we happened to be leaving at the same time. At least I feel safe now, even if he's thirty feet away in his battered Camry.

Slowly, I make my way to my tangerine VW Bug. My dream car, even if it is secondhand and has a gazillion miles on it.

The engine of the Camry ignites, and the headlights flicker on. But the car doesn't leave. I get into my Bug and take a moment to slide my sketchbook securely into my backpack. Ethan is still there, still waiting. Only when I turn on the engine and drive out of the parking lot does his car follow, flashing its lights twice before turning in the opposite direction.

I blink, staring at Ethan's taillights too long in the rearview mirror. Huh. Maybe he was waiting to see me off safely, after all.

You never know what can happen, small town or not.

Chapter 2

I walk into my house to the smell of my favorite meal. *Nam phrik ka pi.* Sliced eggplant dipped into beaten eggs and then fried, paired with a spicy sauce made from tamarind, chilies, lime, fish sauce, and shrimp paste. There's no mistaking the scent because it smells like nothing else in this world.

My mouth waters, and instantly, the Asian boy conversation with Izzy, Ash's parents' fighting, and Ethan's chivalry disappear from my mind. A plate of hot rice and fried eggplant always makes me feel like everything's going to be okay.

I burst into the kitchen, my hair swinging against my shoulder blades. My grandmother is ladling slices of eggplant out of a pot of boiling oil and transferring them to a colander lined with paper towels. The slices are perfect. Fried to a golden brown, bits of egg curling around the edges. I snag a piece, bouncing the still-hot slice against my palm before taking a bite.

Yum. The egg is crisp and savory, the eggplant center soft and mildly sweet.

"Khun Yai, it's like you read my mind." I place a kiss on her cheek. "Are you sure you weren't a fortune-teller in a previous life?"

But she doesn't smile, and she doesn't call me *luk lak.* She doesn't bat my hand away, and she doesn't ask me if I have homework. Instead, she looks at me the way she did during the first few months after my father's death.

"I was cleaning your room," she says in Thai. Even though

her English is more than passable after four years in this country, this is how we always talk—her in Thai and me in English. And yet, we still manage to communicate perfectly. "I found an application for the Illinois Institute of Art." She waves her spatula at the offending form on the kitchen table.

Fear flashes across my stomach, and the eggplant lodges in my throat like a ball of packed rice. "You don't need to clean my room," I mutter. "None of my friends' parents do that. Over here, kids pick up after themselves."

"Do not change the subject, Kanchana."

Uh-oh. My formal name. Not one of her endearments, not even my nickname, Kan, which my dad came up with himself in an attempt to create an American name. That's probably the only reason I didn't nix the name long ago: It's one of the few reminders I still have of my *Por*. Too bad he didn't know my elementary school years would be marked by my classmates elbowing each other and snickering. "Hey, Kan, did you use the *can* yet today? I drank a whole chocolate milk at lunch. Boy, do I need to use the *can*."

"It's *Kan*," I would say between clenched teeth. "Rhymes with Ron."

This, somehow, made them laugh even harder.

"I thought you were going to apply to medical school next year. Follow in your mother's footsteps." Khun Yai turns off the stovetop and moves the pot of boiling oil to a cool burner. "We even decided on the list of twenty schools you would consider. This art institute wasn't on the list."

"No, *you* decided," I say, wondering how far I should go. How much I should confess. She's already found the application. Is she ready to hear the truth—or at least part of it? "You can get a bachelor's degree in fashion design there. And I . . . never wanted to be a doctor, anyway. The sight of blood makes me sick."

She lifts her eyebrows, adding lines to her already lined forehead. "Really? How come you never told me?"

Maybe this time, she'll understand what it's like to be me, a girl straddling two worlds and fitting into neither. Maybe I should admit I've been designing clothes in secret for years. That my job at Miss Patsy's is not as assistant/first aider but as seamstress/costume designer. Maybe she'll see into my heart, where my hopes and dreams lie. . . .

"No matter," she says crisply, turning to the colander and moving the slices of eggplant to a platter. "You'll be a college professor, then."

Maybe not. My shoulders sag. Of course, she would default to the second most revered profession in the Thai culture.

"A college academic?" I ask. "On what subject?"

"Does it matter?"

"That's generally the way it works, Khun Yai. You become a professor because you want to spend the rest of your life studying a subject you love. Not because a PhD makes you look good to your neighbors!"

She sighs and sticks the platter in the oven to stay warm. She begins to arrange raw vegetables on a plate, to serve with the *nam phrik*.

"It's my dream to design clothes, Khun Yai," I say in a soft voice. I'd never reveal as much to Mae, but this is my grandmother. She strokes her soft hands over my hair when I'm sick and gets up early to cook me *jok* for breakfast. "Don't you want me to follow my dream?"

She makes a face like she's had a bad mango. "You and your American passion. Dreams are useless if you can't pay the bills. Provide for your family first. Give them real security. Once that's done, you can dream all you want. Look at your mother. She cross-stitches in the evenings. I watch soap operas. You can design clothes in your spare time."

"Those are hobbies, Khun Yai. They aren't careers." How do I explain this to her? How do I convey the feeling I get when I turn a pile of raw materials into something beautiful, something real? "I'm happy when I'm designing. I feel like my truest self. Like this was why I was put on this earth."

"Oh, please." Khun Yai doesn't roll her eyes; she's much too elegant for that. But I can see the roll in the hand on her hip, hear it in the lilt of her voice. "You are outdoing even the Americans. I hate to say it, but if you continue with this line of thinking, I won't be able to give you our family heirloom."

I gape at her. "You would break tradition over something so minor?"

"It's not minor, and you know it." She straightens to her full height, which is barely over five feet. I've got five inches on her, towering over her the way I loom over everyone in an elevator in Thailand, male or female. "My *Khun Yai* wanted the necklace bequeathed to my eldest granddaughter. But this granddaughter also needs to be a good Thai girl. Someone who understands and respects our culture and values." Her eyes laser into me. "Not someone who questions her *Khun Yai*'s advice. Not a girl who wears tight jeans and low-cut blouses. Not someone who runs around gossiping about boys instead of doing her homework. That's not what this necklace stands for. My *Khun Yai* wouldn't have wanted her necklace to go to a *farang*."

My cheeks burn. A foreigner. I may be the daughter of Thai parents, but I was born and raised in America. Which means I'll never be Thai enough. I'll never be good enough.

We stare at each other. I love my *Khun Yai*. I always have. She gave up her life in her native country to move to the States four years ago. And she did it for me. Well, it was also for my mom, in order to help her raise her child. But it was mostly for me. Her affection for me is without question.

And yet, the gulf between us right now feels as wide as the ocean between Thailand and the United States. I don't know how we'll ever cross it.

"Set the table," Khun Yai finally says. Ultimatum issued. Subject closed. At least for the time being. "Your mother called. She's bringing home a guest."

"One of the doctors?" I grab the silverware from the drawer. "Dr. Stanley or Dr. Roberts?"

"She didn't say."

I lay the spoon and fork at each place setting, making sure they match. There's nothing I can do about the water glasses, however. My grandfather, when he was alive, was a hard man. He had to be, I guess, to leave his small Chinese village and immigrate to Thailand in search of prosperity. He didn't allow us to eat soy sauce with our food, and we weren't allowed to have water glasses at the table. All drinking was done after the meal, so we never had a need for matching glasses.

"What if the guest doesn't like Thai food?" I ask. I'm not trying to be belligerent. It's not like we're talking about *pad thai* here, something that's accessible to the American palate. As delicious as it is, *nam phrik ka pi* is notoriously smelly to *farangs*.

"Then, I will grill him some steak." She opens the refrigerator door, revealing enough meat to feed our family for a week. "But first, he will try my Thai food."

I groan. For his sake, I hope our guest chokes down the eggplant. Khun Yai will be the gracious hostess, as she always is. But inside, she'll be judging him. The surest way to offend her is to refuse to eat her food. Or to have too delicate an appetite. Or to impose any sort of weird restriction. We eat rice morning, noon, and night, so Khun Yai considers carb-free diets to be pure madness.

The garage door grinds open. Mae is home.

She walks into the kitchen, her white medical coat still fresh and unsullied even after ten hours of work. A white girl trails behind her, dragging a bulging suitcase that's about to split at the seams. Khun Yai and I exchange startled looks, our strife forgotten. We assumed *guest* meant one of my mom's colleagues.

The girl is about my age, with mousy brown hair and muddy brown eyes. Even if she smiled, I'm not sure you could call her pretty. Her features are plain, her clothes plainer. A deep scar zigzags down her left cheek, like Harry Potter's bolt of lightning, although it is not as pretty, not as neat. She studies the floor like it might open and swallow her at any moment.

"Khun Mae, Kan," my mother says. "This is Shelly. She's going to be staying with us for a while."

Chapter 3

Shelly Ambrose hardly heard Dr. Som's words as the woman explained Shelly's situation to her daughter and mother. She didn't *have* to listen because she knew the facts by heart.

Shelly's mother had died a couple months ago.

Shelly didn't have any living relatives.

Shelly was eighteen years old and thus ineligible for the foster care system.

Shelly needed a place to live until she graduated from high school and found a decent job.

With nowhere else to turn, Shelly had reached out to the woman the late Mrs. Ambrose had claimed was her angel: the doctor who'd performed an emergency C-section that saved both her and her baby's lives. Shelly had never met the doctor herself, but Mrs. Ambrose had kept in touch with her over the years, and Dr. Som had been a constant reference in their conversations. The doctor's last name was actually Pongsai, Shelly's mother had explained, but since it was too hard to say, everyone just called her by her first name.

These facts should've evoked a deep emotional response from Shelly. And maybe, once upon a time, they did. But not anymore.

She'd once seen a documentary on sand tiger sharks. When they were embryos, these sharks ate their half-formed brothers and sisters to make room in the womb. They had to, so that they could grow large enough to fend off predators after their birth. It was survival of the fittest at its most bloodthirsty.

She got that. She lived in an unfeeling world, and in order to survive, she couldn't afford to get sentimental about anyone's death. Even her mother's.

So instead of listening to Dr. Som's words, she stared at the girl. God, Kan was put-together, with her casual but elegant clothes and the confident tilt of her shoulders. Nice, too. She'd been a little stiff when Shelly first entered the room, but as soon as she heard about Sheila Ambrose's death, her lips softened. She stepped forward and placed a comforting hand on Shelly's arm and didn't stare at her scar at all. "I'm so sorry."

"Yeah," Shelly said, struggling to find the right tone, one that was appropriately mournful and not too pathetic. "I'm sorry, too."

She stuck her hands in her pockets, stroking the paper she always carried with her. As soft and wrinkled as a used tissue, it was one of the notes she'd received in the sixth grade.

You would've thought she'd been the most popular girl in school, judging from the number of triangular notes tucked into her desk on a daily basis.

That is, until you opened them.

The boys were awfully creative, she had to give them that. Each note featured the same stick figure with her bucktoothed grin and the lightning bolt scar on her face. And in each drawing, she was killed in a different way. Blown up by dynamite. Punctured by thousands of rounds from a machine gun. Carved by a knife all over her body, little zigzag scars decorating her arms, legs, and torso. But as varied as the drawings were, the lines written underneath were always the same.

You're too ugly to live. Please die now.

It was the *please* that killed her. The word that turned the cruel taunt of a bully into a polite request from society. If she died, the school, the town, the world would be better off.

Please do not trespass. Please refrain from littering. Please die now.

She never told the teachers about these notes. She never told anyone. She was too ashamed.

"Come on." Kan put her arm around Shelly's shoulders and guided her to the table. "Khun Yai made a special Thai meal for you. It's kind of an acquired taste, so don't worry if you don't like it. We can make you a steak. Or I'll sneak you a peanut butter chocolate chip granola bar. They're my favorite. I've got a stash in my room."

Shelly let herself be led. Why wouldn't she like it? You could serve her silkworm larvae and she'd happily scarf it down if it had been prepared for her. She didn't think anyone had cooked a meal especially for her, ever. Certainly not her mother.

Kan made a big fuss over getting her seated and asking her how she liked her water. She radiated kindness. She was the kind of girl Shelly normally hated because such generosity was never directed at her.

Until now.

"Khun Yai doesn't approve of ice," Kan whispered. "She thinks it messes with your system. But if you like cold water, the way most people do, I get you some. Khun Yai doesn't have her glasses on. She'll never notice."

Shelly couldn't believe she was being asked to express a preference in her drinking water, of all things. It was . . . nice. As though someone actually cared.

She'd been so alone since Sheila Ambrose had died. When she was a kid, and she could hear moans coming from the room her mother shared with her latest boyfriend, she would wish for aloneness. Her wish had finally come true—but it hadn't turned out like she had expected.

This aloneness didn't silence the screams inside her, the ones caused by a series of floating heads—the sneering sixth-grade boys, her vividly imagined but absentee father, and the man who said it wouldn't hurt even as he picked up a blade and sliced a lightning bolt into her skin. Why? For no reason other than he was high—both he and her mom, who had lounged on the couch and laughed while her boyfriend mutilated her daughter.

This aloneness didn't bring the peace she craved.

Instead, it was sharp and pointy. It hurt as much as the knife that carved up her cheek. It woke her in the middle of the night and made her wrap her arms around her knees, not only to still their trembling, but also because it was the only time anyone, anywhere, would hug her.

Kan's arm around her shoulders might've been a reflex. The casualness with which she catered to her might've been instinct. But to Shelly, this girl's behavior was more than simple courtesy.

It meant hope. It meant everything.

Chapter 4

"Can you tell me about your name? Is it...a nickname?" Shelly's tone creeps into the room and looks both ways, as though she expects to be slapped down any moment.

We're in my bedroom after dinner, and if it were anyone else, I might bristle. I might wonder what, exactly, was implied. But since it's Shelly, since she ate every last bite of the *nam phrik ka pi,* since she holds her shoulders in a way that makes me want to scoop her up and keep her safe, I laugh. "Ugly, isn't it? No one could pronounce my name, so my dad chopped it off when I started kindergarten, not realizing how weird it sounded. I guess it just kinda stuck."

"It's not ugly at all. I think it's unique." She sits on my bed and looks around, her eyes devouring the brightly patterned squares of fabric, my collection of chandelier earrings, the form-fitting jeans I pair with blouses of my own design. "What's your real name?"

"Kanchana."

"So pretty. Just like you."

I blink. She thinks I'm pretty? Nobody thinks I'm pretty, except maybe Ash. But she's my best friend. She has to think that. My other friends' compliments always come qualified in some way—like Lanie's comment about my hair.

"You're pretty, too," I say.

Shelly shakes her head in such a way that the hair falls perfectly over her cheek, hiding her scar. Clearly, she must've practiced the movement. "You don't have to say that. I know it's not true. I do like pretty things, though." She reaches out, her hand hovering over a fabric square on which I painted several images of the Eiffel Tower. "Can I touch it?"

"Of course." I tie the fabric around her neck, making sure one of the towers is on full display. "Gorgeous."

She studies herself in the mirror, her fingers grazing over the fabric as if she can't believe it's real. Not once, however, does she look at the reflection of her own face, with the scar on her cheek. Her eyes fix on the scarf, as if that's the only object worth seeing.

My heart cracks. Once upon a time, I looked into a mirror that way, too, when a gold necklace was draped around my neck. I'm not sure what Shelly's story is, other than the tragic death of her mother. But something about this girl makes me want to protect her. To banish whatever demons lurk in her past.

"You know, I've always wanted to go to France," she murmurs. "Ever since I saw *The Phantom of the Opera*. It's my dream that someday, I'll sit at a little café on the Champs-Élysées."

I stare. "That's my dream, too," I blurt out. Not a single one of my friends has this same fantasy. They don't even understand why I have this wish. "I'll go to Paris Fashion Week, and then I'll relax at that café and eat a croissant—"

"And sip espresso from one of those tiny white cups—"

"And watch the people walk by," I finish.

We grin at each other. "You know I don't even like espresso?" Shelly laughs. "It's way too bitter. It just sounds so sophisticated."

"Me, either! I also don't like wine, but I've heard that in France, wine is cheaper than soda."

"Maybe by the time we get there, we'll have developed a taste for both those things," she says wistfully.

"Probably. I mean, look at the way you scarfed down the *nam phrik ka pi*." I reach out and pick up her hand, wondering if I should continue. Oh, what the hell. I've spent too much of my life keeping my thoughts to myself. Might as well tell them to someone who might actually understand. "I think we're going to be great friends, Shelly. I'm so sorry for your loss, but I'm happy . . . I'm happy I got to meet you."

"I'm so glad," Shelly says, giving me a beautiful smile. "You don't know how glad that makes me."

But in the morning, I'm not so sure my family shares my feelings. My mom calls the high school in order to register Shelly, but Khun Yai barely says a word to her. She kisses me on the cheek, but when Shelly says hello, she just grunts.

I almost drop my spoon. My elegant, gracious Khun Yai, grunting at a guest? I thought I'd sooner see elephants fly.

But when Shelly sits at the table in front of her bowl of rice porridge and runny egg, Khun Yai stands abruptly and leaves the room.

"What's wrong with her?" I ask my mom, who has just hung up the phone.

Mae pinches her nose. I can see the blue veins underneath her skin. "We had an argument. She doesn't . . . agree . . . with all my decisions."

"What decisions?"

She clamps her mouth shut but darts a look at Shelly, who's shoveling *jok* into her mouth as though it's her last meal. Does that mean she doesn't want to talk in front of Shelly? Or that the disagreement concerns . . . Shelly herself?

I tense. What if Khun Yai convinces Mae to kick Shelly out?

Mae smiles warmly at Shelly. "You're all set for school. Kan will take you by the front office before first period to pick up your schedule." She drapes her coat over her arm and drops a kiss on my head. After a moment's hesitation, she does the same to Shelly. "Bye now. You girls have fun today, okay?"

"She's nice," Shelly says, after we hear the garage door close.

"My mom? Yeah. Everyone loves her, especially her patients." I fiddle with my spoon. "Sometimes, though, I wish she'd spend a little less time helping everyone else. And a little more time with me."

Holy crap, did I say that out loud? I've felt this way for months, maybe even years, but I've never told anybody, not even Ash.

I brace myself for Shelly's scorn, waiting for her to tell me that at least my mom doesn't drink or curse or hit. Instead, she just squeezes my hand like she knows exactly what I mean. We exchange a smile, and then she excuses herself to get dressed.

Five minutes pass. And then ten. At the fifteen-minute mark, I knock on the guest bedroom door and push it open. She's sitting on the bed, still wearing her nightgown.

I walk inside. "Shelly, what's wrong?"

She bites her lip. "I only have the clothes I came in last night. Your mom put them in the wash, but they're not dry yet. I checked."

Shocked, I stare at her battered suitcase in the corner, the one I thought was going to burst at any moment. "What's in there, if it's not clothes?"

"Oh." She hops off the bed and lifts the top of the suitcase. I see a bunch of ugly rocks. No, not rocks. Porcelain paperweights shaped like rocks. Painted different colors. Ugly colors. The colors nobody wants. They remind me of the artwork that little kids try to sell at garage sales.

"They were my mother's," she says. "She wasn't an artist—but she wanted to be. Every weekend, she would lug these damn things to craft fairs all over the state. Every once in a while, she'd actually sell one. Pity buys, probably. I mean, look at them. Would you want one on your desk?"

There's no way to be tactful. "Nope."

"Exactly." Her lips curve, even as they tremble. "I thought for sure she'd get better over time. But she never did." She nods toward the suitcase. "Go ahead. Pick one up. You've got to see for yourself how heavy these suckers are."

I reach for a paperweight. She's right. I can't imagine carrying one of these for more than a few minutes. An entire suitcase of them must be backbreaking. Idly, I run my finger along the edge. It is jagged and decorated with a splash of brilliant red.

"They held an estate sale of all our stuff and sold everything. If I hadn't grabbed these paperweights, they would have gone in a Dumpster somewhere." She moves her shoulders. "Maybe that's where this junk belongs, but I can't bear to part with a single piece. It's been months since she died, and I still think about her every hour. Every minute."

Her face crumples, and so does my heart. I step forward and fold her into my arms. She presses her wet eyes into my shoulder, and still, I can't wrap my mind around how much she must've loved her late mother. "Are you saying you packed your mom's paperweights instead of your personal belongings?"

She sniffs. "Yeah. I can always buy new clothes. This was my last chance to preserve my memories."

"That's lovely, Shelly."

"Yeah, well, a lot of good that sentiment does us now," she says. "My clothes have to dry for another twenty minutes."

"Easy." I take her hand and lead her across the hall to my bedroom, to my closet. Nothing could feel more natural.

I gesture to the clothes hanging inside. "Help yourself."

Her mouth drops. "Are you sure? But these are yours. They're part of who you are."

If she only knew. They aren't just part of my identity; they *are* my identity. The only time I don't feel pressure to be one thing or another is when I'm making my clothes. It's the only time I can truly be me.

And yet, as her face comes alive while she fingers my favorite skirt, I wonder if this must be how it feels to have a sister. Sharing clothes, sharing laughter, sharing lives. This must be how it feels not to have to face the world alone.

"Sure thing." I grin. "It'll be fun to fight over that skirt."

Chapter 5

Later, as we walk into the sprawling brick high school and toward the gymnasium for the pep rally, Shelly sticks to me like chewed-up gum. Her head is bent forward so that her hair hides her scar. I don't blame her. I've never been the New Girl, but I've always been the Foreign Girl. I know how it feels to be looked at and scrutinized.

"I love your shirt." She eyes my wrap-around blouse. "You look so tall and elegant. I wish I could pull something like that off. It might make it easier to walk into a new school."

"Of course you could pull it off. You just have to be confident," I say, taking a line from Ash. She tells me this at least once a week.

Shelly looks at me doubtfully. She's borrowed a pair of my old, baggy jeans and one of my ratty athletic T-shirts. I urged her to choose something nicer—the shirt has holes along the collar, for god's sake—but she refused. I thought it was because she didn't want to take advantage of my hospitality, but now, I wonder if the stylish clothes themselves make her uncomfortable.

I give her a reassuring smile. I know it's not easy. I know she's self-conscious about her scar, which isn't nearly as big or hideous as she thinks. But she's not alone. She has *me,* and I can't wait to introduce her to all my friends—and anyone else we come across.

Especially Ethan Thorne. This might be the perfect excuse to talk to him.

Surreptitiously, I scan the hallways, looking for his signature black shirt, the one with the silver stripes along the pocket. He must have half a dozen of the same shirt, as his physics partner gleefully reported to the rest of us after she snuck a look in his closet.

And then, I remember Ethan wouldn't be in the halls, since the pep rally is featuring a special performance by the college ballroom dance team.

We enter the gym, and I scan the bleachers, looking for my friends. Lanie pops up, waving her hands like she's signaling the Coast Guard. "Kan! Over here! We saved you a seat."

Shelly and I make our way up the bleachers, passing a group of guys, mostly from the basketball team. They're huddled over a magazine.

It's got to be one of those men's magazines, judging from the way they're snickering, making obscene gestures . . . and sneaking peeks at me.

Heat rushes to my face. What? Why are they looking at me? Unless they're not. Unless I'm just being overly sensitive again. Yeah, that must be it. I'm the last person you would associate with those kinds of pictures.

But then, Walt Peterson jumps out of the group and makes a jerking motion with his hand. He's not directly in our path, but his eyes track us as we walk by.

Gross. I grip the straps of my backpack tighter and walk faster. Clearly, their behavior has nothing to do with us, but I don't want this to be Shelly's first impression of Foxville High.

"Let's pretend we didn't see that, okay?" I mutter to her. "Oh, look! Here are my friends now." We join Izzy, Lanie, and Ash. "Hey, gang, I want you to meet Shelly. She's going to be staying with us for a while."

They give her warm smiles and say enthusiastic hellos. I'm not surprised. They've practically appointed themselves the unofficial welcoming committee at Foxville High. When Melissa Finch moved here last spring, they walked her to class with such regularity, I was afraid she was going to put in a restraining order.

A piercing whistle shatters the air, and the girls around us start clapping and whooping. Startled, I glance around and realize that Ethan and the rest of the ballroom team have just descended upon the gym floor.

Mesmerized, I stare. Man, they're good. The girls' costumes are sequined and skimpy. The boys' outfits are less showy, but each flash of their muscular arms more than makes up for the lack of sparkle. The dozen or so couples move together, fluidly and perfectly in sync. It's better than *So You Think You Can Dance*. I don't think there's a single one of my friends who doesn't wish she could be down there right now, moving in the arms of a sexy dance partner.

Such as Ethan.

His movements are as fluid as water, and his hips rotate in ways I didn't know hips could rotate. He's wearing a tight black shirt, a shinier version of his regular uniform, and his small, secret smile feels like it's directed right at me.

The show is over way too soon, and at least half of the audience are on their feet, stomping and clapping. Ethan blows kisses up to the stands and runs off the dance floor.

Around us, the crowd begins to dissipate, but my friends linger. Izzy fixes her lip gloss, Lanie frantically flips through her chemistry notes, and Ash is talking to Shelly, a crease between her brows. Weird. Ash only gets that crease when she's concerned about something.

Before I can figure out why she's frowning, I notice a couple of the basketball guys staring at me.

Me. Not the new girl. Not Shelly.

What? I bring my hand to my mouth. No food stuck in my teeth, at least not that I can feel. I twist my body and look down my back. No toilet paper coming out of my pants, either. So why are they staring?

"Hey, Kan." Brad Summers comes up behind me. "I was wondering. Would you like to go to prom with me?"

I blink. Didn't he just ask Ash out on a date? Why is he asking me to prom? "Excuse me? Is this a joke?"

He flushes. "Of course not. I was just thinking I'd like to get to know you better."

"He means he thinks you're hot!" one of his friends calls out. The entire group of boys cracks up.

"Let's just say, his eyes have been opened to your natural beauty." Walt smirks. He puts a hand by his head and the other on his waist, elbows out, pinup style. "Can you pose like this? Show the rest of us what good old Brad sees?"

The blood drains from my face, taking all the warmth out of my body. My hands, my neck, my cheeks—everything is ice cold. What is he talking about?

"Or how about this?" Walt bends forward, placing his hands on his knees and bunching his chest. "Squeeze those titties together."

Brad's retreating now, shooting death glares at Walt. "Shut up, dude. Just shut up."

Someone makes a grab for the magazine they were studying, and it flies onto the floor in between the sections of bleachers.

We all stare at the magazine for a moment, and then Shelly runs over and picks it up. Returning, she shows me the centerfold. Oh dear god. Scantily clad models with long black hair and slanted eyes pose provocatively.

This must be the Asian edition. The fantasy of a certain segment of the population. And one of the reasons I hate the word *exotic*.

"You know, Kan, in all the years I've known you, I never thought of you as sexy." Walt strides forward, his pecs all puffed out. "But I've changed my mind; I think I like exotic women. But prom's too big of a commitment. How about Friday night, in Stevie's basement? There's an old couch there that would suit someone like you."

I'm rooted to the spot, my mind a frigid cage. I don't think I could move if my fashion career depended on it. Someone like me? Walt chose those words deliberately. He wants to make clear that, unlike Brad, he's not actually interested in me. He wants this date for one reason alone.

"You're a pig!" Lanie spits out. "Get the hell out of here before I throw up on you."

Shelly moves into the aisle and stands in front of Walt.

He sneers. "You're in my way, freak. Move."

"With pleasure," she says. Before I can blink, she whirls in the air, kicking out her leg. Her foot connects with Walt right in the jaw, and he collapses in a heap in the middle of the bleachers. Someone screams—Izzy, no doubt, with her nails-on-a-chalkboard screech—and everyone stares at Shelly, openmouthed.

She snatches up the magazine and chucks it into a trash can at the end of the bleachers. She's never met any of these boys in her life, but she looks them each in the eyes, even Walt. Especially Walt, who is clutching his cheek and moaning like a little boy.

"That's what happens to assholes who disrespect my friend," Shelly says. Tossing her head, she strides down the aisle. "Come on, Kan, let's go." I scurry after her.

Chapter 6

"I still can't believe you did that!" I say. It's been three hours since the takedown, and we're sitting in a quiet corner of the cafeteria, eating identical lunches of rice and roast red pork that Khun Yai left on the counter for us. "That was the most kick-ass thing I've ever seen."

Shelly pushes her rice around like it's nothing, but a pink glow tinges her cheeks, right across the scar. "I've been taking tae kwon do since I was a kid. You know how people say swimming is the most important skill you can learn? Well, my mom said that was bullshit. She never had the best advice for me, but for once, I thought she was right. You can stay away from the water, but you never know when a thug might jump you in the middle of the street."

"Or when a jerk might need taking down at a new school."

The pink deepens to a red flush. "You think Walt's okay?"

"The nurse said he was fine." I wave a stalk of green onion in the air. Dipped in vinegar, it's a perfect accompaniment to the roast pork. "He probably just went home because he's a big baby."

"At least I'm not in trouble."

Nobody is. Not Shelly, not me, not the boys. A teacher came running after she heard the commotion, but no one would confess to anything. The boys, probably because they felt complicit, even if Walt acted independently. My friends, mostly because they didn't want Shelly punished.

"I wanted to show the teachers the magazine," Lanie whispered to me in math class. "But when I went to fish it out of the trash can, it was already gone. Did *not* want to get into a 'he said, she said' with Walt. He'd blame it all on Shelly, for sure. What do you think? Should I say something?"

I wasn't sure. My head was still spinning. I didn't want Shelly in trouble, either, so I just told Lanie to leave it alone.

Now, I glance at the table in the exact center of the cafeteria. My usual table, with Ash, Lanie, Izzy, and the others. I wanted to sit there, too, but Shelly said she couldn't deal with small talk after what happened that morning. Which was fair. So, instead, we chose a table in the corner. It was the least I could do.

Still, my eyes keep drifting to the center table throughout our lunch.

"Is Ash your friend?" Shelly asks, following my gaze.

"Yes. She's my best friend." I shove a spoonful of rice in my mouth. "Ever since we were in kindergarten and she wrote my name over and over on a piece of paper because she liked the way it sounded. You'll love her."

"Really?" Her eyebrows climb up her forehead. "She didn't say a single thing to Walt this morning."

"She didn't?" I think back to the scene in the bleachers, but everything was so chaotic, I can't picture what Ash was—or wasn't—doing. "Maybe she didn't have a chance."

"Oh, she had a chance, all right," Shelly says knowingly. "It's easy to be friends when everything is smooth. But when life gets a little bumpy, you find out who your true friends are. And Ash didn't stand up for you when you needed her."

"Ash isn't like that," I protest. "She's always the first to come to my defense."

"The fact of the matter is, Kan, you're sitting here, and she's sitting over there. And she hasn't once glanced in your direction."

But you made *us sit over here,* I want to say. But I don't because Shelly has a point. Even if we aren't eating lunch with them, shouldn't Ash come over to say hi? Shouldn't she catch my eye to give me an encouraging smile? I know I would, even if Ash were having lunch on top of the flagpole.

"She's jealous of you," Shelly continues. "I've only met her this morning, and I can already tell her type. She's used to being the center of attention, the prettiest and most popular girl around. Didn't you say this Brad guy had asked her out? Now that he's interested in you, she can't stand it."

I stare at Shelly. I don't know what to say. I don't *think* she's right. But maybe . . . maybe she's more perceptive than I want to admit. Maybe she sees things as an outsider that I don't notice because of my long years of friendship.

Before I can respond, a junior girl approaches us. "Why did I have to pick today of all days to sleep in?" she moans. "Walt Peterson, kicked in the jaw. That's about the coolest thing I've ever heard."

Shortly after her departure, a guy stops by to invite Shelly to run for the student council. "We could use someone like you," he says.

Then, another girl strolls by, giving Shelly a high five.

Shelly keeps shaking her head, a dazed look in her eyes. "You don't understand," she whispers to me in between the admirers. "This doesn't happen to me. No one ever pays attention to me."

"Better get used to it. We're so bored of one another, you'll get attention just by being the new girl. But a new girl who puts bully Walt Peterson in his place?" I smile gleefully. "You won't forget me when you're the most popular girl in school, will you?"

Her eyebrows pinch together. "Don't say that. I would never forget you. I'd rather have one real friendship than ten shallow ones. No matter how popular it makes me."

I drop my teasing tone and squeeze her arm. "I feel the same way, Shelly." I glance at the center table once more. As always, Izzy and Lanie are shrieking over something that Ash has said. And they still haven't looked in my direction once. "I feel the exact same way."

Ten minutes later, I'm in the girls' restroom, bunching my now-straight hair into a ponytail, eliminating one more way that I look like the centerfold models, when Ash bursts into the room.

"Oh," my closest friend says, looking like she wants to flee. She takes a step back. From *me*.

I swallow hard. So it wasn't my imagination. Ash was deliberately avoiding me in the cafeteria.

We're not as tight as we used to be back in elementary school, when we practically lived at each other's houses. But she was still the first person I called when I got the job at Miss Patsy's. She's the only person in whose arms I've wept on the anniversary of my father's death.

And now, she won't meet my eyes. She doesn't ask why I didn't sit with them in the cafeteria. She doesn't give me a hug and ask how I'm doing after this morning's events.

Instead, she runs her fingers over her sparkly necklace and crosses her tight-jeaned, brown-booted legs, as though she's posing for a magazine. Maybe even the one the guys were perusing this morning. Except not—because she's not Asian. Can't forget that.

I check my watch. Our next class starts in five minutes. "Well?" I say, when it becomes clear she isn't going to break the silence. "Did you want to say something to me?"

"Why didn't you say no when Brad asked you to prom?" she asks finally, her voice small. "You know he asked me on a date a few days ago. I told him I'd think about it, and I was going to give him my answer today."

I blink. And then blink again. "He wasn't exactly my main concern at that moment. Walt and his disgusting antics were."

"Walt is gross. Everybody knows that." She pushes her hair back impatiently. "You don't understand, Kan. I told all the girls that Brad likes me. What are they going to think now that he's invited you to prom?"

"They're not going to think anything." I put my hand on her arm. "Are you . . . interested in him? Is that what this is about?"

Her shoulders droop. "Maybe. I don't know. It's just that things at home have been so hard lately. Brad was the one bright spot of my day. And now, you've ruined everything."

I reel backward, my sneakers scuffing the floor. *I ruined*

everything? I know Ash is having a tough time with her parents. I know her reputation's always been important to her. But how can she possibly say that? "Excuse me. Are you actually blaming me for what happened?"

"Yes. No. I don't know." She crosses to the sink and turns on the faucet. The water spurts into the sink, but she makes no move to touch it. "I shouldn't have said that. It's just that the whole school's talking about the incident. And they're all talking about how Brad prefers you over me."

"That's not my fault," I say quietly. "I'm sorry it turned out that way, but I can't apologize for it."

"I just wish you had shut it down sooner."

I don't say anything. Neither does she. All we can hear is the gurgle of the water as it flows down the drain. The years of our friendship flit in the air between us. The laugh-until-our-stomachs-hurt conversations, the talk-until-our-batteries-die phone calls. She texted me 756 times the week Charlie Rosen broke up with her last spring. I know because Khun Yai marched into my room, waving the phone bill and asking when I found the time to study.

My mind drifts to the summer I wiped out on my bicycle. The skin at my knee had been scraped away so completely that I could see a glistening white bone. I took one look at the bone and almost fainted.

"Look at me." Ash had gripped my hands. "You're going to be okay, but I have to go get help. Don't freak out, okay? Just lie here and look at the sky. I'll come back. I promise I won't let anything bad happen to you. Okay?"

I was so scared I couldn't talk, but I nodded, and she raced away, her feet kicking up the gravel. Even though the temptation was great, even though I wanted to look down at the bone, I kept my eyes on the blue, blue sky. I gave my pain to the clouds, the way they did in stories, and before I knew it, Ash was back. An ambulance roared up the street a few minutes later, and they took me to the ER and patched me up.

I was laid up the rest of the summer. All the other kids hung out at the pool, but not Ash. She stayed by my side, painting her nails, reading books, playing solitaire. I knew then that I was right to trust her.

The entire memory flashes through my mind, and I turn back to my best friend, ready to make amends. I don't care if it's not my fault. I just want to reach out and hug her. She's hurting, and I'm hurting, and we should just look past our misunderstanding and hurt together. Because that's what friends do.

But even as I'm lifting my arms, she reaches out and turns off the water. The silence accentuates the air, as if setting the stage for what's to come.

"I've got to tell you, Kan, there's something weird about your new friend," she says. "Something not quite right. It's her first day of school, and already, she's leading you into bad situations. Walt deserved it, don't get me wrong. But kicking him in the face? That's freaking assault. We would've been better off telling the teachers what he was saying."

I stiffen. Shelly's words float through my mind, and all of a sudden, I can remember the scene from that morning clearly. Lanie had her hands on her hips, pissed as hell, and Brad was slinking backward from the group, trying to blend in with the bleachers. And Ash . . . Ash was just standing there. Her hands hanging limply at her sides. Not saying anything. Not doing anything. Just like Shelly said. "At least she stood up for me," I whisper. "You did nothing. When life gets bumpy, you find out who your true friends are."

Her eyes flash. "Are you saying I'm not a true friend?"

The bell shrills. We look at each other for a long moment, and then she spins on her heel and stalks out of the restroom.

The door bangs. And I wonder if our friendship will ever be the same again.

Chapter 7

Later that day, I drop Shelly off at the superstore, so that she can shop for new clothes, and stop by my house to freshen up before heading to Miss Patsy's. Khun Yai is in the kitchen, making sticky rice, when I emerge from the bathroom.

"She has no idea what she's doing," she mutters to herself in Thai as she pours rice into a glass tray and covers it with a couple inches of tepid water. "This is not going to end well. I could throttle her for putting us through this."

"Throttling, Khun Yai? Isn't that a little violent for a Friday afternoon?" I grab a diet soda from the fridge. "Who's got you so upset?"

The tray jerks in her hand, and water sloshes over the edge. Recovering quickly, Khun Yai wipes up the spill and lifts her cheek to me. I give her a kiss, which is how I always greet her.

"Your mother, that's who. She thinks she's making things right, fixing the sins of our past, when really, she's just making the situation worse."

"What sins?" I take a drink from the soda. "Are you talking about your disagreement?"

"Never mind, *luk lak*." She pats my hand. "This is between your mother and me. Where's the *farang*?"

"Don't call her that," I say automatically. "I dropped Shelly off at Walmart. You need to pick her up in an hour; I have to get to the dance studio."

She purses her lips. "I'll do it, but I'm not happy about it."

I put the soda down. "Is this because she's white? Please, Khun Yai, don't be like this. She's a nice girl." I pause. I want, more than anything, to tell her about the nudie magazine. Surely, she'd have some good advice for me. At the very least, she could give me a hug and tell me she loves me. Maybe it's juvenile to still need such affirmation, but I do.

But if I tell her about the magazine, she'll just be even more adamant that I not spend any time with these *farang* boys. "Shelly's been a good friend to me already, and she needs us. Even if she's white."

She sighs. "It's not her race. Believe me, *luk lak,* this goes much deeper than you understand."

"Well, then, explain it to me."

"I can't." She lifts her shoulders helplessly, but she doesn't fool me. Khun Yai hasn't been helpless a day of her life. If she's pretending now, that means she's hiding something.

"You can't? Or you won't?"

Instead of answering, she covers the tray and sets it aside to soak for a few hours. She begins to hum an old Thai song about a farmer and his crush on a girl from the salt fields. I should know the tune; I performed it at Khun Yai's seventy-fifth birthday last year in Thailand. Our entire extended family attended—over a hundred people—and I was so nervous my knees literally knocked together. I didn't know knees actually did that. I thought it was just an expression. But I got through the song, and my relatives walked away so impressed with the Thai pronunciation of the *farang* granddaughter that they didn't even think to criticize my singing ability—or lack thereof.

But Khun Yai isn't reliving fond memories now. She's telling me, in no uncertain terms, that our conversation is over. And so, I leave the house, my mind spinning with questions.

What does Khun Yai have against Shelly? And how could it possibly relate to the sins of my mother's past?

I arrive at Miss Patsy's dance studio. Now that I've gotten the girls' measurements, I don't technically need to work on-site. But Miss Patsy offered me free reign in the spare classroom, which has a ton of advantages. It's got great afternoon sun. It helps me keep my extracurricular activity a secret from Khun Yai. Best of all, it's right across the hall from where Ethan Thorne teaches dance classes.

After the day I just had, I could use a little of Ethan's company. And if he doesn't talk to me, at least I can look at him.

When I walk into the dance studio, however, the place is deserted. I remember all of a sudden that Miss Patsy cancelled classes because she is out of town.

I sigh and am about to retreat to the classroom, when I hear voices. Two voices, to be precise. One female, the other male—and disturbingly familiar.

"No, not like that," the girl says. "Watch me."

"Maybe if you hadn't made me wear this outfit, I could concentrate," Ethan grumbles.

"We have to practice in our new costumes sometime."

The voices are coming from the main classroom, the one with a large, potted plant right in the middle of the doorway. Miss Patsy put the plant there on purpose, so that parents could peek at their kids without making them nervous.

Which means there's no reason for my palms to be slick. No reason for my heart to thunder in my throat. I'm not a Peeping Tom, am I, if I'm using the plant for its intended purpose?

I crouch down and part the leaves. And my mouth goes dry.

Ethan pats his forehead with a white towel. He has on black pants and a white tuxedo shirt open halfway down his chest. A bright red bow tie is draped around his neck, as though he got interrupted in the middle of dressing—or undressing, as the case may be. The girl with him is a college student with long blond hair swept up in a ponytail. His dance partner, I'm assuming. I recognize her from the pep rally.

The girl is fiddling with her iPod and wears an even more daring outfit than the one she was wearing this morning. The short red dress has a plunging neckline and is covered in sequins.

Music blares out of the iPod. She turns, the skirt flowing out gracefully, and pulls Ethan into a Latin dance where the steps are slick and the movements are slow. Sensuality oozes from both of them. I feel like I'm watching sex on the dance floor.

The heat creeps up my neck and warms my cheeks. Maybe I shouldn't be watching this, his hand on her bare skin, her eyes half-closed. But I cannot rip my gaze away. Is that his girlfriend? The way he's looking at her, she's got to be his girlfriend.

No one's ever looked at me like that. I squirm, my elbows digging into the soil of the plant. I don't know what I would do if someone did look at me like that.

And then, the music ends and the two of them break apart.

"You're too slow," the blonde snaps. "You were half a step behind me the entire song."

Ethan rolls his eyes. "Whatever, Jules. You were the one rushing the beat. Maybe you just want to get out of here so you can see your girlfriend."

"At least I have someone. Any girls show interest in your ugly face yet?"

"Ha ha." He takes a long pull from a water bottle. "You have no idea. They can't get enough of me."

"Doubtful. High school girls are smart. I would know. I used to be one."

She lies facedown and straightens her arms overhead, twisting her stomach and rotating her shoulder to the floor. He imitates her stretch. Her blond ponytail falls onto his shoulder, but he doesn't seem to notice, as though he's as familiar with her body as he is with his own.

Maybe this is my cue to leave. She's not his girlfriend. That's all I really need to know. My stomach limp with relief, I start to stand when he speaks again.

"There is this one girl . . ." He shifts to a kneeling position, with one knee up and one knee down.

I freeze, midcrouch, and fall back onto the floor.

Jules, like Ethan, moves into a quad stretch. "What's wrong with her that she's actually interested in you?"

"She's not interested in me. We've never even had a real conversation."

My breath catches. He's talking about me. Right? How many other girls does he not have a conversation with?

I clench my teeth. *Don't be silly, Kan. He probably doesn't talk to half the girls at school.*

Jules groans. "Oh, please. Don't tell me you're gaga over some girl just because she's cute."

"I'm not gaga," he says. "But face it. This thing called physical chemistry? It's real."

She wrinkles her nose. "I guess something's got to account for all those girls yelling your name at dance competitions. If only they knew you smelled like sweaty socks."

"Better than a sweaty butt." He gives her a playful shove, and she falls to the floor, giving up on her stretch.

"Go on." She grabs her water bottle.

"Well, she is cute, but it's more than just her looks. She has this . . . passion. This focus when she throws herself into her work. That's sexy to me. And it makes me wonder . . ." He lowers his voice. "It makes me wonder how it would feel if she put that attention on me."

She snorts, and water comes up her nose. "Oh, you have it bad, don't you?" she asks, wiping a hand across her face. "But I approve of your reasons. When are you going to ask her out? Or, you know, talk to her?"

"Tonight, maybe. I heard she was going to Derek's party. I'll be there, too. And . . . we'll see."

"I guess we will." She pulls him to his feet. "Until then, Romeo, break time's over."

She taps a button on the iPod, and the music starts playing again. I get to my feet and back away from the plant, unreasonably hurt. I have no plans of going to Derek's party tonight, so I'm not the girl he's talking about.

I gather my tote bags of fabric and walk woodenly to my car. There's no way I can stay and work here now. I'm such a fool. I should've known it wasn't me.

Should've known there was no way I had a shot with blond, blue-eyed Ethan, not when he has a plethora of other girls from which to choose. Girls who aren't the only Asian student at school. Girls who don't have squinty eyes and puffy hair. Girls who look like everybody else.

In my seventeen years in Foxville, Kansas, it's never been me. Why should anything change now?

Chapter 8

I decide to make Shelly a shirt. The idea comes to me as I'm driving home from Miss Patsy's. I need something to occupy my hands, and besides, I want to thank her for standing up for me. The girls' costumes can wait. They would make me think of Ethan, anyhow, and I really don't need him crowding my mind.

Shelly's in the living room when I get home, watching reruns on the television. I make up some excuse about needing her as a model for an emergency project and take her measurements. Not even stopping for dinner, I grab a peanut butter chocolate chip granola bar and retreat to the room above the garage.

This is where I work when I'm not at Miss Patsy's. I renovated the space last year and commandeered it as my own. I'm not sure what Khun Yai thinks I do up here. Meditate, maybe. Study, definitely. But she rarely comes up to check on me, and I always make sure the sewing machine and dressmakers' dummies are stowed away in a closet when I'm not here.

Guiltily, I think of Shelly, spending her first Friday night in Foxville alone. But she'll forgive me when she sees the shirt.

I use the purest white cotton I can find and design a wraparound style with a daring, low neckline. It's not Shelly's usual style, but I'm determined to prove to her that she *can* pull it off.

I work late into the night—and then get up early to continue working. By midmorning, I've slept a total of three hours, but I have a brand-new shirt to show for it.

A thrill shoots through me. I've made countless articles of

clothing—some I'm proud of, others of the more experimental variety—and I feel a deep sense of accomplishment every time.

I did this. This shirt wouldn't exist if it weren't for me. My hard work and skill brought it to life.

Humming lightly, I carry the shirt to Shelly's bedroom, not expecting her to be there. The sun is shining brightly, and the clouds are wisps of cotton in the sky. She's probably off enjoying this beautiful weather.

But when I knock and then push the door open, she's sitting on her bed, staring at nothing, much as she was yesterday morning. Except this time, her eyes are narrowed and her mouth is twisted. I almost don't recognize her. She looks consumed by rage.

My heart skips a beat. "Shelly! Are you . . . okay?"

With effort, she rearranges the planes of her face and attempts a smile. "It's nothing. I was just thinking about my mom."

"Oh." I step forward. Should I give her a hug? I want to, but the lingering traces of her anger make me hesitate. I settle for rubbing her shoulder instead. "Do you want to talk about it?"

"Nah. It's not good for me to dwell so much in the past." She shakes her head, as if putting and end to the subject. "What's up?"

I hand her the neatly folded shirt. That should make her feel better. "Look what I made you!"

"Oh, Kan, for me? You shouldn't have." She unfolds the shirt carefully, almost reverently, and holds it up. "It looks just like yours." She beams at me.

I smile back, even as bubbles of unease pop in my stomach. I'm glad Shelly can transition so quickly from anger to gratitude . . . but the end result feels like whiplash.

I push the feeling away. That's probably just my fatigue talking. I'm so tired I can barely stand up. "Thanks for sticking up for me. I'm lucky to have a friend like you."

"I've never owned anything so beautiful." She strokes the fabric. "But I'm sure it will look awful on me."

"It won't. I promise."

She looks uncertainly into the mirror, clutching the shirt to her chest.

The white fabric is too plain against her pale skin. Too stark. She needs a splash of color.

Red, perhaps. The color of passion, the color of life. Immediately, I think of Ethan, half-undressed with a red bow tie draped around his neck.

My cheeks flame. That's the color of passion, all right. The color of hips moving in a slow, sensual way. The color of steamy looks and smoldering silence.

And . . . red and white is also a basic color pairing, so I just need to stop being so ridiculous.

"You need a bright red accent," I say. "Something in your hair or around your neck."

I move to the dresser, where I spy a few pairs of brightly colored earrings. "How about these?" I hold up a dangly red pair.

"Oh, um, they were having a sale at Walmart. I never wear things like that, but I . . . I couldn't resist." She ducks her head. "I think being around you has inspired me to be more fashionable. Try to, at least."

"They're perfect."

She takes a deep breath and puts on the earrings. "I'm being silly, I know. If you went to all this trouble to make me a shirt, the least I can do is put it on." She strips off her blouse, and I look away to give her privacy.

My eyes fall on another piece of jewelry: a BFF heart necklace hanging on a knob of her dresser. Did she pick this up at Walmart, too? Upon closer examination, I see that there are two necklaces, rather than one. The kind that Ash and I used to wear in the fourth grade—but different, too. Together, the two halves form a heart, but the bottom of each heart has this weird, jagged edge that looks almost like a key. What's even stranger is that both halves of the heart are present.

I pick up one of the halves and turn the pendant over. *R & S, best friends forever* is inscribed on the back. So, clearly not from Walmart. *S* is clearly Shelly, but who is *R*? And why does Shelly have both halves of the necklace?

"Well, what do you think?" Shelly's voice intrudes on my thoughts.

Startled, I hang the necklace back up and flush, although I'm not really snooping. I mean, she's standing right there.

Clearing my throat, I walk to her and tie the crisp bow by her waist. "See? It fits you perfectly. I knew it would."

"I can't believe that's really me." She twists back and forth in front of the mirror.

"You look downright sexy."

She shakes her head, and the earrings brush against her cheeks. "Are you sure? Is this shirt too, um, classy for me?"

"No way." I pool her hair on top of her head and secure it in a messy bun. "You wear this outfit with skinny jeans and tall boots, and you're as sophisticated as anyone."

She admires the new hairstyle in the mirror. "I don't even recognize myself," she says wonderingly.

I shrug and smile. If there's one thing I'm good at, it's fashion. It doesn't care about your race or which world you fit in. It just is.

"You have no idea how it feels to be me," she continues. "How it feels to be . . . ugly."

I've been ugly all my life, but now's not the time to mention my own insecurities. Not when I'm trying to build her up. "You're not ugly. Far from it." I lick my lips, not sure how to proceed. "Do you think so because of . . . your scar?"

She nods.

"I think you look beautiful, just as you are," I say. She shakes her head, as though she doesn't want to hear it, so I keep going. "But if it would make you feel better, you could cover the scar up with concealer. You have lots of admirers, Shelly. Didn't you see all those people who came up to you yesterday? I don't think you realize how much people like you."

An expression I can't read crosses her face, and she yanks the earrings off. "No, Kan. I'm not like you. Even if I didn't have this scar, I wouldn't be tall and pretty. I wouldn't be popular like Ash. People like her make me feel like I'm a speck of dirt. I could get blown away in the wind, and nobody would care."

"The Ashes of the world shouldn't matter, Shelly. Don't let someone else determine how you feel about yourself."

She closes her eyes, breathing deeply, as if she is battling with invisible demons. I wish there were something I could do to help. Something to lessen the pain.

"I think I just need to hear that every day," she says, in a small voice. "Until I can convince myself it's true."

"Well, I'll be happy to tell you."

"Could you . . . could you say it again?" She takes a shuddering breath, sticking her hands deep into the pockets of her pants. "All of it. Especially the part about Ash." She ducks her head. "You must think I'm really pathetic."

"Of course I don't." I look right into her eyes. "Shelly, you are beautiful and strong and kind. Don't ever forget that, and don't ever let anyone tell you otherwise. Don't worry about Ash. Her opinion doesn't matter. You determine who you are. Not anyone else." Now if I can only internalize such lessons for myself.

She grabs my hands. "Thank you, Kan. That means a lot to me." She takes a breath. "I'm sorry if I seem needy. I had a . . . bad experience with my last friend. We were as close as sisters, and I supported her in everything. I thought she supported me, too. But then she got a new boyfriend, and she ditched me right when I needed her most. Right when my mom died."

"Oh, Shelly." My heart wrenches. She must be talking about the R in the BFF necklace. "I'm so sorry you had to go through that."

She grips my hands even tighter. "You wouldn't do that to me, would you, Kan? You wouldn't get a boyfriend and drop me? I don't think I could go through that pain again. Not so soon."

"Of course not."

"Do you promise?"

I pause. The promise feels a little dramatic, but again, it's harmless. I'm not likely to get a boyfriend anytime soon, and besides, I would never forget about my friends.

So, I smile at Shelly and squeeze her hands. And say the words I hope I don't regret: "I promise."

Chapter 9

After Kan left the room, Shelly looked at herself in the mirror for the millionth time. Her new friend was a magician. With a few twists of the hair, a selection of earrings, and a new shirt, she had transformed Shelly into someone different. Someone better. Someone new.

She almost didn't even see the scar on her cheek anymore.

She picked up the BFF necklaces, the ones with the two halves of a broken heart. As always, the sight of the two parts nestled together made her feel sad. The necklaces weren't supposed to be reunited. They were supposed to hang around the necks of two separate people. Two friends, two sisters. Two girls coming together to make a whole.

But there was no reason to feel sad. Pretty soon, the other necklace would find its rightful home again, around the neck of someone loyal and true. Someone who wouldn't betray her, the way the last girl did.

Maybe that person would be Kan.

She inhaled sharply, the wish spurting through her veins. Oh, please, let it be Kan. Let it be this sweet, sophisticated girl, who was everything Shelly wasn't and wanted to be. It would be a simple enough matter to turn the *R* into a *K*. Before the *R*, after all, there was a *P*. And before the *P*, there was a *B*.

She was lucky, she supposed, that the girls who entered her life had such interchangeable first initials. Although you'd be hard-pressed to call her lucky at anything.

Shelly wrapped her hand around her half of the heart pendant, squeezing until she could feel the jagged edge slicing into her skin. She just had to hold on a little while longer, and then she wouldn't feel so alone anymore.

She wouldn't feel this darkness wrapping around her, threatening to choke the very life out of her.

All she wanted was for one person to understand her. Someone to glimpse her pain and ease it, for a little while. Someone to look at her the way she'd caught the boy in the tight black clothes sneaking glances at Kan in the cafeteria. Not that Kan noticed. But Shelly supposed if you had lots of admirers, you wouldn't pick up on one appreciative glance.

Kan had said that *Shelly* had lots of admirers. Ha. Nobody had ever looked at Shelly that way, ever. She would know, because she wasn't a complete and total fool.

That was the first time Shelly wanted to punch Kan. To hit her so hard her teeth would go flying out of her mouth, and then, maybe she wouldn't be so pretty anymore. She hoped, for Kan's sake, that her new friend wouldn't be the same as her last one. But she wouldn't. Shelly was sure of it. Yes, Kan had made the statement about the admirers, but she had also made Shelly a shirt. A lovely, lovely blouse, sewn with Kan's very own hands. It fit like a dream, and it made Shelly feel something she had never felt before. Beautiful.

Even before the scar on her cheek, she'd never felt beautiful. How could she? She'd been ugly from the moment she was born. Nobody cooed at her. Nobody patted her head. She had been treated like a household pet—and not even a valued one. She was a rodent who wandered through her mom's living quarters, scrounging for food.

When she was six years old, her mom had a boyfriend who would come to their apartment. He spent most of his time in the master bedroom, where he would make loud grunting noises. When he did appear, he would slouch on the couch with a hand down his pants, and if Shelly walked by, he would pelt her with popcorn. "Who'd your mom screw to end up with such an ugly kid? Didn't know she was into bestiality!" He'd then roar as if he'd told the best joke in the world.

So, *beautiful* was not a word in her vocabulary. Until now, when Kan had given her a glimpse of the fairy tale.

Was it possible? Could she become the girl she had always wanted to be?

Like with everything else, only time would tell.

Chapter 10

The sound of frying bacon wakes me up. Except it's still dark outside, and there's no accompanying smell of grease. Crap. That's not bacon, after all, but a torrential rain pounding against our roof. Exactly what I need on a Monday morning.

With the exception of my brief moment of euphoria when I finished Shelly's shirt, I spent the entire weekend sulking. Wrapping egg rolls with Khun Yai and replaying the scene with Walt Peterson in my head. Lying listlessly on my bed and imagining Ethan hooking up with another girl. I was so mopey even I was beginning to get bored.

I wanted to turn things around this week—but now, this weather is like a slap in the face. *You think you're going to have a good day? Yeah, good luck with that!*

I drag myself out of bed and to my computer. It's too early to be awake, but my mind is so cluttered that going back to sleep is out of the question. Idly, I type in a search for Sheila Ambrose's death. I'm curious about Shelly's past, about what she's been through. But I don't know how to bring up such a sensitive subject with my new friend.

My hand hovers above the ENTER key. This information is in the public domain. I'm not really prying into her privacy if I take a peek. Right? Maybe. Ugh, I don't know.

I press the button before I can change my mind.

And wish I hadn't.

Article after article about Sheila Ambrose's demise pops up. I guess when you die in a spectacular way, all the newspapers in the area turn into tabloids and rush to report on the juiciest details. I'm surprised I hadn't heard of her death, but the Ambroses' hometown, Lakewood, is a few hours away.

Sheila Ambrose was found in a church early Sunday morning, hanging from a rope attached to the second-floor balcony. She was wearing a wedding dress, complete with a mesh veil, lace-up ballerina heels, and even a garter with tiny sprigs of blue flowers. A suicide note was tucked in her bodice, one that explained her dissatisfaction with her earthly life and her desire to be united with her one true love and savior: Jesus Christ.

Oh, man. I bring my hand to my mouth. No wonder Shelly seems so desperate to hang on to our friendship. The one person who should've loved her most chose to leave her alone in this world.

But there's more: the one detail over which the newspapers went wild. Sheila Ambrose was never married. She never had a wedding. She never owned a wedding dress. This meant, of course, that in preparation for her suicide, Sheila had to shop for the gown. She had to compare varying lengths of veils; she had to choose among garters with bits of lace or silk or flowers.

I click through the articles, my nausea like a stone at the pit of my stomach. The same details are rehashed again and again. And then, on the seventh page of the search results, I come upon a Web site that leaked a photo of her corpse. With the same sick compulsion that draws onlookers to car accidents, I enlarge the photo of Sheila Ambrose's body.

The picture is fuzzy, as though it was snapped from someone's cell phone. Sheila is hanging from the rope, her head slumped forward, the dress on full display. Tiny rhinestones are sewn all over the bodice, and even though the lighting is dim, I can tell the dress would sparkle brilliantly under any kind of bulb.

I scan the photo, taking in every column of the banister, every fraying bit of the thick, twisted rope. And then, my blood freezes.

On the dead woman's cheek is a freshly cut scar. It zigzags from her eyebrow to her jaw like a lightning bolt.

And it looks just like Shelly's.

A couple hours later, the questions are still chasing each other through my mind. Did Shelly's mom cut herself before she died? Why? Is Shelly aware of this little detail? How did Shelly get the scar in the first place? Was it something more than just an accident?

I sneak a glance at my friend as we drive to school. She's dreamily looking at the rain slicking down the window. Unlike me, she's been smiling and whistling for the last two days.

There's about a zero percent chance that I'm going to ask her these questions, unless she brings up the subject herself. I may be nosy, but I'm not completely insensitive.

We arrive, and I pull into my assigned parking spot. The rain had subsided briefly, leaving the sky cloudy and gray. But now, the clouds break open again and start dumping buckets of rain on us.

"Race you inside?" Shelly asks me, with an impish smile. Before I can respond, she opens the car door with a squeal and makes a mad dash for the building.

Slowly, I get out of my car. I would wait until the worst of the storm passes, but if I get another tardy, I'll have detention. That would make my life just perfect.

I don't hurry, though. Being drenched can hardly make me feel any worse, and maybe it will ease the questions pounding my brain. I take my time locking the car door. The water runs freely down my face, plastering my clothes to me.

And then, abruptly, the rain stops. Or, at least, the water no longer pelts my face. I glance up and see the underside of an umbrella. Whipping my head around, I look directly into the eyes of Ethan Thorne.

My breath catches. He's wearing his trademark black shirt, and he's close to me, so that he can stand under the umbrella, too, and not get wet. His chest is inches away from my face, and the shirt hugs every contour of his torso.

Warmth travels up my body, and suddenly, I'm overheated in my thin blouse and leopard-print scarf. If he keeps looking at me like that, with his eyes hot and his lips solemn, I might go up in flames.

Without a word, he begins to walk toward the school, and I shuffle forward to stay with him and the shelter of the umbrella. The concrete bites through the thin soles of my shoes, and flecks of rain blow against my already wet skin.

It's not easy for two people to walk underneath an umbrella side by side. Our shoulders keep bumping, and both of us keep straying outside the circular canopy and into the rain. This is so awkward. I wish I weren't lurching around like a giraffe with a broken leg. I wish—

He wraps his arm around my shoulders, and I about die. My heart tries to sprint out of my chest, and my mouth dries. I'm tucked against his body, nestled against the very muscles I was admiring. They look good, but they feel even better, all warm and firm and solid. He smells like Irish Spring, and his hand is on my shoulder, near my hair. I can feel a slight tug on my roots. Is he playing with my hair? Good god, I want him to play with my hair.

Stop it, I order myself. *He's not interested in you. He met another girl at the party on Friday night. For all you know, he kissed her. He's just being courteous now. It's raining. He had an umbrella. End of story.*

But with his arm draped over me like a cozy sweater, and my head practically snuggled against his chest, I can't be logical. I can't listen to reason. It's all I can do to hold myself together.

Too soon, we reach the roof that hangs over the school's entrance. He removes his arm from my shoulders—slowly, reluctantly, or is that my imagination?—and shakes out the umbrella, so that water droplets fly all around us.

We're dry now underneath the ledge, but a foot away, the rain continues to pour down. The pelting against the roof sounds like a drumbeat, underscoring the chaos shooting around inside me. I can hardly see the row of parked cars through the blur of the drops. It makes the moment even more intimate, as if the rain is a sheet separating us from everything else.

I look into his eyes, those gorgeous blue eyes that look even darker today. Stormier, as though they're reflecting the weather.

Silence blooms between us, but it's not empty. It's filled with those eyes, so deep and bottomless. With his warmth that I can still feel. With his lips. They linger above mine, just inches away.

I open my mouth to thank him, to quip something witty about the weather. Hell, to express my approval that he wears these shirts every day. Before I can connect my brain cells to my mouth, however, he nods, touches a finger to my nose, and then disappears into the mob inside the school.

All without saying a word.

Chapter 11

My hands drift to my nose. Did that really happen? Did he actually touch me? The moment was so fast, so transient, I can't tell if I imagined the whole thing.

I rise on my toes, attempting to pick Ethan's muscular back out of the crowd. I can't find him. If he was ever here—and he *was*, I'm not so far gone that I made up the whole encounter—then the people have absorbed him like bees converging on a honeycomb.

No matter. My nose tingles, and I can still feel a delicious, invisible weight on my shoulders. If you put me under a black light, I swear I'd be shining. Imaginary or not, this contact will keep me smiling for the rest of the day.

The warning bell rings, and I realize that the crowd has dissipated. I'd better hurry if I don't want to be late. I round the corner, heading toward my locker, when Walt Peterson materializes in front of me. Deliberately, he steps into my path so that I plow right into him.

So much for my smile.

"If you want a piece of me, just say so," he says. His hands move to my hips, ostensibly steadying me. "You don't have to pretend to bump into me."

"Get your hands off me," I snarl.

He leans in close, so that I can feel his hot breath against my face. "You're a spicy one, aren't you, Kan? No wonder Brad prefers you to your plastic friend, Ash. I'd do you, too."

He backs away, his eyes flickering over my body, a lascivious grin on his face. Heat rushes to my cheeks, and my hands begin to shake. His words make me feel like I need to scour my body with boiling water, but I know it has nothing to do with me or even Ash. He wants payback for Shelly kicking him in the jaw. I should've spit right in his face. I should've kneed him right in the groin. I should've screamed until a teacher came running.

But I didn't. I don't want to get Shelly into trouble. Maybe if we ignore Walt, he'll just go away.

I lean against a locker, breathing hard. When my heartbeat starts to resemble something close to normal, I continue down the hall.

Before long, I glimpse a knot of my friends gathered around Ash. She's model-tall and towers over the rest of the group by several inches, so I clearly see her red-rimmed eyes, the mascara running like ink down her face.

My steps falter. What's going on? Did Walt harass her, too?

We may have had an argument, but I still care about her. Damn it, she's still my friend. I don't want her crying and hurt. I don't want anyone hurt—least of all, this girl who's been on my side since before she knew my squinty eyes were different.

"What happened?" I ask. "Is Ash okay?"

Izzy flips a hot-roller spiral of hair out of her eyes. "As if you didn't know. We only texted you ten million times! Guess you were too busy with your new friend to care."

"I didn't get a single text this weekend." I fish my phone out of my backpack and show them. When I go into the zone, like I did when I was making Shelly's blouse, I banish my phone to a distant corner of the room. Normally, I surface to a gazillion messages, but not this time. I assumed my friends were keeping their distance—and I didn't mind. After what happened Friday, I wasn't quite ready to pretend that everything was fine again.

Lanie takes my phone and scrolls through the messages. "She's right. There's nothing here."

"Let me see that!" Ash comes out of her stupor and grabs the phone. "It wasn't just me, you know. We *all* texted you, multiple times. Are you sure you didn't delete your messages?"

My stomach flips. "Why would I do that?"

"I have no idea, but I needed you this weekend, Kan." Her voice drops, the brashness and bravado disappearing. "I *needed* you."

I soften. I can't help it. I can't look at my old friend, listen to her kitten-like whimpers, and not forgive her. "I'm sorry, Ash. I have no idea what happened to those texts. Is this about Brad?"

"No, it's not about Brad," she says, her face crumpling. "It's my mom. She has cancer. That's why she and my dad have been fighting so much. They've been dealing with her diagnosis and trying to figure out how to proceed."

My throat convulses, trying to draw in a breath. Oh god. Not a disgusting boy, after all, but the *c* word. The disease so nasty it unites us all. The same killer that stole my father.

"Oh, Ash, I'm so, so sorry," I say again. But the words were inadequate when my father's body was lowered into the coffin, the round torso I'd known all my life deflated like a beach ball. Words couldn't bring my father back to me then; they didn't allow him to sneak into the kitchen one last time for his favorite snack, honey-roasted peanuts.

Those same words are inadequate now. But maybe hugs aren't. So I step forward, and I wrap my arms around Ash, and I hold on, as tightly as I can.

"How can you forget about me already, Kan?" Ash mumbles in my ear. "You've known her for five minutes. I told you before: The girl is bad news. We've been friends for fifteen years. I'm your best friend, Kan. Not her."

I spend the rest of the day trailing after Ash, rushing to meet her in between classes, leaving flowers in her locker, buying her favorite foods—salt and vinegar chips and ice cream sandwiches—from the cafeteria.

Shelly rolls her eyes when she sees me juggling my backpack and the overflowing lunch tray. "Seriously, Kan? Do I have to remind you how she turned on you last Friday?"

I bite my lip. "You don't understand. She's hurting right now, and I want to be there for her."

"You were hurting, too. You're hurting now. Did you tell her what Walt did to you this morning? I bet she couldn't care less. I heard her talking about you in class. She was telling the other girls that you think you're all that, now that you've straightened your hair. She's threatened by you, Kan."

I rest the tray on the table, fighting the wave of nausea that's rising in my throat. "She said that?" It doesn't sound like Ash, but maybe she was still upset from last week. Maybe Shelly misheard her. I shake my head, telling myself it doesn't matter. "That's not important right now. Friendship is something you give, not something you trade for."

"It's not even a real cancer, anyhow."

I sink into the seat across from her. "What?"

"Lanie told me Ash's mom has thyroid cancer. Highly treatable, highly curable. She's going to be just fine, but that doesn't stop Ash from milking it for all it's worth."

"That doesn't mean it's not real." I clench the table. "That doesn't mean she's not scared."

"Please." She grabs an apple from my tray, but instead of taking a bite, she kneads it between her hands. "Ash is manipulating you. Can't you see that? She wants you to feel sorry for her, and it's working! Look at you. You're running around without any lunch, all because her mom got diagnosed with a disease that's ninety-seven-percent curable. Most likely, she'll have one little operation, and then she'll be just fine."

"How do you know all this?"

"My mom." Her voice hitches, as though she's near tears, and the lightning bolt wavers back and forth. "She survived her bout with cancer, but that didn't mean she was fine. 'Cause there are other sicknesses more dangerous than cancer. I lost her." She lifts her shiny eyes to me. "I don't want to lose you, too."

I swallow around the lump in my throat. Ash isn't the only girl who's hurting. She's not the only one who needs me. But while Ash has a half dozen friends around her all the time, Shelly has nobody.

She shrugs out of her raincoat, and that's when I notice she's wearing the white wrap-around blouse. Again. For the third day in a row.

She blushes. "It's clean, you know. I wash it out in my sink every night. I don't want you to think I wear dirty clothes."

"Of course I wasn't thinking that!" I exclaim. "I'm just glad you like it."

She smiles. "It's the nicest shirt I've ever owned."

"I'll make you another," I say. "A different color this time. What would you like? Tangerine? Lime green? Sky blue?"

"Oh, gosh. I'd love any color you made me. But honestly, you don't have to do that, Kan."

I look at the salt and vinegar chips, the ice cream that's already starting to melt. I'll have to buy a new set of snacks for Ash. But for now, I can be a good friend to Shelly.

"I want to. But for now . . ." I rip open the bag of chips and offer her one.

"What are you doing?" she asks.

"Having lunch," I say. "Ash is hurting, but you're right. It's not so important that I can't eat. What do you think?" I gesture to the tray. The apple's the healthiest item on our table. "You want to eat some junk food with me?"

She beams, and for a moment, she looks completely beautiful. In spite of the scar. Maybe because of the scar. "I'd love to."

Chapter 12

Shelly and I are nearly inseparable for the rest of the week. We drive to and from school together. We meet up at lunch and sit at our own table, eating identical meals that Khun Yai prepares for us. And, after I work for a few hours at Miss Patsy's studio, we talk and giggle and eat granola bars late into the night.

As I lie in her bed, my cheek snuggled against her pillow, I feel a cocoon weaving around us, protecting me, protecting us from the world outside. From Walt's continued nastiness at school, from Ethan's interest in another girl. Each conversation adds more threads; every laugh pulls those threads more tightly. It's us against the world, and no one—not Khun Yai, not one of my friends at school, not one of the bullying boys—can poke a hole through our shield.

I no longer find Ash after every class. I start escorting her every other class and then twice a day. After a few days, I stop altogether. It's not that I don't care about my friend. I do. But she always has so many people around her—girls willing to drop everything and fetch her lunch, carry her books, surprise her with stuffed animals and balloons—that my efforts begin to feel irrelevant. I'm not sure she even notices me. She sure as hell doesn't need me.

Not like Shelly. *She* laps up and appreciates my every word and gesture. She makes me feel valued, important, needed. She makes me feel the way I used to in the early years of my friendship with Ash.

I still haven't asked her about the matching scar on her mother's cheek. I'm not sure why. Maybe I don't want to upset her. Maybe I'm scared to disrupt our fragile new friendship. It's always on the tip of my tongue, and always, I squash down the words before they can form.

There's no rush, I tell myself. *Maybe, when you become better friends, you won't even have to ask. Maybe she'll tell you herself.*

On Friday, I head to Miss Patsy's, but I'm a lot later than usual. Shelly wanted me to work in the studio over the garage, so that she could hang out with me. When I explained to her why I couldn't—Khun Yai would be suspicious if I stopped going to the dance studio—she was so hurt that I had to get a soda with her at the ice cream parlor in order to reassure her that I still love her, that our friendship still means a lot to me.

Hours passed before I was able to extricate myself, and I didn't even tell her the real reason I wanted to go to Miss Patsy's. Because, well . . . because Ethan is also there every night. Every night, he waits for me to leave, holding the door open for me, sitting in his car until I turn on my ignition and drive away. Every night, he follows me out of the parking lot, flashing his lights twice to say good-bye.

He never actually talks to me, and with each day that passes—each hour, each minute—my skin heats a little more and my nerves vibrate a little faster. Today, I'm determined. If he won't make the first move, then I'll approach him. I'll sidle up to him after one of his classes and make a joke about the little girls' dancing prowess. Hell, I'll even discuss the weather if I have to. *Beautiful day, isn't it?/Oh, yes, not a drop of rain./ I like the rain. Especially when there's a hot guy holding an umbrella over my head.*

I'll talk to him today. I swear it. Otherwise, I'll have to live through the weekend before I get another chance.

When I walk inside the studio, I hear shrieks coming from the classroom. Business as usual. Weaving through a crowd of chatting parents, I stop outside the door. Someone's moved the potted plant, despite Miss Patsy's wishes, and I can see clearly into the room. It's almost the end of class, and they look like they're playing a game. Ethan stands in the center, and the little girls hop around him as though he is their mother hen. Nothing new. And then he pumps his fists in the air and wildly shakes his butt. I raise my eyebrows. Very interesting.

He's telling a story. Two giraffes, a brother and sister named Luca and Lucy, are fighting over the bathroom. Lucy knocks on the door, jumps up and down, and crosses her legs. She has to pee in the worst way, but Luca refuses to come out. He's very busy doing important things, he claims. Such as shaking his butt.

The girls squeal with laughter and surge closer to Ethan. Some of them are mimicking his actions, and the others are begging him to please, please, please do it again. He complies, waggling his eyebrows, adding some theme music as he swings his butt back and forth. "Doo doo doo . . . shaking my butt . . . doo doo doo . . ."

The girls double over, clutching their stomachs, tears rolling down their faces.

I'm grinning, too. I can't help it. He looks ridiculous. Not at all smooth. Not at all suave. With more than a passing resemblance to Donald Duck.

Finally, the story ends.

"All right, girls, that's it for today," Ethan says, and I smile even harder. He's actually breathless from the storytelling. "I'll see you next week."

"Will you tell us another Luca and Lucy story then?" one of the girls asks.

"It's my favorite part of class!" another one chimes in.

"I tell all my friends the stories during recess," boasts Shirley, a redhead with lustrous spiral curls. "Now I'm the most popular girl in school."

This touches him, I can tell. He lays a hand gently on each of their heads. "We'll see. Now you're all *duck, duck*. When I get to *goose*, I want you to run outside where your parents are waiting, okay? Duck, duck, goose!"

The girls aren't prepared. I'm not prepared. As they stumble and dash for the door, I attempt to back away from the door. Not quickly enough.

"Oh! Miss Kan!" Shirley almost plows over me. "Were you watching us the whole time? Don't you just love that story?" she chirps.

Busted. I try to smile, but heavy weights pull down on my lips. Especially because I see Ethan out of the corner of my eye. Listening to every word. Crap, crap, crap.

"Yes, it was wonderful," I say to Shirley. Maybe I'm only imagining the warmth engulfing my cheeks? "I, uh, wanted to see how the dance was coming along. The costumes are almost done."

"I can't wait to see them!" She gives me a big hug and runs to her mom.

For the next few minutes, there's a flurry of activity as the girls peel off tights and the parents locate water bottles. I look for an opportunity to slink away, but several of the moms approach me, to ask about the progress of the recital dresses or to say that little Annabelle really prefers purple to pink—is there any way to change the fabric?

So, I'm still standing in the same spot, inches from the doorjamb, when the last mom-and-daughter pair say good-bye. And when they leave, it's just the two of us. Me . . . and Ethan.

I peek at him, expecting him to be packing up his iPod or practicing his dance moves or, hell, studying for his chemistry test. There must be a million things he could be doing. Instead, he's leaning against the wall, arms crossed. Looking at me.

Damn. My cheeks heat up instantly, like one of those induction cooktops.

"Sorry, I didn't mean to spy on you," I blurt out. He doesn't respond—surprise, surprise—but he pushes off the wall and begins to walk toward me. "I was checking on the girls. Wanted to see how far they've come." He keeps walking. My words keep spewing. "You know they'll want to try on the costumes as soon as they've learned the routine."

He's ten feet away now. Five feet. Dear lord, is he going to walk all the way up to me? "You were telling the story, and I probably should've stopped watching, but I couldn't help it. You were so cute—" I break off, horrified. "Not *you*. I mean, the story was cute." Sweat pops out on my forehead. "I know it was for the kids, but I adore those types of stories. Like Junie B. Jones." He's right in front of me now, inches away. Oh god. I talk even faster. "You wouldn't believe it, but in one of the books, she took a fish stick to school for pet day. . . ."

He puts both hands on my shoulders. "Kan," he says. It's the first time he's said my name. Every single one of my nerves lights up.

"I don't mean to be presumptuous," he continues, "but would you mind if I kissed you right now?"

Chapter 13

My brain short-circuits. "Um—yes—please—if you want—" I manage to stutter.

I must make some sort of sense because he smiles. And then he brushes his lips to mine.

Holy moly macaroni. He's kissing me. He's actually kissing me.

My heart stops. My thoughts go up in smoke. He tastes like cinnamon. Big Red chewing gum. The kind I used to chew as a kid. The flavor of my toothpaste. Oh, geez, I'll never brush my teeth the same way again.

His arms wind around me, and we stagger to the sofa. The one filled with cracker crumbs, the one on which the moms were all sitting just a few minutes ago. We fall onto the couch, kissing. His hands cradle my head, and my arms . . . hang by my side. I need to move them. But where? How?

Hesitantly, I bring my hands to his chest. Nice. Then up to touch his face. Even nicer. His cheeks—so smooth; his ears—so warm; his hair—silky and bristly at the same time.

I'm drowning here. Emotions I've never felt swirl around my stomach, and my skin feels tingly all over, like I'm moments away from exploding. Oh god, I hope I'm doing this right. I hope he feels one-tenth of the tsunami he's creating in me.

One of his hands moves to cup my face, holding me like I'm the most precious thing in the world. The other slides down my back, leaving a trail of lightning and stopping at the inch of bare torso where my shirt has come untucked. I almost come apart. The only way to hold myself together is to pour everything I have into the kiss.

I don't know how long this goes on. A few seconds, an eternity. I'd gladly stay where I am for the rest of the night—the rest of the year—but then, the door rattles, and we spring apart. It's Miss Patsy's husband, who doubles as the janitor, here to mop the floors and pick up any trash the kids left behind.

"Hi, Mr. G.!" Ethan says, his voice a little hoarse. Is that how he always sounds—or is the scratchy quality from kissing me? Honestly, I haven't heard him speak often enough to know.

I don't think I can talk yet, not so soon after this full assault on my senses, so I just lift my fingers and wave hello.

"Hi, kids." Mr. G. looks at us curiously, and I flush. He probably thinks I'm not talking because I'm struggling with the language. When I first started working at Miss Patsy's, he complimented me on my English, like he was a proud grandfather, and I didn't have the heart to explain that I was born and raised in America.

Oh, please. Don't mention my English now, in front of Ethan. Don't ask how I speak it so well, or recommend ESL conversation groups offered through the community college, the ones that Khun Yai takes. I will just die.

But instead of looking at us, sitting in the dark now that the sun has ducked behind the trees, the older man peers at the floors. "Not too bad. You should've seen the mess those little girls left last week."

"They had a quick lesson on picking up after themselves today," Ethan says. How he's doing this is beyond me. I doubt I could string a sentence together, and he's sitting here having a full-blown conversation.

"Thanks, son. I appreciate that." Mr. G. pushes his cart into the bathroom, his keys jangling with every step. Judging from previous nights, we have a good twenty minutes before he comes back out.

Ethan turns to me and grins. "Why are you so far away? Come here." He tugs me over, until my legs are draped over his lap. If possible, I flush even more. I'm not sure what just happened. I don't know what we did or what it means, but I'm pretty sure right here is exactly where I want to be.

He lowers his head and nuzzles my neck. I shiver, and little zips of awareness pop all over my skin. "My name is Ethan," he says.

I giggle. "I guess we've never been properly introduced. I'm Kan."

"I know. It's a beautiful name."

"It's not a beautiful name." I wince. "It sounds like a metal can of food. I've been made fun of for my name my entire life."

He lifts his head and looks right into my eyes. "What is it short for?"

I blink. Other than Shelly, no one's asked me that question for years. My friends don't ask because they've always known it. Everyone else, because they don't bother to think of it. *Kan* is just a weird name for that weird girl from that weird country. End of story. No need to dig any further.

"Kanchana," I whisper, breaking the name into its distinct syllables. Kan-cha-na.

"Like I said. Beautiful. Interesting. Unique. Just like you." His mouth is right there, hovering above mine. I can't resist. Like a magnet, I'm pulled, pulled, pulled into his lips. I feel like I could kiss him forever. I want to kiss him forever.

But I don't even know him. I've waited forever to have a conversation with him. I can't let this moment pass because I'm too distracted by kissing. Right?

I wrench my mouth away, breaking the force fusing us together. It's almost painful.

"Oh my god." He takes a shaky breath and leans his forehead against mine. We stay like that, inhaling and exhaling, and I feel like we're sharing something more intimate than air.

"I've been dreaming about kissing you forever." He pulls back, but he's still close enough that I can count his lashes.

"You have?" I wrinkle my forehead. "Since I straightened my hair?"

He picks up a strand of my hair and lets it slide through his fingers. "Since way before then."

"What about the girl you have a crush on? The one you went to Derek's party to meet?"

His brows rise, and I realize what I've just said. "I was here last Friday, and I, uh, I guess I overheard you talking to your dance partner," I say haltingly and then groan. "Oh, geez, I know how this looks, but I swear to god I'm not stalking you. Much."

He bursts out laughing. "I think it might be the other way around. I went to the party hoping to run into you. All your friends were going. I assumed you would be with them."

"Really?" My veins flow with honey, and I smile so big it might permanently bisect my face. Me! He went to the party to talk to me! "But why did you have to wait for the party? You've had plenty of other chances."

He ducks his head, and I feel his warm breath against my neck. "You're kinda intimidating, you know that?" he asks.

"I am not. I'm the least intimidating person I know."

"No, you are. You're always so focused. When I walk you to your car, your eyes are dreamy, like you're still thinking about your work. I didn't want to interrupt your profound thoughts with something totally boring."

"My eyes were dreamy because I was thinking about you!" I say foolishly. But snuggled in his arms, with him smiling down at me, I don't feel foolish at all. "So you kissed me instead? Very creative. You know what they say. A picture is worth a thousand words. Which would make a kiss . . ."

He catches my lips between his teeth. Minutes later, he lifts his head. "What was that?"

"I think we may have had a lifetime of conversations already," I say weakly.

Chapter 14

We leave. There's nothing else we can do, really, with Mr. G. jangling his keys and rattling his cart. In fact, he seems to be making even more noise than usual, as if to give us adequate warning. Which makes me blush all the way to my toes.

Ethan drives toward the park on the edge of town, the one with picnic tables and a rusty but functional playground. He glances at me across the darkened interior of the car. "If we turn right, we'll be heading to the reservoir. That's where all the kids go to make out."

I swallow hard. "Is that . . . where we're going?"

"What do you want?"

I'm going to be stabbing myself with a needle later. I know I am, but . . . "I want to talk."

He turns left. "Done. Don't get me wrong. I'd like nothing better than getting you in the backseat . . . or the front seat . . . or hell, even the hood of the car would do." He gives me a fake leer, and I giggle. "But I'd like to get to know you, too."

He pulls into a parking space, and we walk to the swings, hand in hand. The playground is deserted, and the air is tinged with the leftover scents of someone's barbecued dinner. The moon hangs above us, a round, white orb to hold the blanket of stars in place.

We sit down on adjacent swings.

"Dare you," he says, the hint of a dimple in his left cheek. My breath catches. I've never noticed his dimple before. I want to reach out, to touch his cheek, but the game is on. "Whoever touches the moon first wins."

It's a ridiculous dare, like one of his Luca and Lucy stories. And just like the stories, it sucks me right in.

"You've got it." I pump my legs, harder and faster. My swing climbs higher and higher. I laugh. The wind flows through my hair, and I feel like a butterfly, riding on the breeze. I can't remember the last time I felt so free.

I'm about to declare myself the winner when he kicks his foot into the sky, his shoe slicing through the middle of the orb.

"I won! I touched the moon." He leaps out of the swing and pumps his fist. I wouldn't be surprised if he started shaking his butt.

"Cheater." I jump onto the ground next to him.

"It's my game; I get to make the rules."

"Does that actually work?" I ask incredulously.

"Not when I was a kid. I never understood why girls didn't fall all over me when I dipped their hair in glue." He tangles his hand in my hair and holds it up to the moonlight. "My plan was to glue tissue-paper flowers to the ends of their braids. It would've been epic. But not a single one let me finish." He shakes his head sadly, and I burst out laughing.

He gestures to the *m*-shaped jungle gym. "Race you to the middle."

We take our positions on opposite sides, and on the count of three, we climb ten feet off the ground to the first crest before lowering ourselves to the valley in the middle. We arrive at approximately the same time, bump noses, and start cracking up. I can't remember the last time my stomach was this achy and glowy at once.

I lie back on the jungle gym, the curve of the structure a perfect cradle for my back. "No boy ever dipped my hair in glue," I say. A few clouds have drifted over the moon, so both the stars and the shining white orb are dimmed.

He mimics my position, but opposite, so that my feet are by his head and vice versa. "They couldn't bear to mess up your hair."

"Nah. They just didn't think of me that way. I was like an alien from outer space."

He nods slowly. "I can see how you would feel that way. How *others* might make you feel that way. But I never thought you looked different. I thought you looked like you. And I like that. More people should look like you."

"They do. Just go to Thailand. They all look like me over there."

"Somehow I doubt that." He grabs my sneaker. I feel the jolt all the way through the canvas. "I doubt that very much."

"How do you deal with it?" I ask suddenly. "You're different, too. The way you dress, the way you act. I mean, you're super talented, but it can't be easy for you, being a ballroom dancer. The guys must give you a hard time." I stop, wondering if I've assumed too much. Projected too many of my own feelings onto him.

He shrugs. "It's not that bad. I've been friends with those guys forever, Walt, Grant, the whole group of them. Doesn't mean they don't think I'm weird. But they give me a pass, mostly because of my mom."

I swallow hard. I know his mom passed away a few years ago in a car accident. We all do. In a town like Foxville, you know everybody's business, even if you've never talked to them.

"She died when I was thirteen," he continues. His voice is perfectly even, perfectly normal, but I take his hand anyway. I know how it feels to lose a parent. I know what it's like to walk around with a gaping hole in your heart.

"Before she died, though, she was the nicest mom in the world. All my friends loved her. She always had cookies for us, and she just listened, you know? Not just to me, but also to Scott, when he got his first girlfriend in the seventh grade. Walt, when he messed up his knee and had to sit out an entire football season.

"She was a ballroom dancer, and she used to give all of us dance lessons. The guys grumbled and complained—but they went along with it. And you know what? I think we all liked it, even Walt. And then she died."

He looks down at our hands, at our interwoven fingers of

dark and light skin. In the dimness of the night, however, I can hardly tell the difference in our skin color.

"Her death . . . was hard on me," he says slowly. "I'm not going to lie. I don't know how I got through the year."

I tighten my grip.

"After she died, I found a note she had written to me." He tilts his head back, back, back until he's looking at the generous dusting of stars. "She told me to find my joy in life. To find the thing I loved more than anything else—and to do it. No matter what anyone else said. That's when I started dancing for real. For hours every day. At first, because it made me feel close to her. And then, because I truly loved it."

I can't breathe. My heart is saturated, and my head is full. It's like he's speaking directly into my soul. "That's how I feel, too, when I'm designing and making my clothes."

"I can tell. When I look into your eyes, what I see there . . . well, it reminds me of my mom."

I blink. And then blink again, because my vision is all of a sudden blurry. "Wow. That's the nicest thing anyone's ever said to me."

He smiles and tugs me forward. I fumble along the bars, and after a bit of rearranging, I'm sitting next to him, shoulder to shoulder and hip to hip.

"That's why the guys leave me alone, even after we drifted. You know, they still bring flowers to her grave every year."

"Even Walt?" I choke. I try to imagine Walt Peterson kneeling by a grave, a bouquet of fresh flowers in his hands, settling down for a talk with the departed. And I just can't. I can only picture him with a nudie magazine in his hands, sneering and making obscene gestures.

"Yeah. He's really not so bad. My mom would say there's a good guy hiding underneath. He's just taking his sweet time being found."

"Could've fooled me," I mutter.

"I'm not defending the guy. I heard what he did to you, and that was a complete asshole move." He pauses. "If he bothers you again, will you let me know?"

"Would you actually do something about it?" I ask, more than a little awed.

"Of course. He has to learn he can't treat girls that way. I'd talk to him or to the authorities, whichever is more appropriate." He picks up my hand, studying my fingers as though he's memorizing the creases across the knuckles. "So, um, the other day, Greta Greenley asked me to prom."

"Really?" I say, struggling to sound casual. "What did you say?"

He slides a sidelong glance at me. "I told her I was interested in someone else, that I was hoping *she* would go to prom with me."

"And, uh, who would that be?"

He smiles, so sweetly it makes my heart painfully sticky. "Kanchana, will you go to prom with me? I promise I won't step on your feet."

"Yes." I lunge at him, almost knocking both of us off the play equipment. "Although I can't promise I won't step on yours."

Chapter 15

I float into my house, my lips curved. It's after midnight. Khun Yai gives me a curfew on school nights, but she pretty much lets me come and go as I please on the weekends. We got into vicious battles about it at first—no good Thai girl would be out so late—but I never get into any trouble, and I don't go anywhere other than Ash's house and the dance studio. So she finally relented my junior year.

The house is dark. Still. If I stop and listen, I might hear the quiet, even breathing of the women most important to me—my mom, Khun Yai, and more and more, my new friend, Shelly. But I don't listen. Instead, I clap a hand over my mouth as giggles threaten to geyser out.

Ethan. Oh my god, that kiss. The way I almost drowned in his embrace. Our conversation at the park. Turns out Ethan is a super nice guy *and* a good kisser. Who knew?

My head bursting with song, I walk into the living room. There's no way I can sleep yet. Might as well watch some television. I flip on the lights.

Shelly's asleep on the couch, an open book on the carpet. The coffee table holds a bowl filled with popcorn balls in every color of the rainbow. Red, orange, green, blue. There are even a few multicolored ones. The bowl wasn't here before. Shelly must've brought it in.

Smiling, I grab an afghan off the back of the couch and tuck it under her chin. I'm about to head to my bedroom when she stirs and sits up. Her eyelids are red and puffy, as though she cried herself to sleep.

"Oh." She blinks at the overhead lights. "I must've crashed while I was waiting for you. I should get to bed."

She stumbles off the couch and begins to lurch toward the door. I grab her arm. "Shelly, wait. Have you been crying? What's wrong?"

She won't look at me. "It's nothing. It's just . . . I thought you would be home a lot earlier."

"I was at Miss Patsy's," I say. "And then . . . I went to the park. With Ethan."

"You don't have to explain yourself to me. I mean, I'm not your mother." She takes a hitching breath. "But I would've told you if I was going to be home late."

"I'm sorry, Shelly." Guilt winds through my veins. She's right. I should've told her.

She flicks her eyes over my body. "What are you wearing?"

"Oh." I hug myself with the long sleeves of the oversized sweatshirt. "I was a little cold on the way home. Ethan let me borrow this."

Her mouth twists into a sneer, and the scar on her cheek seems to gape at me. "Were you really cold? Or did you just want a guy's sweatshirt to wrap around yourself so that you could rub it into the faces of all the single girls?"

"Shelly! What's gotten into you?" I drop my arms. "I'm not trying to rub this in anyone's face. How could you say that? The last thing I was thinking about was you."

She flinches like I slapped her. "Oh god, I'm such a fool. Forget I said anything." Her expression stricken, she starts to walk away again.

I take her arm again. "Let's talk about this. Please."

She stops but doesn't turn around. "Obviously, I was wrong. Now that I know how you really feel, I won't burden you anymore."

"You're not a burden!" If she won't look at me, I'll make her, damn it. I grab her shoulders and spin her around. "Shelly, we're friends. Good friends. You defended me against Walt Peterson. I won't forget that," I say quietly. "You proved from the beginning you would be there for me."

She's facing me, sure, but her eyes are trained on the collar of my shirt. "I even made you popcorn balls."

She gestures to the bowl on the coffee table. "Khun Yai told me a story about how your dad took you to the county fair. How you wanted those brightly colored popcorn balls more than anything. How you took your first bite and thought it tasted just like—"

"Magic," I finish for her, squeezing my eyes shut. "I thought my dad was just like Jack from 'Jack and the Beanstalk,' trading a few coins for a bit of magic. I tossed my last popcorn ball out the window that night, and when I woke up, my dad had planted a bean stalk in that very spot." I open my eyes and focus on Shelly. "I miss him."

"I know. That's why I made the popcorn balls. Because I wanted you to have magic in your life again."

My heart twinges. Shelly's so sweet. As far as I know, I'm her only friend. And I took off with Ethan without giving her a second thought.

"I waited and waited, and finally, I had to admit to myself you weren't coming. I thought you'd gone to that party all the kids at school were talking about. I thought you were hanging out with Ash and Izzy and didn't want me around."

"Oh, Shelly," I say. "That's not it at all. I wouldn't have gone to that party without you, and besides, I doubt Ash is really in the mood for partying. You should've texted me." I fish my phone out of my pocket. I have a couple text messages from Lanie. At least, my phone seems to be working now.

Putting it away, I lick my lips. "Ethan . . . kissed me, and I've never felt anything like it. We went to the park and just talked. It was amazing, Shelly. He really seems to understand me."

"I understand you," she mumbles.

I squeeze her hand. "Yes, you do. But you have to admit, this is different."

"I wouldn't know," she says haltingly. "The only dates I ever have are in my dreams. You know my fantasies of going to Paris one day? Well, I've planned out every detail of my perfect date there, too. Tall white candles, heavy gold-rimmed china, decadent French food. But it doesn't matter what my dreams are. Doesn't mean they'll ever come true. Doesn't mean anyone will ever put me first in their life." She buries her face in her hands, her shoulders shaking.

"Hey. Look at me, please." I nudge her shoulder, and she lifts her tear-stained face. "I messed up tonight. But it won't happen again. No boy is going to come between us. I promised."

She widens her eyes. "You still plan to keep your word?"

"Of course. I don't make promises just for the hell of it, you know."

A smile ghosts across her lips, but I can tell she's still hurt. My heart contracts even more. "I'm here for you, Shelly. How can I prove that?"

"Well, there is one thing. . . ." She glances over her shoulder, although no one else is here. "Never mind. You're going to think it's silly. Forget I said anything."

"I won't. We're friends, right? You can tell me anything, and I won't think you're silly."

She takes a deep breath. "Okay. Fine." The words tumble out. "It's something I've always wanted to do, ever since I was a kid. Problem was, I never had anyone to do it with."

"What is it?"

"I want us to be blood sisters."

A chill creeps up my spine. Blood sisters? As in, my blood mixed with hers? This is unsanitary at best, deadly at worst.

"You hate the idea, don't you?" she moans. "Forget it. I knew it was silly. . . ."

"No, no. You just surprised me, that's all." My mind spins, as I try to think of how to respond. "I don't have anything against the idea, in theory. But you know all that stuff we've heard, about AIDS and other diseases and infections. Maybe I'm just being silly. . . ."

"Hey, it's a valid concern. And I could tell you I'm clean, but you can never be too sure, right?" She wrinkles her forehead. "I've got it! We can do our own modified version. We'll drop our blood onto a clean surface and let the liquid mix there. That way, we've performed the ceremony, but we're still protecting ourselves. What do you think?"

"Um . . ." *NO!* my mind screams. Every cell in my body rebels against the thought. Mixing our blood is just gross. And weird. There's nothing in me that wants any part of this. I rack my brain, searching for a reason, any reason at all that won't offend her.

"Look, I know we only met a couple weeks ago," Shelly says in a small voice, "but I feel this connection with you. Like we were always meant to be friends. This ceremony represents that. You're my sister, through and through."

I take a deep breath. This idea she's suggesting is more than a little creepy. But Shelly's been through such a rough time lately. It's not going to kill me to drop a little blood on a cutting board. If it makes her happy, I should just say yes. It's not that big a deal . . . even if it makes all the hair stand up on my neck.

"Okay, fine," I say, before I can change my mind. "Let's do it."

Chapter 16

A few minutes later, we're in Shelly's room. I haven't been in here since last night, and the tops of the dresser and nightstand are spotless. No scatter of earrings. No BFF necklaces.

My smile wavers. Did she clean off the surfaces because of me? Because I didn't come home when she expected, and she no longer wants to share that part of herself with me?

"I finally had a chance to put my things away," Shelly says with a light laugh. "You must've thought I was such a pig, leaving my stuff everywhere."

I relax my shoulders. Apparently not. Apparently, I'm just reading too much into a simple action.

We raid the kitchen and bathroom and come up with the supplies we need. Small paper plates. A needle. Matches. Alcohol wipes.

Ten times, I open my mouth to tell her I've changed my mind. And ten times, I see the happy smile on her face and close my mouth again.

Suck it up, Kan. It's a few minutes of your life. Just get it over with, and you can forget it ever happened.

We arrange everything on her bed, and with practiced movements, Shelly lights a match and sterilizes the needle. She then pushes two of the paper plates, a packet of alcohol wipes, and the sterilized needle toward me.

"Prick your finger, and let some blood drop onto both plates," she says. "This way, we can have before and after specimens. Our blood, before and after it's combined."

She presses the needle into her pointer finger and in quick succession, drops the blood onto two of the plates. She smiles, pleased. "Your turn."

"Okeydokey." I inhale deeply through my nose. I know I agreed to this. I know this ceremony is important to her. But right now, all I want is to be tucked in my bed, dreaming about Ethan.

I grit my teeth. The sooner I stab my finger, the sooner I can make that happen.

I run the alcohol wipe over my pointer finger and pick up the needle. Ew, this is so gross. I can't stand blood.

"You can do it," Shelly says. Even in the dim light of the room, I can see her eyes shining. "It's like a flu shot. One prick, and then you're done."

I nod, but my fingers shake. Sweat dots my upper brow, and the room slowly begins to spin. I put the needle down. "Do we really have to do this? Maybe we can just say we did. That's almost as good, right?"

She pats my shoulder. "Listen, Kan, when I said I understood you, I wasn't kidding. I really do. Give me your hand."

I curl them into fists. "Why?"

"I'm going to do it for you. Don't be scared. Just close your eyes, and I'll take care of it. We'll be done before you know it."

"Do you know how?"

"It's not open-heart surgery, Kan. Gimme." She waggles her fingers at me.

Taking a deep breath, I put my hand into her palm and close my eyes. It's just a little blood. *Prick.* This is the girl who kicked a boy to defend your honor. *Squeeze.* She's asking for so little in return. *More squeezing.* You can do this. You can do anything for a little while. *Even more squeezing. Holy hell. How long does it take to get out two drops of blood?*

"Finished," she finally says. "You can open your eyes now."

"How many samples were you making? A hundred?"

"I wanted to be sure we had sufficient before and after images. Here, take a look." She presents me with the plate with our two drops of blood commingled, as proud as a new mom.

I stare. A bright red blot is shaped like a squished-together dumbbell. With two blobby ends. Two bodies. Two heads. It's like we just created a strange new creature, one that's made up of half her and half me.

That doesn't make me proud. Not one little bit. Instead, it makes the chill crawl up my back, one long spider leg at a time.

Chapter 17

Shortly after the blood ceremony, Kan mumbled something about the late hour and retreated to her room. Clearly freaked. Shelly didn't mind. She had everything she needed from her new blood sister—and then some.

She waited until she heard the shower running and then snuck into Kan's room and swiped her phone. It was a simple enough matter. She had been doing it every night. She took the phone out of curiosity, as part of an education that had started years ago. What on earth did people say to one another? How did they sound so natural and relaxed? How was it possible to be spontaneous and yet so witty at the same time?

She had never had a friend. Not really. Not a true one where she could let down her guard and be herself. Not a best friend whose menstrual cycle lined up with hers. That was when you knew you were really close. That was when you knew the two of you could be sisters.

She and her mom had moved around a lot when she was a kid, and at first, that's what she had blamed. She never stayed in place long enough to make lasting relationships. But then later, as the moves stretched farther apart and she remained friendless, she had to admit that wasn't the problem.

Maybe the problem was her. Her grotesque face, with her jagged blemish. She was the only common denominator, after all. Although she'd observed plenty of friendships and had learned to fake it over the years, she didn't get it—the spark that bonded two people, the germ of connection that turned an acquaintance into something more.

She stood on the outside, and her classmates' glee made a wall so thick there was no way she could penetrate it. So, she pretended to laugh. Did her best to be one of them. But she always suspected that deep down, they knew. With their matching clothes and their mascaraed lashes, with their high-pitched giggles and confident tosses of the hair, they saw right through her façade to the fraud she was underneath.

How could they not? In an aquarium full of guppies, with their swishing tails and brightly colored scales, she was the plain, gray one, whose deformed body was bent at a right angle.

It was even worse digitally. She read their little jokes when she snooped on social media, the sarcastic remarks, the profuse displays of affection. She scrolled through Kan's text messages and read as far back as the history would allow. She read and read and read, until her eyes dried and she had to switch her contacts for glasses, and then she propped Kan's phone up on her knees and read some more.

She studied the quick, back-and-forth conversations, taking them apart as though she were studying for a test. There was nothing she couldn't learn, and this social *thing*—having friends, being popular, knowing how to make people laugh—was just another subject for her to master. And this time, she was determined to get it right.

She'd made a mistake with the last girl. She'd been so excited about their friendship, so hopeful. The girl had been so kind and understanding.

In retrospect, Shelly had to admit, the relationship was doomed from the beginning. There were red flags she should've seen. It was like their friendship was a wet clump of sand, and for a while, she was able to hold it close to her chest. For a while, it was the most tangible relationship she'd ever had. But then, the sand began to dry out, and clumps began to slip through her fingers. As much as she tried, she couldn't hold on any longer.

She learned, then, she couldn't wait for the sand to dry before she took action. She had to mold the friendship right from the beginning.

And so, a few days ago, she had pressed the DELETE button on Kan's texts. Tapping it once had given her a rush of power. Tapping it twice made her feel like she was, at long last, a player. By the time she'd deleted all of the messages, she felt something she hadn't felt since Sheila Ambrose's death. Something that had been sorely missing from her life these last few months.

She felt like herself again.

After the blood sister ritual, when she got back to the safety of her room, she unlocked Kan's phone with a simple triangular swipe over the numbers. Really, that girl had a lot to learn about security—and inputting her code into the phone where others could see her. A new text popped up. It was a message from Ethan.

I miss you already.

Her fingers hovered over the screen. She could almost believe he was talking to her. He didn't use any names, after all. And the message had arrived when the phone was in her hands. Besides, she missed him, too. She didn't know Ethan, to be sure, but she missed having someone like him in her life. She missed having a first kiss. Hell, a first smile or a first conversation would do.

It wasn't fair. Kan and the others—they took these milestones for granted. Whereas for Shelly, having a boy's interest would be a once-in-a-lifetime miracle.

Without warning, tears soaked her eyes, and she gasped for air as if her lungs had sprung a leak. Just as quickly, she wiped the wetness away and forced her breathing to become steady. She hadn't cried over Sheila Ambrose's death, and she wasn't going to cry now.

Kan was going to be her new best friend. She shouldn't mind if Shelly took a few blades of pleasure for herself, when she had a whole freaking lawn of it. There wasn't a limited supply of text messages, after all, and Shelly was certain that if Kan knew, she would be more than happy to give her new blood sister this experience.

That settled, Shelly leaned back against her pillows and began to text Ethan back.

Chapter 18

Needles jab me everywhere, poking, prodding, pricking. In my cheeks, down my back, along my legs. Like a thousand acupuncture needles, but worse. Because these needles aren't designed to relieve pain—but to draw blood.

Fountains of blood spurt from the millions of tiny holes all over my body. Splattering the white walls. Pooling on the white tile. Drenching the white sheets.

Drowning me.

I gasp and choke, clawing at the blood, trying to push it away. But there's too much liquid, too much wetness. I can't see, I can't breathe, I can't—

I jerk awake. Sweat pours down my face, and the drenched sheets tangle about my legs. Panting, I look around my bedroom, from the brightly colored scarves draped over my desk chair to the hand-painted wooden bangles on my dresser.

A dream. It was only a dream. Blood's not gushing out of me. Shelly only pricked me once, on the finger. The nightmare has nothing to do with our bloodletting ritual last night.

Or does it?

Shivering, I lie back in my bed and pull the comforter over my shoulders. I feel . . . unsettled. I shouldn't have agreed to the ceremony. It may be harmless kid stuff, but it also creates another bond between Shelly and me, one that feels too intimate. Too soon.

Ash's words echo in my head. *How can you forget about me already, Kan? You've known her for five minutes. We've been friends for fifteen years.*

Time makes no difference in a true friendship. I know that. But now . . . I'm not so sure. I don't really know anything about Shelly. I didn't know about her fixation with blood, for example. I didn't know she would get so upset because I forgot to call.

I drift back to sleep, and the next thing I know, the sun is streaming across my body. Oh no. I slept through my alarm. What time is it? I grab my phone from my nightstand, but the battery's dead.

That's weird. I always plug in my cell to charge before I go to sleep. But I couldn't find it after my shower, and I was so exhausted I just fell into bed. If my phone was missing, though, how did it end up here, back on my nightstand?

Frowning, I sit up and pull my hair into a ponytail. Is it possible that Shelly had something to do with my phone? First, the texts from my friends go missing; now, this. Tendrils of unease curl around my stomach as I think about our blood-mixing ceremony last night. That girl is definitely . . . strange. Normally, I don't like that description. Because *I'm* strange—I've been strange all my life—I know that. And yet, something about Shelly isn't sitting right with me.

I glance at the clock again. Great. Now, I'm *really* late for my weekly egg-roll-wrapping date with Khun Yai.

Every Friday night, Khun Yai mixes together a filling made from ground beef, shredded cabbage, vermicelli noodles, fish sauce, powdered garlic, and black pepper. And every Saturday morning, at eight a.m. sharp, she and I wrap the filling in egg roll skins. She then deep-fries them in vegetable oil and takes them to her ESL teachers at the community college.

"You don't have to bring a gift every single time," Mae has told her more than once. "They work for the college. They get paid."

"They don't get paid very much," Khun Yai would shoot back.

"Besides, they're teachers. They deserve our highest esteem and respect."

When I burst into the kitchen, Khun Yai is already at the table, scooping a bit of the meat and cabbage mixture onto the middle of the egg roll skin, her wrinkled hands moving deftly. I'm not surprised. Khun Yai's not the kind of person to wait for anyone.

But she's not alone.

Shelly sits across the table from her, in *my* seat. Her hair is pulled back from her face, the scar on full display. She dips her fingers into a bowl of beaten eggs and then runs them along the diamond-shaped edge of the egg roll skin to create the adhesive. That's my responsibility.

My eyes fly to the clock above the stove: 8:36. I'm thirty-six minutes late. A travesty, through Khun Yai's bifocal spectacles. Doesn't mean she has to give away my job.

"What are you doing?" I ask Shelly, fighting to keep my tone neutral even as part of me wants to shove her out of my chair.

"Oh, Shelly is helping me wrap egg rolls," Khun Yai says in English, since Shelly is present. "Like a good granddaughter."

There's something in the air, something . . . strained about her words, and it's not just the switch in language. Khun Yai is hiding something. Is she mad at me for being late? Nah. I've been late before, and she's never minded. Is it the issue she has with Shelly? Clearly not, or Shelly wouldn't be sitting here, wrapping egg rolls.

"You decide not to help me this morning?" Khun Yai continues.

I flush. "Of course not. I would never skip out on this. I look forward to it all week. I love your stories—" I break off. As part of our ritual, Khun Yai tells me stories about her childhood. Stories about how she helped her mom at the dessert shop. About how Khun Ta fell in love with her and skipped lunch so that he could spend all of his *baht* on tapioca balls and coconut cream.

But I don't say any of these things. Shelly's eyes are a little too wide. She's leaning forward a little too much. Listening a little too hard.

And for some reason, I don't want to share these stories with Shelly. They're my bond with Khun Yai, not hers. She's already co-opted my egg-roll-wrapping session. I'm not going to give her this part of Khun Yai, too.

"My alarm didn't go off," I finish weakly.

"I thought I heard your alarm this morning." Shelly begins to seal another egg roll, but she glops on too much egg batter and the skin sticks to the plate. "But then the ringing stopped, so I assumed you turned it off." She shrugs apologetically. "I didn't check because I thought you needed your beauty sleep. I mean, since you had such a late night and everything."

"Your night was just as late." I stare at the Band-Aid on her finger.

"Yes, but I'm not as pretty as you. So I need less sleep." She smiles, but I'm in no mood for her woe-is-me act.

"Well, I'm here now. So you can get out of my seat." Maybe it's the dream. Maybe it's just my regret for participating in that silly ritual. But for the first time since we've met, my tone is harsh.

"Kanchana, you are rude." Khun Yai stands and brings the metal mixing bowl to the sink. "We are finished. There is nothing for you to do."

I look at the egg rolls piled high on the silver platter. Some are fatter than the others, and the diamond fold is off-center on almost every one. "Do you want me to rewrap these, Khun Yai? You always yell at me when I don't wrap them tightly enough. . . ."

"Very rude. Shelly is doing a good job, for her first time," she says grudgingly, as though it pains her to admit it.

Any other day, I would've been proud of her for putting her prejudices aside and trying to embrace a white girl. Not today.

"There are bubbles under the skin," I say. "They won't fry properly. Ever since I was five years old, you've taught me—"

"Enough." Khun Yai covers the platter with plastic wrap, and I know the subject is closed. "I need to talk to you. Where were you last night?"

"What . . . what do you mean?" I stutter.

"It is a simple question. Even my English is good enough that I cannot mess that up."

"I told you. I was at Miss Patsy's."

She looks at me over the top of the bifocals. "After the dance studio. You came home past midnight."

I dart an angry look at Shelly, who shakes her head in return.

"No, do not look at Shelly. I have ears. I know when my own granddaughter is arriving home. You may not have a curfew, but that is because you said I could trust you. Do not make me lose my trust, Kanchana."

"Fine." I blow a breath up through my hair. "I was at the playground. At the park."

"You were with . . . whom? A boy?"

I cross my arms and uncross them. I look at the peeling wallpaper with its baskets of fruit, the light blue tile that clashes horribly with our yellow refrigerator. I really don't want to answer her question. She's not going to like it, and I'm not going to like her not liking it.

But lying isn't an option, either. Not if I want any kind of a future with Ethan.

"Yes. A boy," I say slowly. "His name is Ethan, and he helps Miss Patsy teach dance classes."

She puts her hands on her hips. "It is not proper for you to be seen at night with a boy."

"We were on the swings, for god's sake! Not making out in his car."

She doesn't blink at me taking the lord's name in vain. Good thing we're Buddhist.

"What if someone saw you driving to the park?"

"Someone?" I shake my head. This is an old argument, but that doesn't mean we won't keep repeating it. "Who, exactly, are you talking about?"

"It does not matter who. It is not proper."

"Khun Yai, you barely know anyone who lives in Foxville! Why do you care what they think?"

"It is not a matter of knowing them. It is a matter of what is right."

Shelly watches us, fascinated. She's breathing quickly, taking in our drama as though we were characters on a TV show. I'd snap at her, but Khun Yai would get even more upset. A proper Thai girl, I am not.

But neither is Shelly, I want to shout.

"Fine." I relax my shoulders. All of our arguments end this way, with me acquiescing. "I won't ride around with him in the dark anymore. Satisfied?"

"No, I am not." Khun Yai smooths a hand over her bun. Back in Thailand, she went to the hairdresser twice a week. Here, she does her hair herself—with the occasional help from me to dye the parts she can't reach—which means it's never as smooth as she likes. "If my granddaughter is running around with a boy, I want to meet him. You will invite him here for dinner tomorrow night."

"I can't do that," I sputter. "They don't do that here. You don't bring a guy home until he's your boyfriend. And Ethan's not my boyfriend." At least not yet.

"He better not be your boyfriend. No boyfriends until college, remember?"

I drop my eyes. "Yes."

"But if you spend time with him, I need to know he is a good boy, from a good family. Invite him to dinner tomorrow. I will make him real Thai food. We will see what kind of boy he is."

"But Khun Yai—"

"This is not a request, *luk lak*. Invite him, or you will quit your job at Miss Patsy's."

"All right, geez." I roll my eyes to the ceiling. No good Thai girl would act this way, but none of us are under any illusions about what I am and what I'm not.

I stomp out of the kitchen, and Shelly creeps out after me. When we're halfway down the hall, I whirl around. "What do you want? Haven't you caused enough trouble?"

She recoils, and guilt snakes through me. I take a deep breath and then another. The thing is, Shelly hasn't done anything wrong. It's Khun Yai I'm upset with, for holding me to these impossibly high standards. And me. For not being the kind of girl she can unconditionally love.

"Ethan seems like a nice guy," Shelly ventures. "Just explain it to him. I'm sure he'll be happy to come here for dinner. Khun Yai's food is terrific."

"It's embarrassing. Whatever . . . this . . . is, it just started. I can't sic my weirdo family on him before he even decides if he really likes me!"

"If he's truly the right person for you, he won't think your family's weird," she says quietly. "I don't."

I sigh. She's right. If Ethan and I are to have a future, he'll have to meet my family sooner or later. I just didn't realize it would be this soon.

That's when I see Shelly's blouse. I can't believe I didn't notice earlier. Must be because I was so distraught about the egg rolls. It's a flowy, emerald green number, with cutouts along the shoulders—Ash's birthday present to me last year.

I swallow, but the silly lump won't go down. I did say she could borrow anything in my closet. Only, that was before she bought her own things. And I never wear that shirt to wrap egg rolls. "Is that my shirt?"

She flushes. "Oh. I, uh, didn't think you'd mind. All my clothes are in the wash, and you have so many."

I blow out a breath. Shelly is my friend. My blood sister. I offered her my clothes. She hand-washed the shirt I made her in the sink, so that she could wear it three days in a row. I'm overreacting. It's just a shirt. I don't care if Shelly wears it. I don't.

"It's just . . ." How did she get it out of my room without me knowing, anyhow? "Next time, just ask, okay?"

She nods, her eyes open as far as they'll go. "Of course, Kan. Anything you say."

Chapter 19

My cell phone lies on my desk, mocking me. It is rectangular, slim, and encased in bling-bling gems. I want to hurl it as hard as I can across the room.

Instead, I sweep it up and press the cool surface against my forehead. I have to call Ethan. There's no way around it. Tomorrow is Sunday, and I won't see him at Miss Patsy's before then. I really don't want to call him on the dreaded *next day*, the day after we kissed for the first time. I might as well tattoo on my forehead: *Eager, much?*

But I have no choice. So I tap in the phone number he gave me. He answers on the first ring.

"I was just thinking about you," he says, his voice low and warm.

"You were?" I gape at the phone. A few seconds later, I regain my senses and plunge ahead. "Now listen, before you say anything, I want you to know I'm not stalking you. I have a reason for calling you, really I do."

"You don't need a reason for calling me, Kanchana," he says. "In fact, I was about to call you myself."

"Really? You're not just saying that?"

He pauses, and I flush, thankful we're not on a video call. "You *are* just saying that!"

"All right, I am. But not because I didn't want to. I . . . um, had fun last night." His voice dips low into my stomach.

"Me, too." I smile my words and wonder if he can hear it.

"I had fun kissing you. And I, uh, had fun later, too. When we were telling each other bedtime stories."

I'm still smiling—how can I not smile when I'm talking to Ethan?—but my lips curve one degree less. Did we tell each other bedtime stories? We talked about our pasts at the playground, but I wouldn't have called our conversation "bedtime stories."

No matter. I've got more pressing concerns. I take a deep breath. "I have a favor to ask. It's a little strange, so feel free to say no." I squeeze my eyes shut. "My grandmother wants you to come over for dinner. Tomorrow night."

He pauses for a moment. "Okay."

My eyes fly open. "Okay? Aren't you going to say it's a little early? I mean, we're not even dating yet, and we only kissed last night."

"Well, it's true we only kissed last night. But I was hoping we were dating."

Oh. My. God. This boy. I don't think my lips have ever gotten this big a workout. "You mean it?"

"Absolutely. And if your mom or grandma wants to meet me, I'm happy to have dinner with them."

I shake my head. It can't possibly be this easy. "One more thing. My grandmother can't know we're dating. We're just friends from the dance studio."

"Friends?" He rolls the word in his mouth suspiciously, like it might be poisonous.

"Yeah. You know, friends who go to the park together. And swing under the stars. And climb the jungle gym, and—"

"Kiss under the moonlight?"

I pinch my arm. Nope, I'm definitely not dreaming. "Yeah. That kind of friend."

"That, I can live with," he says.

One day later, I'm pretty sure if I'm living any kind of a dream, it's a bona fide, wake-up-screaming nightmare.

Khun Yai insists on serving *miang kum* for an appetizer. Now, I love *miang kum*. It consists of taking a green leaf called a *chaplu,* which Khun Yai grows herself in our garden, and filling it with a variety of chopped ingredients, such as lime (with the peel on), shredded coconut, roasted peanuts, dried shrimp, ginger, onion, and chili pepper. The mixture is topped with a tamarind and cane sugar jam, and the entire leaf is popped into your mouth for a delicious, sweet-and-savory bite.

But just because I like it doesn't mean my friends do. In fact, the first time Khun Yai served this dish to Ash, she whispered to me that it smelled like dead cat.

"Please," I had begged Khun Yai after Ash left. "Don't serve this stuff. My friends want nachos and pizza and chicken wings."

She had wrinkled her brow. "But that is, how you say, trash food. And I know why they call it trash food. Because that's where it belongs. Why wouldn't your friends want good, authentic Thai food? It isn't easy to find, you know."

I sighed. "They just don't, Khun Yai. Why don't you make my friends your egg rolls? They'll like that, I promise."

"Fine," Khun Yai humphed. But that's what she served my friends from then on, and that's what they loved. So much that her egg rolls became famous in Foxville, and my mom was constantly asked if Khun Yai would cater retirement parties and birthday celebrations around town.

I wanted her to make egg rolls for Ethan. I hoped and prayed she would make egg rolls for Ethan. But no such luck. An hour before he is due to arrive, the scent of tamarind jam perfumes our house.

"What's that smell?" Shelly asks, sniffing the air.

I drop my head into my hands. "Don't ask. And don't say it smells like a dead cat, either."

"Oh, I don't think it smells bad," she says. "Just different."

What she doesn't know is that I've been different all my life.

Being with Ethan is showing me that difference is not necessarily a bad thing. And yet . . . I'm not quite sure I'm ready to embrace it, either.

Chapter 20

Shelly is in the kitchen helping Khun Yai, playing the part of the dutiful granddaughter. I can't help but notice the awkwardness between them. Khun Yai is perfectly kind and courteous but there's something forced about her words.

A pause that's an instant too long, movements that are a little too stiff. But whatever's going on, I don't have time to dwell on it. Especially since Ethan is coming in fifteen minutes, and I still haven't changed out of my yoga pants.

I fly into my room. I want to look nice, but at the same time, I need to stay casual, since it's only dinner at home.

I'll pair my tight black jeans, the ones with the coated sheen, with an off-the-shoulder turquoise blouse I made last fall. Perfect. Khun Yai doesn't love the shirt, but I can make sure it stays on my shoulders, not baring too much skin during dinner.

As for Mae? Not only will she not comment, she won't even be here to notice.

My hands slow as I fumble through my clothes. Mae got called to the hospital half an hour ago, and Khun Yai was not pleased.

"You want me not to go to work because some boy is coming to dinner?" I'd heard my mom ask incredulously through the paper-thin walls.

"It's not just some boy," Khun Yai said. "It's the boy Kanchana likes. Shouldn't you make sure he's a proper young man?"

"Kanchana is a very responsible girl. I trust her to choose appropriate company."

"She needs parental oversight."

"And you're doing such a good job of it." There had been a pause, as though my mom was leaning over and kissing Khun Yai on the cheek. "You always have. I don't know where we would be without you."

"I wonder if I've made a mistake, coming to stay with you," Khun Yai said slowly. "It's allowed you to ignore your own child in favor of your work. If I weren't here, maybe you would pay her a little more attention."

"Oh, Mae. You know this is what we Thai mothers do. We have *Yais* so that the *Maes* can work. Where do you think Kanchana would be if I didn't have a job? Did you ever think of that?"

"I don't fault you, *luk lak*." The Thai endearment rolls off Khun Yai's tongue. She calls me that all the time. I don't think my mother has said it to me once. "I'd just like you to spend more time with your daughter, that's all."

"You spend time with her, Mae. You give her plenty of love. It's the same thing."

"It's not the same, and you know it," Khun Yai said. "Nothing can ever replace a mother's love."

Their voices faded away then, or maybe I'd just fled, no longer wanting to listen.

Remembering their words now, my hands fist around a pair of blue jeans. I know my mom loves me—in her own way. But I also know that when my dad died, she threw herself into her job, working such long and hard hours that she didn't have time for anything else. Not for me, not for her grief. Certainly not for herself.

That doesn't mean I don't wake up sometimes and hear her sob in the night. That doesn't mean we don't sit across from each other at breakfast, the silence so heavy it seasons our bowls of *jok* as surely as the fish sauce or the thin strips of ginger.

I take a deep breath and release it slowly. I put on the black jeans and my turquoise shirt and look for my hairbrush. It's not on the dresser. Shelly must've borrowed it.

I dash across the hall and into the bathroom we share. The brush isn't on the sink or in the first two drawers I yank open. Sighing, I get on my knees and open the cabinet under the sink. I pick through rolls of toilet paper, extra bottles of shampoo, and a container of cotton buds. And then, my hands close around a calendar. That's weird. I never keep paper calendars anymore. My life is practically stored on my phone.

I flip the calendar to the correct month. Bright red dots mark the squares of today's and yesterday's dates. I wonder if Shelly is keeping track of her menstruation cycle.

Coincidentally, I also started my period yesterday. Could Shelly and I already be on the same cycle? Nah. She just moved in a couple weeks ago. I would think an alignment between our cycles would take a few months at least.

Then, I notice an asterisk with a scribbled note underneath the red dot. I squint and can barely make out: *Tampon wrapper in trash.*

My breath explodes out of my chest. Wait—what? Did I read that correctly? Is it possible Shelly rifled through the trash can, looking for my tampon wrapper? Dear god, why? Are these notations on the calendar keeping track not of her own period . . . but mine?

No way. No freaking way.

I push the calendar to the back of the cabinet and slam the door closed, stumbling from the bathroom. I . . . need . . . to get out. Need . . . to get away. Need . . . to get . . . air.

But even after I'm back in my room, even after I finally get my breathing under control, I still don't know what to think.

I take that back. I know exactly what to think. It's not just my imagination. I'm not jumping to conclusions. Something is definitely not right with Shelly.

And I'm not sure I want to be her friend anymore.

Chapter 21

"And your parents? What do they do?" Khun Yai asks twenty minutes later. She's been relentless in her questions ever since Ethan rang the doorbell with a bouquet of spring flowers.

Ethan winks at me and assembles another *miang kum* wrap from the platter on the coffee table. He adds every ingredient that Khun Yai set out—including the dried shrimp and the chili pepper and the raw ginger. If Khun Yai notices, however, it doesn't ease the arms crossed tightly over her chest.

"My dad's a plumber. And my mom used to teach dance before she passed away," he says, popping the leaf bundle into his mouth.

"Oh." She blinks. Her elbows drop onto the couch, and for the first time since he's entered our living room, she relaxes her spine. "He is a single father?"

"Yeah. I keep hoping he'll find someone, but it hasn't happened yet."

"How do you manage?" she asks, her voice gentle now. "Who does the cooking?"

"I do. Five nights a week, anyhow. We usually get takeout on the weekends." He assembles another *miang kum* and gives her a winning smile. "You'll have to give me the recipe for this. My dad would love it."

Khun Yai is staring now, her mouth partially open. I hide my snicker. She isn't often caught off guard. After a moment, she pushes off the couch, mumbling something about turning the chicken drumsticks in the oven.

I look up to see Shelly smiling at me, one of the secret, knowing grins we've exchanged in the past couple weeks. The ones I imagined I would share with a sister or anyone else who had an intimate understanding of my family. But I can't bring myself to smile back. Not when she's stealing my clothes. Not when she's rifling through my trash.

Ethan turns to us and holds out a leaf. "Girls? May I make you a *miang kum?*"

Damn. Even his pronunciation is correct. I swallow my frustration with Shelly and focus my attention on Ethan. If I wasn't in like before, I believe I am now. Who would have thought? Me, falling in like with a blond, blue-eyed boy over a plump green *chaplu* leaf. Wild.

Later, I walk him to his car, and my heart feels like it's going to burst out of my chest. The evening couldn't have gone any better. After Khun Yai relaxed, she actually seemed to have a good time getting to know Ethan better. Hell, even I got to know him better. I learned some new facts about him—his favorite subject in school is physics, and he used to play soccer before devoting himself to dance. More importantly, I learned about the way he talked to Khun Yai with genuine respect. I learned about the sincere interest he showed when he asked about her life in Thailand.

"Be careful what you do, because I'm pretty sure Khun Yai is watching us right now," I murmur to Ethan.

"How about a dance lesson? Surely she can't object to that?" He takes my hand and spins me around in a slow circle. I'm a terrible dancer, always have been, but I'm able to turn without tripping over my feet, and I end up right in front of him, pressed against his chest, his eyes and nose and mouth inches from mine.

I swallow hard. There's a lot for Khun Yai to object to. Letting a boy touch me outside on our front lawn, where—god forbid—any neighbor might peek out and see, for example. But his eyes look into mine. The warmth radiates from his chest. His cinnamon-gum scent wraps around me. And I just can't say no.

I nod, wordlessly, and he eases us apart. He trails the pads of his fingers up my arm until he catches onto my hand. He places his other hand on my shoulder blade, and I forget how to breathe. There's just something so intimate about the way he's holding me. His fingers don't move, and yet, I feel like he's caressing me. There's no other word for it.

"This is called the closed dance position, and I'm going to teach you the basic salsa step," he says. "It's an eight-count, where you pause on the four and the eight. Fast, fast, slow. Step back on one, then step in place with your other foot on two. Step forward on three, and then pause. Repeat with the opposite feet. Here, I'll show you. Just follow my lead."

He moves forward, pushing against my palm, and then pulls me back with a slight pressure against my shoulder blade. His grip is at once firm and gentle, commanding and . . . hot. With his little touches guiding me, I fall into the dance. My steps may not be exactly right, but they feel good. They feel really good.

"Look into my eyes," he murmurs. I am perfectly helpless to look anywhere else. "Sway your hips. Follow the natural rhythm of the dance."

The fire burns in me, beginning in my stomach and radiating out to engulf every limb, every cell. Even my fingertips feel hot. I don't know why Khun Yai isn't out here, putting an end to this inferno, but if she's decided to trust me for once, I'm glad.

We dance for what seems like forever, and then Ethan breaks away from me, panting. "I know I'm supposed to be all competent and professional, but keeping my hands where they belong? It's killing me."

My heart thunders, and my blood sings. I want with everything in my being to close the gap between us, but I can't. The curtain in front of the kitchen window doesn't twitch, but that doesn't mean Khun Yai isn't inside, watching.

He moves back, putting a comfortable but electric foot of

space between us. "Right now, Friday night." He groans. "You sure know how to torture a guy, don't you? I don't know how much more I can take."

I lay my fingers on his arm, even though I know it's dangerous to touch him. I may spontaneously combust. "What are you talking about? I didn't torture you Friday night. I don't know about you, but that was the best time I've ever had at a playground."

"I'm not talking about the playground." He steps closer again, and my skin sizzles in response. "I'm talking about later. When we were texting."

I freeze. We didn't text after the playground. Am I missing something, or did we have a conversation that I just can't remember?

"I don't remember texting you at all," I say carefully.

His forehead creases. A long moment passes, and then the lines disappear. "Oh, right. We're not supposed to talk about it. I forgot."

"No." I grip his wrist. "I'm not kidding around. I really don't know what you're talking about."

He rakes his gaze over my eyes, my nose, my mouth, searching, searching, searching. I want to give him the right answer. Problem is, I don't know what the question is.

"What's going on here, Kan?" he asks softly. "Are you . . . ashamed of what we did?"

Heat floods my face. I can't see myself, but I'm pretty sure the color's gone beyond red. Inexplicably, I feel . . . dirty.

"No, I'm not ashamed," I say between gritted teeth. "Because we haven't done anything. I never texted you. Give me your phone. Show me what you're talking about."

He looks at me for a long time, and then he sighs, leans over, and brushes a kiss across my cheek. "You're right. I must've made a mistake. We didn't text."

"Ethan—"

He cuts me off by putting a finger to my lips. "I had a nice time tonight. Can't we just leave it at that? Thank you for inviting me to dinner."

I shake my head. My brain is about to explode. I don't understand what just happened. I want to keep talking about the subject, but I don't know what else to say. I can't *make* him turn his phone over to me. Not when our relationship is so new. Is he confused? Delusional? Was he texting with someone else? Greta Greenley, perhaps, or maybe a former girlfriend?

A dark, insidious thought creeps into my head. Maybe it's not a former girlfriend at all. Maybe it's a person much closer to me than that. My phone was missing. Texts appearing, disappearing. Someone's been messing with my phone. Not just someone—Shelly.

The ramifications of my conclusion make me weak in the knees. But I can't shake the feeling that I'm right. It's got to be her. Nothing else makes sense.

"Will I see you tomorrow?" he asks.

"I hope so," I say weakly. I can't voice my suspicions to Ethan, not yet. Not until I know for sure. "We're, uh, still dating, aren't we?"

In response, he replaces his finger with his lips, in a kiss that's soft enough to be poignant, but not so long it would give Khun Yai a heart attack. "You go back in the house first," he says.

Turning, I trudge up the driveway and into the house, my head still spinning. When I walk into my bedroom, I drift to the window. Maybe if I see him one last time, this confusion will lift like the fog. Maybe he'll look up and catch me watching. Maybe he'll smile and wink, and the unease slithering through my stomach will disappear.

He's still standing by the car, where I left him. And then he turns toward my window, and my hand shoots into the air. Before I can wave, however, another figure comes tripping down the driveway. Shelly.

She runs toward him and jumps, expecting him to catch her. He does, at the last moment, fumbling as though she's taken him by surprise.

I duck before she can see me, not that she's looking, and crack open the window so that I can hear.

"Hi, Shelly," Ethan says, setting her on the ground. He tries with difficulty to untangle her arms from his neck. She is like an octopus, though, and her fingers go back as soon as he dislodges them.

"Thanks for catching me." She laughs girlishly and shakes her hair, so that it covers her cheek. "I always wanted to try that, and I know you're used to catching girls in your dance routines."

"Right." Finally, he succeeds in taking her hands from his neck. "Well, I'm happy to be of service."

"Oh, I'm sure you service the girls really well."

Oh my god, did she actually say that? My ears burn, and I feel like my head is going to blow off. In what world is that appropriate?

Ethan clears his throat, obviously uncomfortable. "Well, I'd better get going. Good to see you." He smiles, and I know he's doing it to be nice. I know he's trying to be kind. Problem is, he's got those all-American good looks and those intense blue eyes. No matter what he says, anything remotely friendly also comes out kinda . . . melty.

"You, too, Ethan. You, too," Shelly says, more than a little dreamily. It takes all of my strength not to march out there and slap her.

Clearly, she's a little infatuated with him. I don't blame her. I mean, he's the whole package—sweet, gentlemanly, hot. But I don't really care what kind of crush she has on him. She'd better stay the hell away.

We both watch as Ethan gets into the car, sticks the key in the ignition, and puts the car in reverse. With one last smile, he backs out and drives away. And I watch her watching his car turn into a tiny speck in the distance.

As though he is her boyfriend. And not mine.

Chapter 22

I go straight to bed. It's close enough to bedtime that Khun Yai won't question it, and I don't want to see anyone. Least of all Shelly.

I don't sleep, though. I can't. Picking up my phone, I scroll through my text messages again. There's nothing, of course. If Shelly used my phone, then she hid her tracks well. If she did text Ethan, however—and I'm pretty sure she did—what could she have said? What could have "tortured" him and ranked right up there with our kiss?

My mind darts in a million directions, each one making me blush more than the last. Dear god. I can't . . . she wouldn't . . .

I take a deep breath. No. I have to get a grip. I don't even know if that's what happened. No use in letting my imagination run away.

Sighing, I throw off the bed covers and tiptoe into the kitchen. It's late, and the house is quiet. I pour myself a glass of water, but as soon as the cool liquid hits my lips, my stomach growls. Guess I was so nervous during dinner I didn't eat much. I rummage in the fridge, looking for leftovers, when suddenly, I hear low voices. I'm not the only one awake. Spotting a light coming from the den, I creep over, a chicken drumstick in my hands.

It's my mom and Khun Yai, speaking in hushed voices.

"She knows," Mae says.

"She doesn't know," Khun Yai says sharply. "She couldn't even begin to guess."

"No, she will. She's on the right track. All it will take is for her to find one more clue, one more puzzle piece, and everything will fall into place."

"We've kept this a secret for seventeen years. The truth won't come out now. I won't let it."

There is silence. I can't see them through the closed door, but I can imagine my mother twisting her fingers together, over and over, as though they are the strings of a friendship bracelet.

"I hope you're right." Mae sighs. "I can't imagine how she'll look at me if she finds out. . . ."

A floorboard creaks as if one of them is moving toward the door. I hurry back to the kitchen. I've only taken a bite out of the chicken, but I've lost my appetite.

What can this mean? I must be the *she* in their conversation. There's no one else it could be. So, what is my mother hiding from me, not just now, but for the last seventeen years? Does it have to do with Shelly? It's got to be about Shelly. Nothing else has disrupted our lives recently. But what?

Neither the cold chicken nor the humming refrigerator nor the dark kitchen has any answers.

As I lie under my covers, conspiracy theories assault my brain from every direction. So far, I suspect Shelly, my mom, and Khun Yai of nefarious intentions. Who's next? Miss Patsy, from the dance studio? Shirley, of the red braids and freckles?

I drag myself to the studio above the garage and take my sewing machine out of the closet. I need a distraction—anything will do. My mind's too frazzled for something as complex as a shirt, but I can handle lining a fabric square. Something bright and cheerful that would make a nice scarf against the plain backdrop of a wrap-around shirt.

A gift. The breath leaks out of my lungs, and my thoughts stop bouncing all over the place. Yes, that's what this will be. A gift for Shelly.

Not because I'm in the mood to give her a present. God no. I almost want to take back the shirt I already made her. In fact, I'm already fantasizing about sneaking it out of her closet. I mean, she "borrows" my clothes. It's only right that I "borrow" hers. Right?

I want to make her a scarf for an entirely different reason. The last time I gave her a gift, she opened up to me. So, this scarf might be just the thing I need to find out more about her intentions. So, it's more like a trick. Or . . . a trap.

I throw myself into the project, pouring every bit of anger and confusion and suspicion into the scarf, until it is the most precisely lined piece of fabric that ever existed.

When I finish, my thoughts are only slightly less jumbled, but at least I have a scarf to show for it.

I go back into the house and walk down the hall, once again on tiptoe. The sun's not yet up, but Shelly's in the kitchen, eating breakfast. Perfect timing. I'll give her the scarf, and maybe she'll drop her guard. Maybe she'll still be drowsy enough that she'll confess everything.

It's not much of a plan, but it's the best I've got.

I sneak down the hallway toward the kitchen, thinking I'll surprise her. When I get closer, however, I hear a noise. No, not just a noise. Moaning.

I freeze. What? Is somebody else in the kitchen?

I shift closer. The chandelier shines a bright light over the table. Shelly is definitely alone. She's eating an orange. No, not eating it. Her mouth is moving against it, her lips flared against the rough skin. Oh dear god, she's not eating it—she's kissing it. The way Ash and I used to practice kissing when we were kids.

I move closer, and finally, I can make out the words she's muttering: "Oh, Ethan. Kiss me some more. That's it, big boy. Oh yes. Yesssss."

Chapter 23

Half an hour later, I'm waiting for my mother outside the master bath in her bedroom. It's the crack of dawn, and she's showering. This is the time she always leaves for work.

"Something's not right with Shelly," I blurt out, as soon as Mae steps out of the bathroom, fully dressed. "She's . . . really creeping me out. You have to ask her to leave."

Mae walks to the vanity and begins to apply her makeup. "I know it's hard to have another girl living here all of a sudden, Kan. But give it a little time. She'll settle into our routine, and you two will get used to each other soon enough."

I take a deep breath and let it out slowly. My thoughts tumble over each other as I try to figure out how to translate my unease into words. "This isn't about growing pains or roommate differences. She's . . . weird. She has a crush on Ethan, and she's acting super inappropriately around him. She's stealing my clothes. And, um, she's been keeping track of my period." Briefly, I tell my mother about the calendar and the notation I found.

Mae raises her eyebrows. "That sounds a little far-fetched. Maybe you're misinterpreting the situation."

"How could I misinterpret it? It was written there, in black and white. 'Tampon wrapper in trash.' "

"But it didn't mention your name, did it?"

I stare. Why is Mae being so defensive? Why is she so determined to take Shelly's side?

"No," I finally admit.

She recaps her mascara and then twists her hand to look at her watch. "Go easy on her, will you? The poor girl just lost her mother a couple months ago. You would act strangely, too. In fact, you did." She picks up an eyebrow brush, making a face at the mirror. "When we lost your father, you disappeared into your books so deeply, I wasn't sure we would ever be able to drag you out."

"That was different. I withdrew from the world. I didn't go around stealing people's phones."

The brush shakes in her hand. "Do you have any proof of that?"

"Well, no." I duck my head. "I just have my suspicions."

"I hear you, Kan. I really do. But you haven't given me anything definite. And I'm not going to kick Shelly out over some vague discomfort you might have. I owe her mom too much for that."

I frown. "What do you mean? I thought it was the other way around. That *she* owed *you* because you saved her life."

Mae puts on powder, her throat moving with every pat. "It's a long story," she finally says. "I don't want to get into it, but let's just say I might've had partial responsibility for things turning out the way they did." She leans over and tucks a strand of my hair behind my ear. "Tell you what. When you have a concrete reason why Shelly shouldn't be living with us, come back to me, okay? And then we'll decide what to do."

She kisses the air by my cheek and is about to walk out the door when I stop her. "Wait, Mae. How exactly did Shelly contact you?"

"I told you. She just showed up at the office one day. I'd stayed in touch with her mom over the years, and Shelly must've found the address among Sheila's things." Mae shrugs. "She said I was her last resort."

"Why did you decide to let her stay with us?"

"What kind of question is that? I couldn't throw the girl out on the street, Kanchana. Besides, like I said, I owe her mom."

I search her face. The tense eyebrows, the pink cheeks. I can't see her eyes because she's bent over her briefcase, fiddling with the combination.

"Are you sure?" I ask.

For a long moment, the only noise is the *click-click-click* of the lock. And then my mom looks up. "I'm sure."

Finally, I can see her eyes. But they no longer reassure me the way they did when I was a little girl and she was the only thing that stood between me and the monsters underneath my bed. Her eyes no longer look like they belong to a confident woman who is always in control.

Instead, they look scared.

For the next few days, I avoid Shelly. I don't have any other choice, really, since my mom refuses to budge about letting her stay. It's not easy, given that we live in the same house. But I pretend I need to be at school early so that I can help the drama club with their costumes, and I stay late at Miss Patsy's.

I just don't know what to say to her. How to act. This girl rifles through my trash looking for tampon wrappers. Play-acts kissing Ethan with an orange. I just can't look her in the eye and ask her to pass the fish sauce.

So I don't. I keep my head down and mumble greetings, and if Shelly notices anything is amiss, she doesn't comment.

I also change the password of my cell phone and start sleeping with it under my pillow. I'm usually careless about my phone, flinging it in a random corner and then forgetting about it, but these days, it's glued to my hands. Paranoid, much? Maybe. But at least, no more strange incidents occur with my texts.

On Thursday, I slam my locker shut, dislodging a flyer that's been stuck to the outside advertising the spring carnival, and catch a glimpse of Ethan. At least, I think it's Ethan. No one else at school has his slim, muscular build—and yet, he's not wearing his signature black shirt. Instead, he has on our school T-shirt, the one that's bright orange and has a fox on it, for god's sake.

"Ethan?" I call. "Is that you?"

He turns, and it's him, all right. His face and hair look the same as always, all slick and suave, and the contrast against the school T-shirt is even more bizarre.

"What on earth are you wearing?" I ask.

"It's my new look." He grins, spreading out his arms. "Do you like it?" His tone is casual and deliberately light. And I want to keep it that way.

We seem to have taken two giant steps backward since our dinner on Sunday night. We're talking, at least, but his thoughts are as opaque to me as they were before we kissed. Our conversations are stiff and unnatural. Neither of us so much as mentions texting, and we sure as hell haven't kissed again or even had another dance lesson.

I want to tell him my suspicions about Shelly. In fact, I'm dying to confide in someone other than my mom. But all of my friends are preoccupied with Ash's grief, and I'm waiting for Ethan's and my relationship to get on stronger ground.

"You look good in everything," I respond. Oh god. Was that too forward? What's wrong with me? "Seriously, though," I rush on. "Why are you wearing that?"

The smile falls from his face. "It's the weirdest thing. After gym class, my shirt was just gone. I'm sure I left it on the bench. I don't know if I dropped it, or if one of the guys is playing a trick on me. . . ."

My stomach lurches. It must be because of me. Ethan's never been harassed before. Walt and those guys are his old friends. They used to eat cookies at Ethan's house and take dance lessons from his mom, for god's sake.

"Walt's punishing you for dating me," I say in a low voice.

"What? Come on. That's not it. Are you talking about the incident with the magazine? He's got to be over that by now."

I shake my head. Walt still bumps into me at least once a day. At least once a day, he still says something gross and disgusting as he walks away. I haven't mentioned any of these instances to Ethan. I know he asked me to tell him if Walt bothered me again . . . but our relationship doesn't need the additional strain. Besides, it's nothing I can't handle myself.

"He cares because Shelly kicked him in the chin, and he associates her with me," I say instead. "I've never been friendly with Walt, but now, he sees me as the enemy."

"Listen, I'm sure that's not it at all. Maybe one of the guys in my gym class just has a crush on me." He waggles his eyebrows mock suggestively. "Maybe he just wants me to walk around school without a shirt."

Despite myself, I laugh. "Well, I can see how that would be tempting. . . ."

He leans forward and touches my cheek. I freeze. This has been happening all week. In spite of our awkwardness, he touches me—at odd moments, in unexpected places. The inside of my elbow when he passes me at school. The small of my back when he comes up behind me at Miss Patsy's. These touches are like the sporadic working bulbs in a string of faulty holiday lights. They sustain my hope that one day we can get back to that brilliant spark we had that night on the swings.

"Seriously, I wouldn't worry about it," he says. "I don't care if I have to wear my gym shirt around for the rest of the day. Besides, I'm not sure there's enough school spirit. . . ." He looks at the streamers crisscrossing the ceiling and the balloons taped to every row of lockers. The school's annual spring carnival is taking place this weekend, and the hallways are bleeding orange and black.

I raise my eyebrows. "You think?"

"Maybe you could wear a school T-shirt the rest of the day, too," he says hopefully.

"I like you, Ethan," I say, grinning. "But not a chance."

Chapter 24

Shelly liked to poke around in places where she didn't belong. She liked to snoop through other people's things. Liked to see who was smoking pot, who had condoms and secret notes in their purses. She liked to scroll through cell phones whose owners were careless enough to leave unlocked. She liked having secrets about people, because she'd learned a long time ago that secrets meant power. Secrets meant you had control over another person. You could make them do whatever you wanted.

After the week she'd just had, when Kan more or less stopped talking to her, when everything she had been working toward had begun to slip through her fingers, she could use a little control again.

It had been unwise to text Ethan. She should've known that Kan would find out. Shelly was all but certain that was why her new friend was giving her the cold shoulder. But she wanted to give Kan some distance, an opportunity to cool down, before she approached her again.

For a week now, she had been roaming the school during her fourth period study hall. It didn't take long for her to learn that her teacher took attendance and then dozed off for the rest of class. A bomb could go off in the middle of the room, and he wouldn't notice. So, Shelly took to slipping to the bathroom a couple minutes after class began—and never returning.

She liked the locker rooms best. They were devoid of the orange and black decorations that covered every inch of the school's walls. Besides, the girls' locker room always had a ton of juicy finds. Why, just the other day, she'd found a key to the school's concession stand and made a copy for herself. You never knew when such things might come in handy. The boys' locker room was riskier but had even higher payoffs.

Such as this morning.

One of Ethan's shirts was lying right on the bench. She hadn't realized he had gym class this period, but she would've recognized the shirt anywhere—a tight black knit with silver stripes along the pocket.

She'd swept the shirt off the bench and brought it to her nose. It smelled just like him, like cinnamon and sweat and . . . just plain Ethan.

She had to have the shirt. It probably wasn't smart—just like texting him wasn't smart. She normally didn't take anything—the concession stand key, for example, she had copied and put back—because it would just alert people to her presence. But she couldn't help herself. She'd spent so much of her life yearning. Wanting what all the other girls had. Just once, she wanted a shirt that belonged to a boy. A shirt she could wear over her shoulders. One she could smell at night before she went to sleep.

If she couldn't have Ethan himself, the least she deserved was his shirt. Right?

This would be the first step toward wrenching back control. There would be another, more definitive action.

But for now, she was pleased with her find. Without another thought, she'd walked out of the boys' locker room, the black shirt with the silver stripes clutched to her chest.

Chapter 25

I don't see Shelly for the rest of the day or the next morning. Either I'm getting really good at avoiding her—or she's steering clear of me, too. It's now Friday, though, which means the weekend is approaching. We'll have to face each other sometime.

After the last bell, I hear footsteps flying around the corner. I look up, expecting to see Shelly. Instead, it's Lanie, who comes to a halt right in front of my locker.

"How did you get over here so fast?" she pants.

I'm stuffing pink tulle in my sewing bag, as I'm heading straight to Miss Patsy's. "What are you talking about? I came from my seventh period class in the next wing, like I always do."

"I saw you headed to the basketball stadium," she says, her face tight. "Sneaking into the concession stand with Walt Peterson, of all people."

With an effort, she relaxes her jaw. I can tell she's trying not to yell or call me a traitor. But the stiffness of her tone says it all.

"It was someone else," I say. "I haven't been near the athletic field the entire day. And Walt Peterson's the last person I'd go anywhere with."

She peers at me from beneath her straight-cut bangs. "You're right," she says finally. "I don't know why I thought it was you. Maybe I'm just tired. Worried about Ash. She's not eating again. Had two bites of an apple at lunch and said she was full. The last thing she needs is for one of her friends to hook up with the guy who's made her life hell."

I freeze. I didn't know either of those things: that Ash hasn't been eating and that Walt's been harassing her, too. I've been hiding out in an empty classroom during lunch all week, catching up on my sewing. The gang would've welcomed me back at our regular table, I'm sure. I just didn't want to risk running into Shelly.

Damn it. I'm a lousy friend. I was so caught up in my own drama I forgot to think of anyone else.

I close my locker door, making a mental note to bring Ash some egg rolls tomorrow. Even when she was trying to fit into a homecoming dress two sizes too small, she's never been able to resist Khun Yai's egg rolls. "I would never do that."

"I know. None of us would. We're friends till the end." She gives me a sidelong glance. "Speaking of boys, though, I've been hearing rumors about you and a certain ballroom dancer. True or false?"

I blush. "True."

"And his kisses, on a scale of one to ten?"

I glance around the hallway. Student council members are already beginning to set up for the spring carnival tomorrow, ripping down the streamers and flyers and replacing them with oversized arrows and placards with names of the carnival games.

Ash, Izzy, Lanie, and I have been rating smooches ever since the sixth grade, when Ash had her first kiss with Tyler Beckham. I've contributed three ratings, all derived from parties at someone's house: Lance, 4 (tongue flicking in and out like a lizard); Austin, 6 (bonus points for enthusiasm, negative points for braces); and Monty, 8 (the first time I understood why someone might actually enjoy kissing).

I'm probably past the point of sharing—and definitely beyond the point of rating—but what the hell. For old times' sake, and besides, I'm not actually confiding anything personal. "Eleven," I whisper.

She shrieks and spins me around in a little dance. I laugh as we trip over a few of the streamers that have fallen to the floor. And remember exactly why I've been friends with these girls for so long.

After a euphoric minute or two, Lanie runs off to her cheer-leading practice, and I continue down the hall and out of the building. The crowd's thinning now, although a handful of students are rushing about, intent looks on their faces and carnival supplies in their hands. When I walk toward the parking lot, however, Ash herself crosses right in front of me, her head high and her stride long.

"Hey, Ash," I say. "You'll never guess what Lanie said. . . ."

But she doesn't slow down, and she doesn't stop walking. In fact, she keeps going as though she doesn't see me at all.

My steps falter, but only for a moment. Did Ash just give me the cold shoulder? Nah. Sure, I haven't been as present in her life lately, but we did exchange a few texts the other night. She started out depressed about her mom, but pretty soon we were LOLing about celebrity fashion faux pas.

"Ash, wait!" I call, running after her. She hears me, I know it. But if anything, she starts to walk faster.

What the hell? Ash wouldn't run from me. First of all, we've been friends too long, the incident with Walt notwithstanding. And second, she's not six years old.

I break into a jog and catch up to her. "Hold up, Ash! Why are you in such a hurry?"

She wheels around, her eyes so hard they could shatter glass. "How could you, Kan? Did you know that asshole's been telling the whole school that Brad prefers you over me because I'm a terrible lay?"

My mouth goes dry. "Are you talking about Walt? I haven't gone near him."

"Don't play dumb with me," she says fiercely. "I know you were in a lip lock with that disgusting pig. Come on. You're like a sister to me. How could you betray me like that? It's just gross."

"I didn't do anything," I say, my voice faint. A sense of déjà vu floats over me. I've had this conversation before, with Ethan, just a few days earlier. Once again, I'm accused of doing something I know nothing about.

"Don't." Her face is a mask of hatred and rage. Even the tears in her eyes seem to freeze. "I saw you, Kan. I. SAW. YOU."

Before I can say anything else, she spins on her heel and sprints away.

"Ash, wait. Wait! I promise I don't know what you're talking about. I promise this is all a big misunderstanding. . . ."

But she's out of earshot within moments, and a few seconds after that, she ducks behind the annexed buildings and disappears. I could run after her. But then what? Tackle her and sit on her until she hears me out?

People are beginning to stare. A group of girls from my physics class. The boys' soccer team. Underclassmen I don't know.

I sink onto the sidewalk, my sewing bag spilling tutus and ribbons onto the concrete. What just happened? First Lanie mistook somebody else for me, now Ash. What's going on? Is my ghostly twin walking around? Do my friends need to get their eyes checked? Or am I blanking out and losing whole swatches of time?

Despite the sun beating down on my shoulders, I shiver. Rows of ants seem to march up my arms, leaving a trail of goosebumps in their wake. I don't know how long I sit there, cold and trembling, and then a shadow falls over me.

I look up. And go perfectly still.

It's Shelly. Wearing my electric silver leggings and my plum-colored flannel shirt tied at her waist. A thousand silver bangles clink at her wrists. But that's not all.

Her hair has been dyed black. Straight, straight, straight as a board. A waterfall of silk from her scalp to her shoulders.

Chapter 26

My heart stops, hanging in the air between beats. Ash and Lanie are right, after all. There really are two of me.

She has my hair. She's wearing my clothes. Our builds are similar enough that at a glance, she could be me.

My jaw drops, but nothing comes out. No words, at least. Nauseated, I slap a hand over my mouth. Is this some kind of sick joke?

"There you are!" Shelly exclaims, oblivious to my distress. "I've been looking for you everywhere. You would think we didn't live in the same house. I've been dying to show you my new hair."

She twirls around, and her hair flies into the air in a slow circle. Just like mine does.

The acid climbs up my esophagus.

"Well?" she demands. "What do you think? Khun Yai gave me the name of your salon. Of course, it didn't take them eight hours to straighten my hair, the way yours did. I guess my chemical bonds just aren't as stubborn."

"You, uh, dyed your hair, too." I gulp the air.

She beams. "I've always dreamed of having black hair, ever since I was a little girl. So when the stylist suggested it, I thought, why not? I have a new life now. A new family. Might as well have a new look to match."

She is so excited, so earnest. It just makes my rage flame higher.

"Your hair looks just like mine. From the back, we could be twins," I bite out. I pull my vibrating hands through my hair, wishing I could still the shaking in my heart as easily.

Her lips tremble. "Are you mad?"

Yes. I want to rip your goddamn head off. But that's not going to get me the proof I need to convince Mae to get rid of you.

I roll my shoulders and try to relax. "It's not like I own this hairstyle. I'm just . . . surprised, that's all."

"I'm sorry," she whispers. "I thought you would be pleased. I admire you so much. You know what they say. Imitation is the sincerest form of flattery."

Once upon a time, I might've fallen for the innocent, injured act. Not anymore.

And then, I catch a glimpse of her eyes. And what she did to them. Moving closer, I grab her chin and tilt her face toward the sunlight.

"You have on makeup," I say flatly.

"Oh, yes. Didn't you say I should wear more makeup? I put a bunch of concealer and foundation on my scar. Looks better, don't you think?"

It's less noticeable, at least, although she can't cover the jagged edges and discoloration altogether. "I never thought your scar looked bad," I say. "But that's not what I'm talking about. It's your eyes. You look . . . Asian."

Shelly's eye makeup is not your typical soft brown applied above the lash. Instead, her eyeliner is dramatic and black, and she's extended the line past the corners, flipping it at the end to form a perfect cat's eye. The makeup changes the shape of her eyes. Making them appear tapered at the corners. When they're not. Making her look Asian. When she's not.

The prickles are back full force, and this time, I don't feel like it's a line of ants marching up my skin. I feel the entire battalion.

"Don't you see, Shelly?" I ask, trying to stay calm, trying to explain it to her. "People are mistaking you for me."

"Are they?" She laughs delightedly. "That's wonderful. That's the best compliment I've ever received."

"It's not wonderful, and it's not a compliment," I snap. "Ash is so mad she won't even talk to me. And why are you making out with Walt Peterson? I thought you couldn't stand the guy."

Her smile turns sly. "I did it for you, Kan."

"What are you talking about? What does you kissing Walt have to do with me? He's been nothing but nasty to me since you kicked him in the jaw."

"Exactly." She lifts her chin. Her tone is cool now. Controlled. "Someone had to teach him a lesson, and since you were too scared, I did it for you."

A faint alarm begins ringing inside me. "What did you do, Shelly?"

She checks her watch and smiles. "It's just about time." She inclines her head toward the basketball gymnasium across from the school, the motion long and elegant. "Come along and see for yourself."

Reluctantly, I fall into step beside her, and we cross the parking lot to the athletic field. Clumps of students are beginning to cluster in anticipation of the upcoming game. A bus from the opposing school is parked at the lower end of the lot, and the tall, overhead lights have switched on. I accept a pennant from someone dressed as our school's mascot, a wily orange fox, even though the last thing I feel like is cheering. Each crunch of the gravel seems to settle at the bottom of my stomach.

Whatever Shelly's done, it can't be good.

"You'd think he'd know not to trust someone like me," she says conversationally as we pass Lanie and the entire cheerleading squad practicing a pyramid formation on the lawn. "I assaulted him, for god's sake. What other warning does he need? But boys only think with their dicks. All I had to do was press my breasts against his arm and tell him I wanted to make it up to him, and he would've followed me anywhere. When I took him into the concession stand, I flashed him my thong, and he couldn't take his clothes off fast enough."

The ringing inside me turns into a full-fledged siren. I grip Shelly's arm. "What did you do to him?"

She shakes off my hand as though it were a stray hair. "Oh,

you don't have to worry, dear Kan. My virtue is perfectly intact. I didn't have to compromise my morals."

She stops in front of the concession stand. Rolling counter shutters seal off the front, and the side door is locked with an enormous padlock. Even as we watch, however, a girl with a ponytail threaded through her visor approaches the stand and wrestles with the lock.

"Perfect timing," Shelly murmurs.

Perfect for what? I don't have long to wait. The visored girl dispenses with the lock. The door flies open, and a very flustered and very naked Walt Peterson bursts out.

I gape. His face is red, and his bare, hairy chest and belly jiggle as he turns first left and then right. An empty Twizzlers box is clamped firmly over his private parts.

He spots us and snarls, advancing a few threatening steps. But a knot of students forms almost instantaneously around us. Excited buzzing fills the air, and cell phone cameras flash on top of one another like lightning in a summer storm.

Walt freezes. With one last growl in our direction, he turns and takes off toward the parking lot, his butt cheeks winking with every step.

Laughter ricochets in the air. The cell phones continue to flash, memorializing what will be the most shared photo on social media tonight.

I stumble away from the concession stand and put my hands on my knees, gasping for air. Shelly follows me, looking smug. Her breathing is hardly ruffled, but no matter. I'm gulping enough air for both of us.

"Shelly, this is bad," I wheeze. "Really bad. This isn't teaching him a lesson. It's sexual harassment."

"It's no worse than what he did to you," she says, her eyes sparkling with rage or delight. Maybe both. "Don't worry. I'm not going to get in trouble. No one else knows it was me, and Walt's certainly not going to admit it."

"It's not just about whether you get in trouble." I want to shake her to make her understand. "You took his clothes, Shelly. You exposed him to all those cameras. He'll be completely humiliated, not only by the people here, but everyone online, too. Don't you see? He won't be able to live this down. It will stay on the Internet forever."

Instead of sobering her, my words make her eyes glow brighter. "Exactly as I said. I did this for you, Kan. All of this—for you."

Chapter 27

Shelly twirled in front of the full-length mirror in her bedroom, looking at herself from every angle. Her hair spun out like a veil, as though she were in a shampoo commercial, before it settled back against her cheek, hiding her scar. Never in her life did she think she could look like this. Her hair was no longer stringy and straggly. No longer blond, no longer brown, boring, mousy, and dowdy. No longer the color of straw forgotten in the sun, of dirt on the trampled ground.

Now, her hair was black. Jet black, so black it punched a hole through the white walls. So dark it sucked everything else into its core. She felt mysterious, wonderful . . . and exotic.

She knew Kan didn't like being called *exotic*. Kan thought this meant she was other; she thought it meant she was different. But that feeling was the luxury of someone who hadn't been ignored her entire life.

Kan didn't know what it was like to be invisible. To be plain, average, and unnoticed. Sure, Kan said she felt ugly as a kid. She felt the boys didn't even consider her to be a girl. They thought she was an alien from another planet.

But that was then, and this was now. The second their hormones kicked in, she got plenty of attention. Some of it may have been unwanted, like the boys with their nudie magazine, but in Shelly's eyes, some attention—any attention—was better than none.

She thought back to that afternoon, to Walt's hairy chest, his jiggling butt, and the strategically placed Twizzlers box. She pressed a hand to her mouth, giggling. Shocked whispers had rippled through the athletic field. Students had shrieked gleefully, their eyes Blow Pop round. And afterward, they couldn't get to their social media fast enough, to share their hastily snapped photos. All because of her.

You couldn't say she didn't have power now.

But that wasn't even the best part of the afternoon. The best part was when the two of them walked away from the concession stand, and one of the cheerleaders had called, "Kan!" Simultaneously, they had both wheeled around, and the girl had done a second, and then a third take. Her eyes bounced between Kan and Shelly, as if she was caught off guard by the similarities. As if she couldn't tell which was the real Kan.

Kan hadn't liked that, Shelly could tell. She had turned pale, and a muscle had throbbed at her temple. Shelly wanted to remember that image forever. Because when Kan turned pale, they looked even more like twins.

Shelly dug into her newly purchased bag, with the brand new makeup. All paid for by the checks that were coming from Khun Yai. Oh, the old lady probably felt so relieved when Sheila Ambrose died. She probably thought her deep, dark secret had died with Sheila. Ha. Think again. The payments weren't going to stop just because Sheila Ambrose was dead. Not if Shelly had anything to do about it.

She dotted concealer over the scar and then covered it with half a bottle of foundation. In the dim light, you could hardly see the blemish anymore. At most, it looked like a shadow over her cheek.

She found the thick black eyeliner. Leaning closer to the mirror, she drew a line on her eyelid, extending it past her lashes. There. Now her eyes looked just like Kan's.

She examined herself in the mirror. There was no doubt about it. She looked half-Asian, at the very least. She and Kan looked like sisters. She looked like she belonged in the family.

She put on the outfit she'd taken from Kan's closet earlier that day. The black skirt was pleated and flared, but it wasn't short enough. Shelly rolled the waistband two times. Better. The white tank was more of a camisole—a "layering piece," Kan had called it. The only thing Shelly would layer on top was a long silver link chain.

Blowing her reflection a kiss, she grabbed Khun Yai's car keys—keys the old lady was only too happy to hand over after being threatened with the alternative. She walked through the silent house. It was nearly midnight. Kan was probably in her bedroom, sleeping. She certainly wasn't hiding under the covers, sending naughty text messages to her boyfriend.

That was Shelly's job.

She got into the car. Following the directions she'd memorized, she drove to the next town and pulled up in front of a well-lit house. Rock music pulsed off the walls, people spilled off the porch, and red plastic cups littered the lawn. A frat party. One she had learned about by eavesdropping on the college girls at the grocery store.

For a moment, she sat frozen, her hands clutching the steering wheel at two o'clock and eleven o'clock. She could hear the sixth grade boys jeering, see the spittle that formed at the tips of their tongues. *You're too ugly to live. Please die now.*

Please. Please. Please. Not the words of a bully, but a simple request from society.

She flipped down the sun visor and looked at herself in the mirror. She wasn't that girl anymore. She wasn't.

Three deep stomach-breaths later, she got out of the car and stalked up the sidewalk, swaying her hips. A kid was sprawled across her path, throwing up in the grass. His pants rode low on his hips, and she could see the top of his plaid boxer shorts. She placed a spiked heel in the middle of his back and vaulted over him.

"Hello, beautiful. Where have you been all my life?" a guy said as she sashayed up to the porch. He had curly brown hair brushing his eyebrows and was wearing faded jeans and a dark

T-shirt. If she squinted, he might be able to pass for Ethan's brother. Or at least, a distant cousin. Good enough.

She shook her hair so that it fell over her cheek and tugged at the hem of her tank. Like magic, the guy's eyes drifted to her cleavage. Damn. Who knew it would be this easy?

"Hi," she said in her most seductive voice, looking up at him through her eyelashes. "My name is Kan."

Chapter 28

I don't know what to do. I'm not sure where to go. The image of Walt's naked butt is imprinted in my brain, and the last thing I want is to be under the same roof as the girl who caused his humiliation. This incident with Walt should tip my mom over the edge—but it's my word against Shelly's, and I'm afraid that the story alone won't be enough. It's not the concrete proof that my mom wants.

It's weird. Shelly seems to have this hold over my mom—and even Khun Yai. I have no idea what, but I'll bet anything it's got to do with this secret they've been keeping for seventeen years.

At a loss, I told Khun Yai I was staying over at Ash's and passed the evening driving around Foxville, in my own pathetic version of dragging Main Street.

I end up in the parking lot of the community college, next to Ethan's Toyota Camry. He left his car here in order to travel with the ballroom team to a dance competition, and he should be back sometime tonight.

Or so he explained during the tense conversation we had this morning. A conversation in which he looked at me searchingly, trying to peer under layers that might or might not exist, and I blushed and stammered and tried to figure out how things could've gone so wrong.

I check my watch. Five minutes after midnight. Ethan left school shortly after lunch, and the competition was in the late afternoon. The team would've gone to dinner to celebrate; add two or three hours for the drive. That would make them due back . . . any minute now.

Which is still too long. I alternate between blasting the radio and counting the stars. I prop my feet on the dashboard and dream up new dress patterns. My phone beckons with its array of social media apps, but I don't dare touch it. I don't dare see what everyone's been saying about Walt Peterson. Instead, I twiddle my thumbs—actually swirling one thumb around the other—but that doesn't make Ethan arrive any faster.

After what seems like an eternity, two navy vans pull into the lot, and college-aged guys and girls spill out. They carry armfuls of sequined costumes and kiss each other on the cheeks to say good-bye.

I get out of my car just as Ethan steps under the streetlight, his eyes sleepy and his jeans riding low. I've probably seen him looking this adorable. I just can't remember when.

"Kan? Is that you?"

For the first time all week, I don't think. I run to him and fling myself into his arms. Instantly, the awkwardness that's kept us at arm's length evaporates. We return to the Kan and Ethan on the swings, the ones who pumped their feet higher and higher to kick the moon.

"It's good to see you, too," he says, his breath rustling my hair.

Keeping an arm around me, he walks me to his car and tosses his duffle bag in the backseat. Then, he turns and captures my lips with his.

My brain sizzles, and my heart shoots into overdrive. I'm just as surprised—just as slayed—as I was a week ago.

His mouth moves against mine, and the pavement under my feet tilts, so that gravity pushes me forward and I'm leaning into him. Or maybe that's not gravity at all. Maybe that's just a magnetism that's specific to Ethan.

The force keeps pushing. I continue tilting. So this is how we get back on track. This is how we erase the confusion and misunderstandings. I wish someone had told us a week ago.

I also wish this were why I waited in the car for so long. Just because I missed him. The kiss alone would've been worth it.

I pull back a fraction of an inch. "How did you do? In the competition, I mean."

"Not bad. We got second in the Latin category, but we've got another competition tomorrow, another shot at gold." He brushes a kiss on my forehead, one on each cheek, another one on my nose.

My knees go weak. It would be so easy to let his kisses transport me to a place much more magical than this parking lot, with its flickering street lamps and crumbling parking blocks.

"You'll miss the spring carnival," I manage to say.

"I'll miss you," he says. "The spring carnival isn't really my scene. It never has been."

"Me neither," I admit.

"You know, I've never had anyone wait for me in the parking lot after an out-of-town competition before." He sighs. "Jules's girlfriend comes almost every week. Brynn's had at least three different guys here since the start of the season. And I always go home alone. Uncongratulated. Unloved." He pushes out his lower lip in such a realistic imitation of a little boy that I burst out laughing.

"But that's not why you're here," he continues. "You're not here to congratulate me on a job well done."

"No, I'm not."

He drops a final kiss on my lips. It is so sweet it almost hurts. "So what's this about?"

I swallow hard. Sometime between seeing Walt's Twizzlers box and this moment, the vague thoughts that were chasing each other around my brain have coalesced into a concrete suspicion. And now, I have to say it out loud.

"You know our miscommunication about the text messages?" I wince. I can't help it. The entire week, any time I so much as saw the message icon, my jaw would twitch. "I think . . . um . . ." I take a deep breath, and then the words rush out. "I'm almost positive Shelly stole my phone and texted you, pretending to be me."

For a moment, he goes perfectly still. And then, he pushes off the side of the car. "Oh my god, I knew there was something wrong with that girl."

"You sense it, too?" I rub my arms. "She's creepy, right?"

He paces the length of the car. "Super creepy and freaking inappropriate."

"Yeah, I saw how she was with you. What she said, the way she jumped into your arms. It's like she was trying to flirt with you, but it came across all wrong."

"That's not all," he says slowly. "You know that night we were at your house for dinner? Remember, at one point, I jumped up and excused myself to use the bathroom?"

I frown. "I thought you were just getting bored with Khun Yai's interrogation."

"Not at all. I'm happy to talk to your grandmother, about anything. She wants to make sure I'm trustworthy, and can you blame her? I'm interested in her granddaughter."

The simple admission takes away my frown, and I lean against the hood. "You can call her Khun Yai. All my friends do. Culturally, it's a sign of respect." I pause. "So why did you leave?"

"You were sitting on one side of me at the table, and Shelly was on the other. And she . . . she put her hand on my, um, crotch."

My eyes about bug out. "She did what? Are you sure it wasn't an accident?"

"That's what I thought. I thought she must've been going for your leg or trying to pick up her napkin . . . or . . . or something."

He pounds his fist against his forehead. "But now that you tell me she was the one texting me . . . I don't know." He shudders. "When I think about the things she said . . . the things we did . . ."

I go perfectly still. "What did she say? No, more importantly, what did you *do*?"

He flushes. "You don't want to know."

"Oh, believe me. I do." I walk toward him. "Come on, Ethan. Hand it over."

"What?"

"Your phone!" Frustrated, I push the hair out of my face. "I thought she had stolen my phone, but I didn't know you were doing stuff with her! You're supposed to be my boyfriend. She's my . . . extremely dysfunctional so-called foster sister. I think I have a right to know exactly what you said and did."

Two bright spots appear on his cheeks. "You're not thinking about this clearly. Now that I know it was her, I'd happily stab a knife into my brain if it would erase the memory. But it won't. You don't want the details, Kan. Trust me on this."

"How am I supposed to get past this if I don't know what you did?"

"You're just going to have to try. Please, Kan. Please try."

"I don't know if I can." I huff out a breath. And then another. And another. "At least tell me this: How far did you get?"

"Pretty far," he says miserably.

I squeeze my eyes shut. Images rush through my mind. A waterfall of black hair. Ethan's bare chest. The two of them, in their respective beds. Under the covers. "You . . . you enjoyed it," I say, my voice weak with betrayal.

"I thought it was you."

"How could you possibly think it was me? We had just kissed for the first time that night. What kind of girl do you think I am?"

"I was surprised," he says. "I tried to stop several times, and you—she—insisted. I thought it was harmless, and since I thought it was you, it was sexy as hell. I . . . I guess I just went with it. I'm sorry."

And then, something occurs to me, and I'm light-headed and swaying. "That's why you said you had fun, when we talked on the phone. That's why you were thinking about me all morning. You were talking about *her*. Maybe we wouldn't be here right now if you hadn't . . . *sexted* with Shelly." Damn it, I can't even say the word without blushing.

"Listen to me, Kan. That night has nothing to do with our relationship," he says, his eyes bright. "I liked you before. I like you after. That incident doesn't change my feelings one bit. I don't care about her; I'm not attracted to her. Not even a little bit. The only reason it was hot was because I thought it was you. I swear it."

It's not that I don't believe him. I do. He's as much a victim as I am. But I can't stop the movie reel in my head. The shirt falling off Shelly's shoulders. Ethan leaning back on his elbows. Shelly licking her lips. Ethan moaning.

I fall to my knees and press my hands against my temples. Stop it. Stop it! Stop. It.

The real Ethan kneels in front of me. "Don't let her do this to us," he pleads. "This is what she wants. She wants us to break up. We can't play into her games like this."

Somehow, his words pierce through the endless loop in my head. "You're right. She definitely has some kind of agenda."

I tell him everything then. How I feel like she's been stealing my identity. How she locked Walt naked in the concession stand. I even tell him about the strange hold she seems to have over my mom and Khun Yai.

"First you, and then Walt," I say. "Who knows what other vicious pranks she's planning? We have to stop her before she hurts anyone else."

"How? Can we go to the police?"

I chew on my cheek. "For starters, I'd just like to get her out of my house. I need proof, Ethan. Concrete proof that will make my mom see I'm right. Something more than just my word or yours. I sure as hell don't think we'll be able to get Walt to confess. And my mom will write off the hair style as Shelly looking up to me. For some reason I can't understand, she's brainwashed herself into thinking that Shelly is this sweet, innocent girl. I need to find out more about Shelly."

"How are you going to do that?"

I stand and pull him to his feet, the answer as clear to me as the round orb in the sky. "Easy. I'm going to start with her hometown."

Chapter 29

The inside of Shelly's mouth tasted like ash, as though she'd eaten a carton of cigarettes. Or kissed a horde of boys—and a handful of girls—who had eaten a carton of cigarettes. She'd thought victory would taste better than it did.

Finally, she'd gotten what she'd always wanted. She was the center of attention. When she talked last night, people listened. People cared. So what if they called her by a different name? It didn't matter who she was on the inside. It only mattered what they saw.

She lay flat on her bed, breathing deeply. She hadn't changed her clothes, so she was still wearing the short skirt and white tank that fit her like a second—newer and better—skin. She'd never dreamed she would have the body to wear something like this. She was nearly as straight up and down as her and Kan's hair. But all she needed was a push-up bra, and suddenly, she had all the cleavage she'd coveted.

She felt, once again, like she had made the biggest discovery in the universe. She could be somebody. She could be Kan. All she had to do was pretend. They all faked it, every last one of them. Nobody actually fit in any more than she did. Some of them were just better at pretending.

Her eyes were wet. Did it count as crying if she didn't make any noise? It was like that saying about the tree that fell down in the middle of the forest. If nobody saw her, if nobody noticed, did it constitute sadness?

Through the walls, she heard Kan arguing with Khun Yai. They went around in circles, saying the same things without really listening to each other. Shelly felt like she alone could pierce through the bullshit, the half truths, to what they were each feeling underneath.

Kan was being Kan, headstrong, independent. She thought Khun Yai was hopelessly old-fashioned, entrenched in a world that had changed without her realizing it.

But the truth was, Khun Yai was just scared.

Kan was the girl she had raised because Dr. Som was too busy working. Kan was her precious baby, who was now even closer to her than her own daughter. When Khun Yai had been a new mother, she'd worked outside the home, too. She'd had other stresses, too. But now, as a grandparent, she could focus on one thing alone: the girl.

Khun Yai was scared to lose Kan to other people, to other things. To this culture she didn't understand but in which she had to live. The one that threatened to swallow her little girl whole. Piece by piece, it was taking Kan away, a little more each day, and Khun Yai was terrified that this blond, blue-eyed boy would be the last straw.

Khun Yai's voice thundered through the walls. Shelly couldn't understand the words, because Khun Yai spoke in Thai, but she knew exactly how the older woman felt. She felt Kan slipping away from her, too. The wet sand had dried now, and it was only a matter of time before it crumbled.

She didn't like this feeling. Which meant she had to do something to fix it. No more playing around this time. She had to do something big. Something even more definitive. She had to claim what was rightfully hers.

Kan's life.

Chapter 30

"You're not going," Khun Yai says, her hands on her creaky hips, the fire of battle in her eyes. My mother sits behind her at the kitchen table, working on a cross-stitch of a barnyard scene that will one day hang on our kitchen wall. It's one of her rare mornings off. Normally, she picks up every shift she can at the hospital. She claims that she's just being a team player, but my theory is that she's trying to work herself to death. That way, she won't have to suffer through life as a widow anymore.

I want to pound my head against those rooster-covered walls. Grab my mother's perfectly even stitches and toss them out the window. Maybe then, Mae would weigh in on our conversation. Instead, she seems enthralled with getting the duck's webbed feet exactly right.

I take a deep breath. I proposed what I thought was a perfectly acceptable outing. I need a good excuse to be out of town, so that they can't expect me to come running home should they call. Besides, Khun Yai likes Ethan—at least she's starting to warm up to him. It's Saturday. She should have no problem with me tagging along to cheer him on in one of his dance competitions.

It's just an excuse, of course. I'm planning to go to Shelly's hometown to see what I can find out about her background, but I can't exactly tell Khun Yai or my mom this. They'll just accuse me of going on a witch hunt to villainize poor Shelly.

"What could you possibly have against me going?" I ask. My

mother switches to the green thread and moves on to the pond. Those lily pads, you know. They've got to take priority over your child's well-being. "The competition's during the day. We're not sleeping over anywhere. There's going to be an entire gymnasium full of dancers supervising us, for god's sake."

"You just met this boy, Kanchana," Khun Yai says. "What would people say if you were already going out of town with him?"

"What people?" I shove my hands through my hair. These mysterious, faceless people again! They've been keeping me from doing things my entire life, whether it was hanging upside down on the jungle gym or wearing a slightly transparent nightgown to bed. Maybe I shouldn't get this worked up over a fake excuse, but it's the principle of the matter. I'm responsible. More trustworthy than every last kid at my school. Why can't she see that?

"I went with Ash last summer when we took the ACTs," I say. "We drove two hours to Pittsburg, took the test, had lunch, and then came home. What's the difference?"

"Ash is a girl. Ethan is a boy."

"So?" My eyebrows climb my forehead. "I could have sex with her just as easily in the backseat as I could with him."

"Kanchana." Finally, my mother looks up from her cross-stitch. "Do not speak to Khun Yai that way."

"What way? She's not being logical. I'm simply pointing that out to her."

"I don't need to be logical," Khun Yai says, her lips tight. "I am your elder. I make the rules. You follow them."

"I follow your rules when they make sense." I rise on my toes, as if that will make her more likely to hear me. "This one doesn't. Would you want me to blindly follow a rule I don't agree with? Shouldn't I use my mind and make the correct decisions for myself?"

"It's called authority," Khun Yai roars. "It's called respect. It doesn't surprise me you're not familiar with either, you and your American ways."

"Well, at least in America, girls are raised to think for themselves."

Khun Yai's face turns red. I can see every wrinkle and every crease. "I was right not to give that necklace to you. You are not a good Thai girl. You would disgrace the family heirloom."

My heart twists. That necklace means everything to me, but I won't pretend to be something I'm not. "I don't want it, anyway. Not if it means I have to be a subservient drone."

Mae gets in between us, the damned cross-stitch still in her hands. "Stop it, both of you. I have to leave for the hospital soon, and I'd like to spend my last few minutes in peace."

She looks between us. My arms are crossed. Khun Yai is breathing hard, as though she's just run her first race in decades.

"I'll settle this," Mae continues. "Can you both agree you will abide by my decision?"

We nod, more from surprise than anything else. Mae rarely involves herself in household affairs. In fact, I can't remember the last time she disciplined me—or attended any of my school events, for that matter.

"You both have valid points, but neither of your arguments are relevant." She places a hand on my shoulder. "The truth is, Khun Yai isn't doing well. She keeps forgetting her heart medicine, and as a result, her body's been working too hard. We went to the doctor yesterday. He says we need to keep an eye on her for the next few days." She takes a breath. "I'm sorry, Kan, but I need you to stay home this weekend."

"I do not need a babysitter, Som," Khun Yai says stiffly. "The doctor cleared me, so long as I remember my medicine. And I will."

"Well, I haven't cleared you." She pauses. "I had a dream last night. It's a bad omen. I feel . . . uneasy about this weekend."

"You're not supposed to believe in superstitions, Som. You, with your Western medicine and your modern education. You would not advise your patients like this."

"You are not my patient." Mae stands up straight, tucking the cross-stitch under her arm. "You are my mother. As your oldest daughter, as well as the first in our family to become a doctor, this is my decision. And it is final."

She sweeps out of the room, her head held high, putting an end to the argument. It's a neat trick. Something I clearly need to learn.

"Khun Yai," I say softly, putting my hand on her arm. Her sagging skin is cool and wrinkled. I want to twirl myself in the long fabric of her sarong skirt, the way I used to as a little girl. But I tower over her now—me with my American bones and my American diet—and I could more easily envelop her than the other way around. "Why didn't you tell me you weren't feeling well?"

She closes her eyes, as if suddenly tired.

"It is my job to worry about you, *luk lak*. Not the other way around."

"On the contrary, life is a cycle," I say, repeating her own words back to her. I thread my hand through her arm and lead her to the living room. "Parents care for their kids when they're young, so that the kids can care for their parents in their later years."

"Only when they are old." Her eyes flash bright, even as she allows me to help her onto the sofa and place her legs on the ottoman. "I am not old."

"No, you're not. But you can get sick, no matter what your age is."

"I will be fine, Kanchana," she says tiredly. "Go ahead, go to the dance competition with that boy. But no kissing, no hand-holding, do you hear? I am trying to understand your life. But you must try, too."

I take her hand, touched and surprised that she relented. But I'm not sure I want to go anymore. My investigation into Shelly can wait. Anything can wait if Khun Yai is ill. "We'll play cards. *Pai pong*," I say, referring to the Chinese cards she likes. "You'll have to remind me which characters go with which, but I'm sure it'll come back to me after a few rounds."

"Your mother is overreacting. Compensating for the times

she isn't here. The doctor said I would be fine if I remembered my medicine. I've set an alarm, see?" She holds up her phone to show me. "I'm not completely senile, despite what your mother might think. Besides"—she looks at me conspiratorially—"if we do not, as she says, abide by her decision, do you think she'll ever know?"

"Never." I grin. "She'll be too busy working."

"Exactly. So run along now. I have soap operas to watch." She adjusts her spectacles and picks up her iPad from the coffee table, where her latest favorite Thai soap is cued up.

"I'll watch with you," I insist.

"Fine," Khun Yai says, smiling a little, as if to say, *We'll see how long you last.*

I settle down next to her. The actors are as beautiful as always, and the drama is as intense as always. But pretty soon, I lose track of the many subplots, which Khun Yai expects. I begin to nod off, as she expects. When she once again urges me to leave, I reluctantly agree—also as she expects.

Except what I leave her to do is the last thing she would expect.

Chapter 31

I drive to the community college. The ballroom dancers are already there, loading their gear into the team vans. This part, I wasn't lying about. They really do have a dance competition a few hours away. I just won't be going with them.

I pull into a parking spot next to Ethan, who is sitting on the hood of his car. I get out of the bug, and we look at each other awkwardly, not sure where we stand. Finally, he hands me a thermos. I unscrew the top and take a sip. Hot chocolate and coffee mixed together. My favorite.

"How did you know?" I gesture with the cap.

"Khun Yai mentioned it during dinner, when you were in the bathroom," he says. "She said when you were a little girl, you were desperate to drink coffee like her. So, she would dilute her coffee with hot chocolate until it was sweet enough for you. The taste stuck with you." He brings his own thermos to his lips. "It's kinda sticking with me, too."

"I call it choffee."

"Yes. She mentioned that, too."

I take another sip. The bittersweet liquid swirls around my tongue, and my heart swells, for so many reasons. Because Khun Yai told him the story. Because he cared enough to prepare me the beverage. Because he's drinking the same thing, too. In different ways, and in varying degrees, they both mean so much to me.

Shelly threatened that. In fact, she almost ruined my relationship with Ethan.

I won't let her, I vow. *I'll find a way to move past this betrayal that Shelly tricked him into. I'll uncover her secrets and get her out of our lives. I won't let her do any more harm, to me or anyone else.*

A horn honks.

"Hey, Ethan!" Jules yells. Her hair is wrapped in hot rollers all over her head. "Kissy kissy, and get a move on!"

He searches my face. "Be careful today, okay?"

"I'm just going to talk to a few neighbors," I say. "I won't be in any danger."

"Still." Hesitantly, he brings his hand to my face. "I worry about you. We'll be back late tonight. Too late for you to wait up."

"Okay. I'll talk to you tomorrow, then."

The horn sounds again, low and long. "Ethan! We're leaving in thirty seconds. With or without you."

"Better go." He hops off the hood and looks at me uncertainly. "Thanks for coming to see me off."

"Is this a first, too?"

He pauses. "If you kiss me good-bye, it will be."

What the hell. We have to start over somewhere, and it might as well be here. I rise on my toes and press my lips lightly to his. It lasts all of two seconds, but it is as sweet as a first kiss. As aching as a final good-bye. Will we ever get back to the emotions in between? Those light, nonsensical laughs. The easy, insignificant conversations. Or did Shelly take that away from us, too?

"I'll call you," he says. "No matter how late it is."

The memory of our kiss and the thermos of choffee cause the hours to fly by. I still feel hurt, betrayed. But it's not his fault, and if anyone's worth making the effort for, it's Ethan. And so, I sip the delicious beverage he prepared for me and smile as I make the drive.

The smile fades as soon as I enter the town of Lakewood. It was a simple matter to get the name of Shelly's hometown from the many news articles surrounding Sheila Ambrose's death.

And once I had the hometown, it only took a bit of digging and a couple paid reports to find Shelly's exact former address. Using the GPS on my phone, I navigate to the right neighborhood and park in front of her old house.

There's a Realtor's sign in the front yard. The grass has been recently mowed, and the shutters gleam with what looks like new paint. The driveway, however, is empty, and the lights inside the house are off. Clearly, a new family hasn't moved in yet. Even if they had, they probably wouldn't know anything about the Ambroses.

But her neighbors will.

I sit for a minute inside the car, taking a sip of the now cold choffee for strength. This is way out of my comfort zone—approaching strangers, asking for information that is ostensibly none of my business. But you know what? Having a girl impersonate me and sext with my boyfriend is out of my comfort zone, too.

Squaring my shoulders, I get out of the car and walk to the house across the street. I practice a smile and try to look friendly. I've never been the kind of girl whom people rush over to help. Maybe my eyes are too squinty; maybe my skin is too brown. And maybe I'm just going to have to get over whatever complex I have.

I ring the doorbell, and a chorus of barks fills the air. The door cracks open, and a man's hand waves me away. "Not interested, sorry."

"I'm not selling anything," I squeak out. "I just want to talk. Ask you a few questions about your former neighbors. . . ."

One dog sticks its nose through the crack, and another shoves its ear and half its head below it. I see several more dogs at the window. Nails scratch against the tile. Hundreds of scratches. Just how many dogs are inside, anyway?

The hands grab the collars of the two dogs and pull them back. "Sorry. I don't know my neighbors. And I don't like questionnaires. Or strangers. Bye, now."

Before I can respond, the dogs yelp as though they've been kicked in the stomach, and the door closes in my face.

I swallow hard. No problem. If he doesn't know his neighbors, he wouldn't be able to give me any information, anyway. And with a house full of dogs, who can blame him for not being more sociable?

At the next house, however, I get the same response. This woman doesn't have pets, but she crosses her arms and crowds in front of the door as though I might dive inside and steal the silverware.

"You have the wrong house." She looks me up and down, from my dark blue jeans to the fitted T-shirt I hand-painted with geometric shapes. "I didn't order any Chinese food."

I take a deep breath. *Do not be insulted. Nothing good will come out of being insulted.* "Ma'am, I would love to talk to you about your former neighbors across the street. The Ambroses. Shelly Ambrose goes to my school now."

"The Ambroses?" A muscle ticks at the woman's temple. "They weren't real neighborly. I brought Sheila a casserole once when she broke her foot. Did she return the favor? Nope, even though I lived across the street from her for years. I never got the casserole container back, either. It was one of those disposable plastic ones, but still. I reuse 'em, and it was only polite that she bring it back. When I brought it up, though, she just looked at me like she didn't know what I was talking about. Her daughter goes to your school, you say? Maybe you can ask her for my container."

I blink. "Sheila Ambrose died, you know. I don't think anyone cares about a disposable plastic container."

She huffs out a breath. "Which is why I stopped bringing casseroles to my neighbors."

Another door closes in my face. Wow. With neighbors like these, no wonder Shelly's a little creepy.

Exactly how much remains to be seen.

At the third house, an older woman with a streaky gray bun opens the door. She has a widow's peak, and when I mention Shelly's name, her forehead relaxes.

"I used to babysit her," she says. "She was real quiet. Kept to herself. A little strange. After that girl moved in with the Ambrose family, she got even stranger."

I raise my eyebrows. "Girl? What girl?"

"I think she was a friend of the family. She came to live with them a few months before Sheila died."

"What was her name?"

"Well, I'm not really sure," the woman says, her eyes sharpening. "Why do you want to know? Is Shelly in some kind of trouble?"

"Not yet. But she could be." I take a deep breath. I've got to give this woman something, or she'll shut me out just like the rest of them. "I think Shelly's gotten in a little over her head. She's been impersonating some of the girls at my school. And, um, sexting with their boyfriends."

"Oy." She shakes her head. "You know, Shelly was always a sweet kid. If she's gotten involved in some bad stuff, I blame that entirely on Riley's influence."

"Riley?" I ask.

"The girl who moved in with them. If Sheila Ambrose wasn't so high all the time, maybe she would've put a stop to their friendship. Riley's not the kind of girl you want for your daughter's best friend."

I go perfectly still. The BFF necklaces in Shelly's room. The ones that look just like keys. They had two halves of a heart, each bearing the inscription, *R & S, best friends forever.*

Riley must've been the *R* in that inscription. She must've been Shelly's best friend . . . until something happened. Whatever that was, one thing is clear.

They're not best friends anymore.

Chapter 32

Shelly wore jeans. Not her normal jeans, but the tight, designer ones that were Kan's. She paired them with the white wraparound shirt Kan had made her and slouchy brown boots, which she had filched from Kan's closet.

When Kan wore an outfit like this, it looked so easy, so effortless. As if she pulled it together in a matter of minutes.

It had taken Shelly a good two hours to decide on this precise combination.

She pulled her hair into a ponytail, even though it meant she was showcasing her scar. That's what the other girls did after a wild night out. After Friday parties with fancy hair and makeup, they always spent their Saturdays—even Saturdays that were the social event of the month—dressed down and casual.

How did all the other girls know this? It had taken her ages to figure out this particular nuance, but they all seemed to absorb this knowledge effortlessly. It was like they had read some rule book that she had somehow failed to receive.

She would've asked Kan, but she'd heard Kan leave ages ago, presumably to go to the spring carnival the student council was hosting that day. There would be games and prizes and good things to eat. Laughter and fun and ample opportunities for flirting. At least, this was what everyone at school was saying. Everybody would be there, and Shelly would be no exception.

Even if Kan hadn't bothered to wait for her.

Shelly wasn't surprised, though. Kan had been testy ever since

Ethan had come to their house for dinner. Ever since she might've found out about their sexting session.

Shelly wasn't surprised—but she was disappointed. Kan had promised she wouldn't let a boy come between them. If she were a true friend, she should be willing to share Ethan. She shouldn't begrudge Shelly those small touches and moments. After all, Kan had everything, and she had nothing. It was like a king who hoarded his gold and refused to spare a few pennies for the beggar.

It was well past time for them to switch their roles.

When Shelly arrived at the spring carnival, however, nothing was right. Her hair was perfect. Her clothes were perfect. And yet, her classmates still ignored her.

They walked around her as though she didn't exist, eating their cotton candy, tossing colorful pieces of popcorn into each other's mouths. Everywhere she looked, people were aiming darts at a rack of balloons to win oversized stuffed animals. Or throwing balls at a target to dunk one of their classmates. Or getting henna tattoos on the backs of their hands. They were laughing and talking and having fun.

Fun. The concept paralyzed Shelly. She didn't know how to have fun, not really. She didn't understand it.

God knew, she tried. She attached herself to a group of girls to whom Kan had introduced her. She laughed when they laughed. Groaned at the same parts of the stories where they groaned. She even handed an attendant two dollars so she could spend a useless five minutes jumping inside a bounce house.

It wasn't fun.

She tried as hard as she could to summon the girl she'd been the previous night. The one who had been the center of attention. The one who was just like Kan.

She wouldn't come.

It was because all the students knew her here. They knew she wasn't Kan. They knew she was the girl with the zigzag scar on her cheek. The girl who'd kicked Walt Peterson in the chin. And they didn't admire her, the way Kan said they did. They thought she was a freak.

The longer she stood there, not fitting in, the faster her breathing came. The people and the prizes and the games began to swirl together and spin around her, like she was in the center of a merry-go-round and couldn't get off. This was . . . wrong. It was all wrong. She couldn't do this. She had to get out of here.

Abruptly, she left the group of girls and pushed her way through the crowd. She slammed into a guy, and his popcorn flew into the air, but she kept walking. A girl yelled at her to watch out, but she didn't listen. She needed something. She needed . . . Ethan.

She needed his reassurance, his strong arms enveloping her. She needed to wrap his scent around herself, so that it would keep her safe.

If the boy himself wasn't available, then his shirt would do.

She stumbled through the crowd and ran into the parking lot, crossed to the athletic field, and unlocked the concession stand with her copy of the stolen key.

She kept Ethan's shirt here, in a tiny closet at the far end of the concession stand, along with a box of things she didn't want anyone else to find. The closet held an old mop, which nobody ever used, and poster board specials from years past. Nobody ever went inside, so it was perfect for Shelly's purposes.

But that day, when she opened the door, Shelly knew immediately somebody had been there. Her cardboard box had been moved half a foot, and the cobwebs that normally dripped from the ceiling were gone.

Her heart shot into her throat as she rummaged in her box. Thank goodness, all her things were still there. A bundle of envelopes tied together with a string. The core of an apple that she and Kan had shared, passing it back and forth after every bite. One of the rock paperweights from the late Sheila Ambrose's collection. Photocopies of portraits from the yearbook. And Ethan's shirt.

She grabbed the shirt, brought it to her nose, and inhaled

deeply. Ethan's cinnamon scent enveloped her. She had to calm down. It was going to be okay.

But it wasn't.

The door of the concession stand flew open, and Ash strode inside, gorgeous and intimidating in her tight jeans, casual shirt, and high, glossy ponytail. At least, Shelly had gotten the look right.

"Scoping out the scene of the crime?" Ash asked, her hand on her hip.

Shelly cringed. She normally had better control over her facial expressions, but she was still rattled by the missing cobwebs. "I don't know what you're talking about."

The girl raised her perfectly arched eyebrows. Shelly wanted to ask where she got her eyebrows done. She wanted to absorb every detail about Ash. The tweezed eyebrows. The hair that started dark around the crown and lightened to golden honey at the ends. The expert eye makeup that probably took countless brushes and shades.

Shelly leaned forward, fascinated. She still had so much to learn, so much to know. This girl could teach it to her.

But Ash had other ideas.

"I know you locked Walt in here without his clothes," she said. "And I know what you're doing to Kan, too."

"I had nothing to do with Walt," Shelly said, her mind whirling. Ash was probably just guessing. Walt would never tell anyone what had really happened—least of all, the princess of Foxville High. "And all I've done to Kan is be her friend."

"Oh, really? Isn't that Ethan's shirt?" She yanked the black fabric out of Shelly's hands. "Of course it is. Everyone knows what his black shirts look like. He only wears one every day. Does Kan know you're sniffing around her boyfriend—literally?"

"It's not like that," Shelly said. "I'm looking out for Kan. I'm researching Ethan to make sure he's the right guy for her."

Ash snorted. "Does research involve stealing his shirt? Does it mean blowing up copies of his yearbook photo and drawing hearts all around him?" She gestured toward the cardboard box where incriminating copies of the photo lay. "Yeah, I know all about those, too. I thought Kan was supposed to be your best friend, Shelly. And you're trying to steal her boyfriend. Doesn't sound like a very good friend to me."

Little bubbles began to pop in Shelly's head. As Ash continued talking, the bubbles got bigger and popped harder. "You know nothing about me. Nothing about my relationship with Kan." Shelly struggled to keep her voice even and her face calm. But the bubbles were interfering. They distorted her voice, pushing and pulling at the folds of her skin.

Ash's face hardened. "I know a lot more than you think. Don't forget, Kan was my best friend before she was yours. And I know she's not going to be happy with you sniffing her boyfriend's shirt like it's some kind of crack. I always knew something wasn't quite right about you, and now, I have proof." She took a step closer. "I bet you stole her phone, too, and deleted her messages. Kan said she never received my texts, and I believe her."

She reached out and flicked Shelly's black hair. "What the hell is this? Who do you think you're trying to fool? You'll never be half as pretty as she is because you don't have her inner beauty. I know what you're doing, Shelly. You're trying to isolate Kan from her friends. But it won't work. I'm going to tell her everything."

Shelly racked her brain. This was bad. Really bad. She had to stop Ash. But how?

"You won't do that," Shelly said, trying to sound more confident than she felt. "If you do, I'll tell everybody how you begged Brad to take you back. I listened to his voice mail messages. I'll tell them how you were pleading with him to take you to prom and how he turned you down for a tennis player at the school the next town over."

Ash's cheeks flamed red. But instead of cowering, she lifted her chin. "Go ahead. Say whatever you want. You think I care what anyone in this town thinks? Five minutes after graduation, and I'm out of here. Kan is more important than any of that. She's a good person, and she deserves to know the truth."

She turned on her heel to go. But Shelly couldn't let her do that. Shelly had been working so hard, so tirelessly, and for the first time in her life, she was actually close to getting what she wanted. A true sister. People who paid attention to her. An identity she could be proud of. She wasn't going to let Ash take that away from her. She just wasn't.

Her eyes flew around the concession stand and landed on the rock paperweight inside her cardboard box. She knew she'd kept it there for a reason.

Ash was almost at the door. Shelly snatched up the piece of pottery. She zeroed in on the back of Ash's head. And then she smashed the paperweight right in the middle of that glossy ponytail.

Chapter 33

Shelly's former neighbor tells me to call her Mrs. Watson and invites me to sit on one of the porch chairs. Guess she thinks this story is going to take a while. Or maybe she just wants company. Either way, I'm happy to oblige.

"Before you sit, would you be a dear and go to the kitchen and pour me a glass of lemonade?" she asks. "You can get yourself one, too, while you're at it."

"Sure." I let myself into the house. Knickknacks are crammed on every available surface, and books are piled waist high along the walls. I walk into the kitchen, and there's a pitcher of lemonade on the middle shelf in the refrigerator. Glasses in the very first cabinet I open. Thank goodness. Rifling through someone's memories is one thing. I really don't want to rifle through her stuff, too.

I bring the glasses back onto the porch, and Mrs. Watson downs the drink in a few audible gulps. "I make the best lemonade in the state." She winks as I settle into the chair opposite her. "It's so good people say I'm a witch and have laced it with a truth-telling potion. Seems no one can sit where you're sitting, drink my lemonade, and resist telling me their life's story."

I freeze with the glass halfway to my mouth.

"It's a joke, sweetie!" She laughs, splaying her hands on her belly. "There's nothing in that lemonade but sugary goodness. Besides, I'm the one talking today, not you. I'll admit, though, I always keep a batch on hand in case I have an unexpected guest. There's no magic inside, but boy, does it seem to work. That's probably the only reason Sheila Ambrose confided in me. Our paths didn't cross much after Shelly got too old for a sitter, but Sheila would come onto my porch a few times a year. When she did, every detail of her life came spewing out." She sobers. "It was like she was storing up the words, waiting for a friendly ear. I was probably the closest thing she had to a friend, poor dear."

She eyes my glass. "Come now. Take a drink. I promise you, it's harmless. Besides, I can't be poisoning teenage girls on my porch. What would that do to my reputation in the neighborhood?"

This doesn't reassure me. I doubt the neighbors on this street talk much. I bring the glass to my mouth anyway, in a show of good faith.

I take one sip—and almost spit it back out. "Is this . . . hard lemonade?"

She roars with laughter. "Told you it had a way of making the truths come out."

I set the lemonade down on the porch. "I'm still a minor. And I'm driving later."

"You're as fuddy-duddy as Shelly. Seventeen going on fifty. You two are friends, did you say? I'm not surprised. Well, if you're not going to drink it, hand it over here, girlie. Can't let it go to waste."

I give her the lemonade and she finishes it off within seconds. She could be a competitive drinker. She wipes a hand across her mouth. "Now, what were we talking about? Oh, yes, Riley."

"What do you know about her?" I ask.

"Well, poor thing never had a chance, not with who her mother was." She crosses her arms over her belly. "You see, Riley's mother, Leesa, and Sheila Ambrose had been friends for a long, long time. I used to see Leesa coming 'round when Shelly was a wee thing in pigtails. They smoked pot together back in college, Sheila said. I don't know if either of them ever graduated, but according to Sheila, Leesa was plenty bright. Street smarts, Sheila called it. She said Leesa could have a five-minute conversation with you and know exactly how to get you to do what she wanted. So, instead of getting a regular job, Leesa's spent the last twenty years using her God-given talents for grifting."

"Grifting?" I raise my eyebrows, not understanding.

"You know, con games and the like. She'd move to a new town and find a mark. Usually a rich but not too bright guy. The con might take two weeks; it might take six months. But Leesa would worm her way into the person's good graces—and bank account. She'd walk away with a sizable amount of cash, move to a new town, and start all over again."

"She raised her daughter through this?" There's a sour taste in my mouth, and it's definitely not the lemonade. "That's awful."

"Yep. Apparently, she made the kid take part in her cons, too. Not that Riley was any good at it. They used to get into terrible rows over it, and finally, when Riley turned seventeen, she put her foot down. She didn't want to grift anymore. At a loss, Leesa called her old friend, and Sheila agreed to take the kid in.

"So the three of them lived together—Sheila, Shelly, and Riley—just one big happy family, for a few months. And then, tragedy struck. Sheila killed herself at the church, in a godawful wedding dress, and both Shelly and Riley disappeared. They were both eighteen, so the police didn't bother tracking them down. Some say they took off for the islands, and others thought they just moved to a new town so they could get a fresh start." She grips the armrests and leans forward. "You know what I think?"

"What?" I whisper.

"I think they're out there, conning someone else. Riley would've picked up lots of tricks from her mom, and she could've easily taught them to Shelly." She looks at me pointedly. "Maybe you and your family are the victims."

I shake my head. "No. Just Shelly is staying with us. Not Riley."

"Doesn't mean Riley's not out there, behind the scenes. Calling the shots."

The thoughts whirl in my head. Could Shelly be communicating with an outsider, taking orders from her? For sure. Even in the beginning, when we spent all of our time together, I didn't keep track of her every movement.

But there was the matter of the necklace. *R & S, best friends forever.* If Shelly was working with Riley, why are the two halves of the necklace together? Shouldn't Riley be wearing the other half?

"What does Riley look like?" I ask.

She shakes her head. "I only ever saw her from a distance. Dirty blond hair. Pale skin. Slender build, like Shelly's. Kind of nondescript looking. The type that you never remember in a crowd."

"Last name?"

"Jeffries, I think. At least, that was her mother's last name."

"Do you have any idea how I can contact the mom?"

"Not a clue," she says slowly. "Sheila said they had a home base somewhere, a cabin on a nearby lake, but that's all I know. Leesa didn't even come to Sheila's funeral, which I thought was a shame. Sheila really cared about her, but she's probably off running a con somewhere and couldn't be bothered."

I stand, my mind still puzzling through the possibilities. "Thanks for the lemonade and the information."

Mrs. Watson leans back, her eyes snapping. "Did I answer your questions?"

"Not entirely, but you helped. A lot. You narrowed down my search."

"To what?"

I look at the older woman. At the empty glasses strewn on the porch. The worn but sturdy furniture. Suddenly, every detail sharpens. I see every drop of lemonade clinging to the glass, every splinter of wood sticking out from the furniture.

"I need to find Riley," I say. "She's the key to everything."

Chapter 34

It was the damn shirt's fault. Ethan's shirt. Shelly knew it had been a mistake. She never should've taken it in the first place. If Ash hadn't found it, she wouldn't have gone to the concession stand, looking for her. She wouldn't have threatened Shelly—and Shelly wouldn't have had to do what she did.

When she got home, her fingers were still trembling, even as she carried the cardboard box. Disgust wrapped around her throat and gagged her. But she wasn't feeling her own disgust; it was someone else's. Someone who used to be important. Someone who had, once upon a time, been her entire world. Someone whose name she refused to utter.

Saying her name would break Shelly's heart all over again.

"When you grift, you need to grift with every inch of your body," the person had instructed. "The tells are in the body parts you least expect. Smile not just with your mouth, but also with your eyes, your nose, your cheeks. Pay particular attention to your fingers. So small, so slight compared to the rest of your body, but in times of stress, they have a mind of their own. If in doubt, wear a pair of gloves. They'll do double duty in preventing telltale fingerprints."

Shelly curled her fingers around the box. She wished she'd brought a pair of gloves, but she hadn't thought that far ahead. When she'd woken that morning, she'd had no idea the day would turn out like this.

But Shelly wasn't the kind of girl who dwelled on the past. She believed in moving forward. The only reason she was here now was because she knew how to recover from tragedy. She had to remember that.

She stopped by her room and stashed the box in the closet, which Khun Yai had turned into a prayer space. And then, she headed straight for the bathroom to wash the blood off her hands.

She plugged up the drain and turned on the faucet as hot as she could make it. Once the sink was filled, she dunked her hands in. Instantly, the water became cloudy with blood.

Biting her lip, she scrubbed her hands in the scalding water. Too bad she couldn't have burned her hands along with Ethan's shirt. She had wanted to hang on to the shirt, but she had learned by now that nothing good came out of keeping material things.

"Don't be sentimental," she had been lectured. "Don't get attached to objects. Don't get attached to people. Don't even get attached to your identity. There will come a time when you have to give up all those things."

Shelly saw the wisdom in the advice—but she didn't want to believe it. She still hoped that she could hang on to her identity. She just had to choose the right one.

She had blood underneath her fingernails. Great. The water turned cool, and she drained the sink and started all over again. But the dried blood was damned hard to get out.

Sweat gathered on her neck and dripped into the cleavage manufactured by her push-up bra. This was ridiculous. She had done much harder things in life, things no one else at Foxville High would dream of doing. And she did them without flinching, because she had her eyes on the end goal. She knew what she wanted, and she wouldn't let some dried blood defeat her. She wouldn't.

"Damn it," she muttered. "What's it going to take to get you out?"

"Try using a nail file," a voice said behind her.

Shelly jumped. Khun Yai stood in the doorway, her arms crossed, her eyes running from Shelly's face to her bra.

"Khun Yai!" Shelly snuck a look at the mirror. Crap. She'd been so preoccupied by her hands, she'd forgotten to wash the blood splatters from her face. "How long have you been standing there?"

"Long enough," Khun Yai said.

Chapter 35

Riley might be the key to everything—but she's also a goddamn ghost. Nobody seems to have heard of her. I talked to the rest of the neighbors on the street. Went by the Dairy Queen, where the local high school kids hang out. I even stopped by the coffee shop and library.

Everyone had heard of Shelly and Sheila Ambrose—but no one knew anything about a teenage girl named Riley. Of course, all I have is a name and Mrs. Watson's description. Dirty blond hair. Pale skin. Nondescript. That could be half the girls at Foxville High.

Mrs. Watson has no reason to lie. Right? But maybe she's been drinking too much of her own lemonade.

I might believe that—if it weren't for the necklace. The damn *R & S* necklace.

Riley exists. I'm sure of it. Now I just have to find her.

By midafternoon, however, I give up. It's getting late, and I need to get home before Khun Yai starts to worry.

There's one more avenue that I haven't considered. It's simple and direct—and it just might get me the answers I need.

All I have to do is ask Shelly.

My phone dies as I get in my car, so I don't have my playlist of songs for the drive home. That's okay. I have to figure out how to approach Shelly, anyhow. I need to be casual but firm.

Nonthreatening but cautious. I haven't talked to her since we watched Walt Peterson run away with a Twizzlers box over his privates. Not since I found out she was pretending to be me and sexting with my boyfriend.

Somehow, I need to set aside the anger and hurt of betrayal. Go back to the friendship we used to have. That's the only way I'll get her to confide in me.

I pull onto our street, and my stomach seizes. Something's wrong. An ambulance sits in our driveway, its lights flashing red. People stand on the lawn, and the paramedics are carrying a stretcher out of our house. Someone is lying on it. No, not just someone. Khun Yai.

I jerk the car to a stop in the middle of the road and tumble out of the driver's seat. My legs don't work properly. They've turned into soft pretzel dough, folding in half with every step. I hobble through the crowd, jostling Mrs. Jenson's elbow and tripping over Bobby Cade's skateboard.

"Coming through!" the paramedic yells. "A little space, please. Coming through."

I break through the mob just as the stretcher passes. My hand shoots to my mouth. Khun Yai's face is the color of coconut milk, and an oxygen tube sprouts from her nose. She is still. Deathly still.

My knees give out, and I sink onto the wet grass. I register numbly that Khun Yai must've watered the lawn. She does that every night. It relaxes her, she says. The plants are good company for her thoughts.

"Kan!" Shelly materializes in front of me. Her eyes are worried, and her lower lip is trembling. "Where have you been? I've been calling and calling, but I couldn't get through."

"My phone died," I say faintly. "I didn't bring a charger with me."

She wraps her arms around me and pulls me up. I cling to her. For a moment, I forget about my suspicions. The fact that she sexted with my boyfriend seems juvenile. All I care about is the answer she's about to give me.

"Is Khun Yai okay?" I plead. "Tell me. What happened?"

She shakes her head. "I don't know. When I came home, she was lying on the lawn, and the hose was running beside her, flooding the grass."

"So she fainted? She's been forgetting her medicine lately." I lurch forward, and if it weren't for Shelly's arm around my waist, I might've face-planted on the grass. "Oh my god. This is my fault. I was supposed to stay with her. To remind her to take her pills. This happened because of me."

"We don't know that," Shelly says. She moves her hands to my shoulders. "You need to keep it together. For your mom. For Khun Yai. You can't go off the deep end. Got it?"

I manage to nod.

"Good. Your mom's going to meet us at the hospital, since she's already there, and she wants me to drive so we'll have another mode of transportation." She looks at my car parked in the middle of the street. "We'll take your car. It's blocking the ambulance."

I nod again, helpless to do anything else.

She tugs the car keys from my hand. "Let's go, then."

"We should bring Khun Yai a new outfit," I say, fighting through the haze in my brain. "Her clothes are probably wet. You know how she is. She'll want to change, and she won't like the hospital gowns."

Shelly pats the overnight bag on her shoulder. "Done."

"And maybe some food. As soon as she wakes, she'll want Thai food. Boiled rice."

She opens the bag, so I can see the hot-food thermos inside. "Got it."

"What about her toothbrush? And the rest of her toiletries . . ."

"Kan, you focus on keeping yourself together," she says gently. "I know how hard this must be, for you and your mom. I've got everything under control. Trust me."

I open my mouth to thank her, to tell her I'm glad she's here. Glad she's taking care of everything. But then, I freeze. My eyes fasten on the jasmine plant by our front door. Khun Yai's favorite. She brought the seeds all the way from Thailand, and we celebrated with a takeout dinner the first time the delicate white flowers bloomed. Without fail, it's the first plant Khun Yai waters when she turns on the hose.

Today, the soil underneath the plant is bone dry. Which means Khun Yai wasn't watering the plants when she collapsed. Which means she was dragged there—and someone turned on the hose as a cover-up.

I try to raise the corners of my mouth, but my lips feel like Play-Doh. "What would I do without you, Shelly?"

She beams. "That's what I've been trying to tell you, Kan. That's what I've been trying to tell you."

Chapter 36

We rush to the hospital, only to wait. One long wait in the visitor's lounge to see my mom, to talk to Khun Yai's doctors. Shelly and I huddle on the yellow and orange plastic chairs. A vending machine hums in the corner, and a toddler sits on the scratchy carpet, trying to pull out the fibers while his mom talks on the phone. The intercom blares every few minutes, instructing doctors to get to their places, stat, and the air smells like antiseptic and overly ripe bananas. Better than dirty diapers, I suppose.

I pace the lounge, from the vending machine to the plastic chairs to the kid. Vending machine, plastic chairs, kid. The jasmine plant keeps popping up in my head—and I keep pushing it away. I'm probably jumping to conclusions. Maybe Khun Yai decided to switch up her routine. Maybe she turned on the hose and crossed the lawn to speak to a neighbor. Who knows? A million things could've happened. The cracked soil beneath a jasmine plant proves nothing.

I peek at Shelly from the corner of my eye. Sure, I know the girl is a little strange. But is she capable of attempted murder?

I have no idea. All I know is that I can't trust her. No matter how helpful she seems to be.

After I take a dozen laps around the lounge, my mom appears, still wearing her white coat over her cartoon-printed scrubs.

"Girls!" She sweeps first me and then Shelly into a hard embrace. "Thank you for calling the ambulance," she says to Shelly. "Thank you for being there for my mom."

She turns to me with a searching look. "And where were you when Khun Yai collapsed?"

The lie springs to my lips. "I went to Ethan's dance competition. Even after you told me not to. I'm sorry."

She sighs and holds her arms out to me again. I walk into them, and she presses her cheek against mine. "It's okay."

"It's not okay," I say miserably. "I'm the reason she's here. She probably fainted because she forgot to take her pills, and I wasn't there to remind her."

"That's not why, *luk lak,*" my mother says. I jerk a little in her arms. That's the first time she's ever called me that. All it took was for Khun Yai to get hurt. "Khun Yai is as sharp as any tool in my medical bag. She doesn't take those pills because she's stubborn—not because she forgets." She pulls back and looks at me. "I came home during my lunch hour. Practically forced the pill down her throat. She's worse than you were as a child."

My mouth drops. "So, she didn't collapse because she missed her pill. What happened?"

She hesitates. "We don't know. But there's a lump on the back of her head."

"What?" I feel like I'm grasping wildly in the air, trying to catch the dust motes. Trying to catch anything. "You mean she was attacked?" I think of the jasmine plant, as dry as the desert. And it takes all my strength not to turn and look at Shelly.

Mae moves her shoulders. "Not necessarily. She could've fainted and landed on a rock or some other hard surface. Maybe she had the lump from before. I really don't know. But I'm sure her doctor will come give us his theories very soon."

"Very soon" turns out to be twenty minutes. Twenty long minutes during which Shelly fetches tea and sandwiches for me and my mom. Twenty endless minutes when I bite my tongue and stay as far away as possible from her. I want to tell my mom about my suspicions. But I have no proof, and no doubt she'll react the same way as before.

Besides, I don't *know* that Shelly had anything to do with

Khun Yai's "accident." Maybe she's made some questionable judgments. Maybe her lack of social intelligence has made her cross the line. That doesn't mean she's capable of violence. Probably, she's just a lonely girl wanting a place to belong. Just like me. Just like all of us.

Probably. Maybe. Maybe not.

When the man and woman in white coats arrive, they don't talk to me but pull my mother aside. I lean forward to bring me closer to the trio, and strain to hear.

A few minutes later, Mae comes back, her eyes glossy with tears. "Whatever caused the lump, the impact was heavy enough to burst some blood vessels in her brain, so they're taking her in for emergency surgery."

"Emergency surgery?" I whisper. "That doesn't sound good."

"It's not. But the good news is, if the surgery is successful, she'll likely have a full recovery. We just have to wait."

And wait. And wait.

Hours pass. I doze lightly in the plastic chairs and resume my pacing of the lounge. The harried mom takes the toddler home around midnight, and I pray to Buddha. I'm not religious, not really, but prayer has been instilled in me from the time I was a child. I recite a chant before going to bed every night, and I pray to—or more accurately, talk with—my deceased father.

Prayers such as this: *Please, Por, protect me and keep me safe. Help me be a good girl, to respect and obey my elders, to do well in school.* That's the standard litany I was taught. To this list, I usually add my own selfish desires. *Please, Por, tell Mae to buy me that new pair of shoes. Help me get Mrs. Miley for homeroom, so that she'll let me sneak off and use the sewing machines. Convince Ethan to kiss me.*

Like I said, it's more of a conversation than an actual prayer.

But I pray now to Buddha. As fervently as I know how.

Please, Phra Buddha Chao, let Khun Yai be okay. Let the surgery be a success. I'll be a good girl, I promise. I'll listen respectfully, and I'll never disobey my elders again. I'll do anything. Please. Just let her live.

Finally, the doctor comes out. Only one of them this time—

the woman with the silver-brown bob and the kind eyes. She converses briefly with my mom and then leaves.

Mae shoots me a brilliant smile. "The surgery was a success. Khun Yai is still sleeping from the general anesthesia, but the doctor thinks she'll wake from it by morning. She's going to be okay, Kan." My mother pulls me close. "She's going to be okay."

A weight lifts off my chest, and I take my first full breath in hours.

But just because I can breathe doesn't mean there isn't more waiting. It's past midnight now, and Shelly persuaded my mom to go home and take a quick nap. I insisted on staying, and Shelly volunteered to keep me company.

The visitors' lounge is even drearier at night. The artificial lights flicker above us, and the blinds covering the windows are closed, shutting us in. I haven't seen anyone other than Shelly in the last hour. I zone out, and Shelly doodles with the crayons the toddler left on the side table.

I watch her fingers move across the paper for a good five minutes before I notice what she's drawing. A bloody red heart, broken into two pieces like the BFF necklaces. The bottom of each heart is long and jagged like a key, also like the necklaces.

And like those metal pendants, it's sadder for the two halves to be together than to be apart.

I clear my throat, which is scratchy from disuse. "Can I ask you something? Can you tell me about . . . Riley?"

The crayon freezes. "Where did you hear that name?" Her knuckles turn white. I'm surprised the crayon doesn't break in half.

"I went to your old neighborhood," I say softly. "I was driving past Lakewood on the way to the dance competition, so I stopped by to see where you grew up. I talked to one of your neighbors. A Mrs. Watson?"

"You can't trust Mrs. Watson," Shelly says flatly. She starts coloring again, but she presses so hard that the crayon rips through the paper. "She doesn't have any friends, so she makes up imaginary people and stories."

"She said she used to babysit you. That a girl named Riley came to live with you and your mom for a few months. Is that true?"

Shelly doesn't say anything. She retraces the jagged edges of the heart again and again.

I touch her arm, and she looks at me. Her eyes are dark, fathomless—and impossibly lonely. Despite everything, despite her lies and my suspicions, her look strikes a chord deep inside me. Because I've felt like this, too. I've been alone, too.

"Was Riley who you meant when you talked about your former friend?" I whisper. "Was she the one who hurt you, Shelly?"

She squeezes her eyes shut. "There was a girl named Riley," she says in a dull voice. "And she did come to live with the Ambroses. But she's not here anymore."

"Where is she?"

She bends over the paper and adds more color to the heart. Blue and orange and yellow, so that it looks like there's a fire flaming inside. A single tear drops onto the paper.

"Shelly," I say urgently, leaning forward. Taking her hand. "Where is Riley?"

"I can't talk about it," she chokes out. And then, she wrenches her hand out of my grip and runs from the room.

Leaving me with her broken, flaming heart.

Chapter 37

That name. Shelly hadn't heard it in months. She hadn't even allowed herself to think it. And now, hearing it on Kan's lips brought all the memories back. Every. Last. One.

She kept it together until she reached the ladies' room, and then she fell to her knees on the cold linoleum floor.

Once upon a time, she had been so hopeful with this girl. As hopeful as she now was with Kan. Once upon a time, she believed she had found what she was looking for. The best friend necklaces had hung in their rightful places. One around her neck. And the other around the neck of the girl she thought of as her sister. Her blood sister. Her true sister.

Well, it hadn't worked out. Her so-called "sister" turned on her. She didn't want to be united forever and ever, after all.

So Riley had to die. There was no choice, really. Shelly hadn't wanted it to end that way. There were so many other options from which they could've picked. Happy options. But the girl insisted.

And so Riley died, and Shelly lived.

She took a deep breath. Picked herself off the floor and splashed water on her face. When she looked in the mirror, she could no longer tell whom she saw.

She would give it one more shot. She had to. In a way, she didn't have a choice here, either. She had to find the girl who was meant to be her sister. The one who made her feel like she belonged.

She couldn't live like this anymore. She couldn't be in this hellish in-between place. All she wanted was to fit in somewhere. Anywhere.

Was that so much to ask?

Chapter 38

I jerk awake and look around wildly. Yellow and orange plastic chairs. A vending machine in the corner. Overhead lights that won't stop flickering. That's right. I'm in the visitors' lounge at the hospital, where Khun Yai is resting after her surgery. Her *successful* surgery—but one that might've been unnecessary if I had stuck around.

At the thought, I start shivering, every inch of my body. The thin blanket the nurse gave me does little to help. Blankets can't fight against this kind of cold, the kind that starts deep in your core. When you face yourself in the mirror—and see the truth.

I'm not a good Thai girl. Hell, I'm not even a good grand-daughter, Thai or American. Khun Yai is right to give the sapphire and ruby necklace to someone else. Someone who doesn't fight with her. Lie to her. Disobey her.

I promised my mom I would stay with Khun Yai—and I didn't. She might not have collapsed because of the pills, but if I had been there, maybe I could've prevented the fall. If there was an assailant, if it was Shelly or someone else, maybe I could've scared her off. Or maybe, if Khun Yai had just gotten confused, I could've helped her. Instead, I took off to pursue my own agenda. Sure, I was trying to protect us all by investigating Shelly. But there are other ways of protecting ourselves. Other ways that focus our attention on what's truly important: our family.

I glance around the room and realize that Shelly is no longer here. Good. She's been here with me every minute, whether I wanted her or not. She packed Khun Yai's clothes and her toiletries. She didn't even forget the toothpaste or eyeglasses. She convinced Mae to go home, urging her to rest, and brought me food from the cafeteria, urging me to eat.

In short, she's been keeping us together while the usual backbone of our family, Khun Yai, is unable to. Maybe I should be grateful to Shelly. And maybe she's a freaking wannabe murderer. I'm glad she's gone. Thrilled.

I flex my fingers. They're empty. I've been so used to sleeping with my phone under my pillow that they feel strange not clutching anything.

Where is my cell? I pat my pockets, search the end tables, rifle through every bag we brought. Nothing.

My stomach turns. I've been so careful with my phone, keeping it on my body or in my hands all the time. But ever since I arrived at the hospital, I've been preoccupied with Khun Yai's fate. I plugged my cell into the wall and then forgot about it.

Wouldn't you know it? The moment I let down my guard, my phone disappears.

Along with Shelly.

Chapter 39

It was as easy as boiling rice to swipe Kan's phone. Sure, the girl had been more careful lately, but she must've been really distraught about Khun Yai. She swiped her finger in the square design of her new security code right in front of Shelly. And then, she went to sleep with her cell phone right there, flung on the end table, almost begging for someone to steal it.

Shelly was more than happy to oblige. While Kan slept like a newborn baby, she casually picked up the phone and slipped it into her pocket. Kan hadn't even moved.

Shelly walked to Kan's car in the parking lot. She hadn't even needed to steal the keys because she already had them. Leaving, of course, meant she was stranding Kan at the hospital without a ride. Not that Kan would notice. She would probably watch Khun Yai sleep for an entire week, if it came to that.

Shelly, in the meantime, had better things to do.

She stopped by Kan's house briefly before driving to Ethan's and parking on the street. Earlier, she'd listened to Ethan's voice mail and deleted it.

"Just got home," he'd said, his voice low and deliciously sleepy. "I know it's late, but I wanted to hear your voice. We won, Kan! First place in the Latin division. I can hardly believe it. I want to celebrate with you, as soon as possible. I also want to hear what you found out about Shelly." He'd paused as though he was unsure whether he should continue. "I've been thinking about your lips."

Shelly's toes had curled. He wasn't saying those words to *her*, but she could imagine someday, in the very near future, he would. She had been so stirred up, she almost missed the betrayal he'd revealed in the previous sentence.

Almost.

So, Kan was digging into her past, huh? That's why she'd talked to Mrs. Watson. It wasn't a casual happenstance like she'd made it sound, but a deliberate decision to investigate Shelly. It didn't matter. Kan wouldn't find anything. Shelly had wiped her trail so clean, even Khun Yai would've approved.

She got out of the car and picked up the paperweight she'd packed at the bottom of her bag—just in case. She left the paperweight on the ground and climbed a tree that was right next to Ethan's window. She'd perfected the maneuver by now. Running jump, leap, grab onto the lowest branch and swing her legs up. Good to know all that strength training and gymnastics lessons her mother had made her take were good for something.

She inched along the thick, horizontal branch. *Oh, Ethan, please be awake.*

Normally, she didn't mind watching him sleep, but she needed him awake for what she was planning. Indeed, on a couple occasions, she had passed the night just staring at his chest rising and falling. One time, however, he was playing video games. And another time, dear god, she was lucky enough to catch him practicing his dance moves. His shirt had been off, and his muscles had gleamed under the light. It was all she could do to hang onto the branch.

She wanted, so badly, to watch him while she texted him. To see what her words did to his body. To watch him sprawled out on the bed, to see him sweaty and panting because of her.

But she never had the chance. The first time, the sexting had been a spur-of-the-moment decision. After that, Kan had been warier, had kept the phone closer to her body. Did her blood sister know what had happened? Now that she'd heard Ethan's voice mail, it seemed more and more likely.

She reached the section of the branch where the leaves parted, giving her a perfect view into his room, and there he was, bouncing around the room like a little kid, shaking out his arms and legs. And he was wearing nothing but a pair of boxer shorts dotted with hearts.

Her hand shot to her mouth, covering the squeal that was about to burst out. What on earth was he doing? And could he look any cuter?

She could've watched him all night. Any other time, she would've. But that night, she had a different plan. A better plan. After all, the only thing nicer than looking at Ethan was being with him.

Ripping her eyes away, she fumbled in her pocket for Kan's phone and dialed Ethan's number from memory. By the time she looked back at the window, he already had his cell phone to his ear.

"Hello?" he said. God, that tone. So eager, so excited. It just about killed her.

"Hey, sexy. It's me," she said, her voice barely above a whisper. She'd learned from experience that people heard what they wanted or expected to hear. So long as she kept her voice low, he'd never suspect that she wasn't Kan. "Guess where I am?"

He paused, for so long that she started to wonder if he saw through her ruse, after all. "Tucked in your bed?" he finally responded.

She breathed a sigh of relief. "No, silly. I'm here. Outside your window." She wanted to tell him exactly what she was—and wasn't—wearing. If it were the other night when they were texting, she would've. But she had to tread carefully. He still thought she was Kan, and Kan would never be so forward. "I couldn't wait until morning to see you."

"Seriously? You're here?" His voice was surprised, but more than that, she thought he sounded happy. Happy to see her. She smiled so widely she thought her skin might bust.

"How do you know which one is my room?" he asked.

Her smile faltered. Oops. Was he suspicious? She hadn't realized Kan had never been to his house. He crossed to the window and looked out.

"It's the one you're standing in front of," she said. "Wearing boxers with blue hearts."

His hand lowered to the elastic waistband, and she shivered. "You like?" he asked.

"Very much. Get down here."

"Give me two seconds."

They hung up, and much to her dismay, she saw him pulling on a pair of jeans and his signature black T-shirt. Oh, well. She'd just have to take them off again.

She lowered herself until she was hanging from the branch and then dropped to the ground. Zips of anticipation shot through her stomach, even as her mind was trying to ruin it for her. Ethan was flirting with her . . . but he thought she was someone else.

No. She couldn't think that way. He was responding to her voice, to her words. She had to believe that he knew, on some level, that he was talking to Shelly. Sure, when he got downstairs and realized it was her, he might be surprised. But she would just have to convince him. Convince him she was the girl he truly loved. Convince him he was only attracted to Kan because of her surface.

The surface was nothing. With a little effort, anyone could look like that. Just look at Shelly. She'd been able to imitate Kan with no problem at all.

Ethan loved her. They'd spent that one glorious night texting. She knew what her words did to his body. And she *really* knew what his words did to her body. It was time for them to be together for real.

A few minutes later, the front door opened soundlessly, and a shadowy figure stepped out. She wrapped the knee-length cardigan tighter around herself. It was a rainbow-colored, nubby knit number that was both a statement and a beautiful piece of art. A Kan original. She wasn't sure if Ethan had ever seen it, but it screamed Kan with every loop, with every color.

Ethan started walking toward the tree, and Shelly turned around, so that he would see only the sweater and her hair as he approached. She had to time this perfectly.

The pulse thrummed in her throat. *Don't rush this. You only have one shot. One kiss to prove that you're the girl for him.*

His feet crunched through the grass, and she felt the heat emanating from his body as he stepped up behind her. *Just a few more seconds. Wait until he gets close, really close, too close to get a clear view. Three seconds, two, one . . .*

She whirled around, aiming to capture his lips with hers.

She didn't. Her lips met with air. Ethan had stepped to one side, and his hand shot out to grip her wrist.

"What are you doing here?" he said darkly. "Where's Kan?"

She took a step back, wrenching her wrist from his grasp. He wasn't supposed to know who she was this quickly. He was supposed to have gotten lost in her lips, in their kiss, so that when he realized who she actually was, it would be too late. He would already be enamored with her.

"How did you know it wasn't Kan?" she asked, stalling.

"How did I know?" His eyebrows climbed up his forehead. "How could I not know? She's my girlfriend, Shelly. I knew the second you started talking that it wasn't her. You're nothing like her."

The words were a slap across her face. Fine. She was different from Kan. He didn't have to make it sound like such a bad thing.

"You don't always know," she said, wanting to prove him wrong. Wanting to make him see her under all these layers of deceit. Her true self, the self no one had ever seen, not even her own mother.

Shelly would've revealed her real self to her mother. In fact, she had been dying to. Her mother just hadn't been interested.

"You didn't know it was me texting you the other night," she continued, trying to wrench the conversation back on track.

He went perfectly still. His features gleamed like marble under the moonlight. "That was a mistake."

"A mistake, Ethan? Are you sure?" She took a step forward, and he backed up, as though they were dancing. He was scared of her. Good. She continued advancing, and he continued retreating until his back was pressed against the tree.

He was cornered now. And right where she wanted him—where she'd always wanted him. "You had a good time, Ethan. That's what you told me. You said it was the hottest experience of your life. That doesn't sound like a mistake to me." She looped her hands around his neck, tugging him close. She could feel the vibrations in his chest. "You said you couldn't wait to get your hands on me for real, that the anticipation was driving you wild." She leaned forward and rubbed her lips against his. "Well, I'm here now. You can have me any way you want."

"I don't want you. Did you ever think of that?" He tried to pull away, but the tree was behind him, and there was nowhere to go.

Anger bubbled in her stomach. He didn't get to talk to her like that. "You liked texting me. You got off on my words. Me."

"It wasn't your words. I thought it was Kan texting me! The whole time, I was picturing her. Not you. There was nothing special about your words. If that's all I wanted, I could call any sex hotline. The only reason those words had meaning was because I thought they came from her."

She wasn't going to let him do this to her. That night was one of the best of her life. She'd known, right then and there, that she was going to cherish the memory forever. She wouldn't let him cheapen it just because he felt guilty.

She sank to the ground, groping behind her. Her dreams involving Ethan were crashing around her, fast. But she wasn't going to let him tear down her lifelong dream, too.

The rage built inside her until it exploded, turning her entire world red. She swayed, and for a moment, she thought she might faint.

"You really have no idea." He just kept talking. Talking, talking, talking. He didn't know when to shut up.

But his words steadied her. They gave her something on which to focus. Something toward which to direct her anger. Her hands closed around the paperweight. She hadn't had a clear idea why she was bringing it. But now, she knew. On some level, she must have known all along.

"I'm not attracted to you," he said. "No matter what the circumstances are, I'd never be interested in you. . . ."

For the second time that weekend, she would take back control. In the most definitive way possible.

She swung the paperweight as hard as she could against his head.

Chapter 40

Where the hell is Ethan? I hang up the pay phone in frustration.

Sighing, I amble past the visitors' lounge, glad I don't have to go back inside. Sometime after dawn, the nurse said I could hang out in Khun Yai's room and wait for her to wake.

My mind spins over the same question, again and again. I'm certain Shelly is a thief, but is she also an attempted murderer? I just can't decide on an answer.

It would be nice to discuss my questions with someone. Someone like Ethan. But I couldn't call him until this morning. Khun Yai's lessons are ingrained in me too deeply. What kind of girl calls a boy at two a.m.? Not a good Thai girl, that's for sure. What would those faceless, nameless people say?

But now, it's eight a.m., and he's not picking up. Is it too early? Nah. If telemarketers can call at this hour, then so can I. Maybe he's still sleeping.

I swallow past the lump in my throat. There's no reason to worry. Not yet. It's early, and he's probably just exhausted. He had a grueling dance competition yesterday, as well as two long drives. That would knock anyone out.

I walk into Khun Yai's room and sit in the chair next to her bed. She looks much better now. She's breathing on her own, without the help of oxygen tubes, and her skin has returned to its normal color. She's not sleeping peacefully, though. She alternates between gulping the air and not breathing for long periods, thrashing around as though she's having a nightmare.

I pick up her hand. It feels so small, so wrinkled in mine. Thinking back to our last argument, I bite my lip. That was definitely not one of the last conversations I wanted to have with her.

"I'm sorry, Khun Yai," I say.

Her head moves. Does she hear me? Is she waking up?

"What could I have done?" she mumbles in Thai. "Everything we've worked for, ruined. I couldn't let him destroy his life over a white girl."

Her hand jerks, and I drop it in surprise. She's not talking to me, clearly, but to someone in her dreams. "I had to pay her. I had no choice. I did what had to be done. If I die now, I will just have to atone for this sin in my next life."

Her arms shoot into the air, as though she's waving away a stray dog. "Stay away from me, *farang*. You're not my granddaughter. Family is more than blood. You weren't raised with us, in our culture. I don't care who your father was. You proved you weren't my granddaughter the moment you blackmailed me with those envelopes. No respect whatsoever."

I freeze. I'm her granddaughter, but she's not addressing me. I'm not a *farang*, for one thing. She may despair over my attitude, but I was definitely raised in the Thai culture. The only white girl she's been around lately is . . . Shelly.

Holy crap. The air turns solid. Is this the big secret my mom and Khun Yai have been keeping from me? Is that why the atmosphere between Shelly and Khun Yai is so tense?

I swallow hard. "Khun Yai, you're having a nightmare." I gently squeeze her hand. "You need to wake up. You're talking in your sleep."

Her eyes flutter open, and her gaze darts around the room, to the sterile white walls and empty surfaces, before settling on me. She blinks a few times, and then her eyes clear. "Kanchana, is that you?"

Thank goodness. She recognizes me. "Yes, Khun Yai. You've had a bad fall. We're in the hospital."

"I didn't . . ." she starts to say, and then shuts her mouth.

"What was that?" I ask.

"Nothing." Lines crease her forehead. "I can't seem to remember what happened. One moment, I was watching Shelly wash her hands in the sink. And the next . . ." She shakes her head. "I don't know."

"You weren't watering the lawn?" I ask carefully. "That's where they found you, lying in the grass. The hose was running next to you."

She moves her shoulders. "Maybe I was. I can't remember."

An image of a jasmine plant flits through my mind, the ground below it dried and cracking. Unwatered. Shelly was the last person Khun Yai remembers seeing? Oh my god. Oh my god. Oh my god.

Struggling to control my thoughts, I pour a glass of water from a pitcher on the nightstand and hand it to Khun Yai. This moment is about Khun Yai, not my suspicions. She takes the glass, and I sink to my knees, bending my head. Her frail hand strokes my hair.

"I'm so sorry. I lied to you. And I shouldn't have left you. This wouldn't have happened if I were at home."

She continues to smooth my hair. "Yes, *luk lak*. If you did indeed lie to me, you were wrong. But you need only be sorry for your actual transgression. You did not cause my injury."

So who did? Did she simply fall, or was it something . . . someone . . . else? Was it Shelly?

I shudder. All of a sudden, it's vitally important that I understand what Khun Yai was mumbling. "You were talking in your sleep," I say.

Khun Yai blinks. "Was I? Well, I always said you got that habit from me. We're the same, you know. Your mother always said we were twins, born two generations apart. We're both too stubborn for our own good. We both harbor deep passion in our hearts. And we both talk in our sleep." She pauses. "What did I say? Was it gibberish?"

"You were talking to your granddaughter," I say slowly. "But it wasn't me. You called her a *farang*."

"It was you, *luk lak*. You're my only grandchild born outside of Thailand. Who else could be a *farang*?"

"No, you said the granddaughter was blackmailing you. With envelopes. How can that be me? I don't even know what that means." I rise from the floor, so I can look at her.

But she won't meet my eyes. Instead, she stares at a spot over my shoulder. Since the walls are blank, I know whatever she's looking at can't be that fascinating.

"I'm not young anymore." She moves her shoulders. "Maybe I'm getting . . . confused. There's no accounting for the things I say, especially in my sleep."

"On the contrary, Mae says you're still sharp. I agree." I sit and move my chair closer. "Could you have been talking to . . . Shelly?"

Her gaze could slice through bamboo. "Why would you say that?"

"You don't have that many teenage white girls in your acquaintance, Khun Yai."

She leans back tiredly and closes her eyes. "I must rest now, Kanchana. Perhaps we can talk about this some other time."

I soften. Whether or not she's avoiding my questions, she is my *Khun Yai*. She's suffered a traumatic injury, and she's been through an emergency surgery. The best thing she can do is rest.

"Of course, Khun Yai. The only important thing now is for you to get better."

Chapter 41

Mae arrives an hour later to take my place by Khun Yai's bedside, and I take her car back to our house. I'm desperate to get clean—but more than that, I want answers. And if Khun Yai won't tell me, maybe Shelly will.

But my bug isn't in the driveway when I arrive, and the house is empty. So, where did Shelly go last night, if it wasn't back here? Mae said she didn't see her this morning, but I thought she just hadn't looked.

Mrs. Watson's words drift through my mind. *The con might take two weeks; it might take six months. But Leesa would worm her way into the person's good graces—and bank account. She'd walk away with a sizable amount of cash, move to a new town, and the process would start all over again.*

Is it possible Riley taught her best friend this particular con? Good god, Shelly has my car. Maybe I'll never see my bug again.

I let out a shaky breath. That's it. I'll give her until this afternoon to bring my car back. Otherwise, I'm calling the police.

I go into Shelly's room. Everything looks the same. There's a suitcase of rocks in the corner. A single pair of earrings on the dresser. At least she hasn't moved out.

I walk idly around the room, poking here and there. I don't know what I expect. A bunch of envelopes in the middle of her bed, with a big arrow pointing toward it? If the envelopes are anywhere, they must be hidden.

Taking a deep breath, I pull open a drawer. I don't see anything out of the ordinary. I go through every last drawer, and although I uncover half a dozen of my shirts, I don't find any envelopes.

I walk into the closet, which Khun Yai has converted into a prayer room. A gold Buddha statue sits on one shelf, along with small pots of sand holding burned-down sticks of incense and fresh garlands of jasmine flower. The other shelf holds a framed portrait of my father. Lifting my hands into a prayer position, I pay respect to both Buddha and my father.

And then, I just look at him, my *Por*. He has a handsome face and a square jaw, with a head full of thick black hair. I don't know if he passed away before his hair turned gray—or if he simply dyed it, the way most men do in Thailand. I could ask my mother, I suppose, but I'm not sure the question is worth the glassy-eyed, shallow-breathing person she becomes anytime the subject of my father comes up.

Most of my memories of Por have blended together, but in fleeting moments such as this, I think of his exuberant smiles and his kind hands. I think how he put me on his shoulders and said I'd better hold on tight, so that I wouldn't float away like a balloon.

Could this man have had an affair with another woman, a *farang*? Could he be Shelly's father?

I search and search his face, but I can't see any resemblance. Not even a little bit. I must be wrong, then. Maybe I took Khun Yai's words out of context. Maybe I jumped to conclusions, once again.

I turn to leave the closet when I notice a cardboard box stowed in the corner. That's weird. I've never noticed the box before, and Khun Yai visits the prayer room every day, keeping it relentlessly clean. You could eat mango and sticky rice right off the floor. She would never leave an extraneous box in here.

Which means it's not Khun Yai's box. It's Shelly's.

My skin prickles with goose bumps. I sit on the floor and open the box. An apple core lies at the bottom, along with a bunch of photocopied sheets from the yearbook. They feature not only Ethan's face, but also portraits of other boys in our class. Last, but not least, I see a stack of envelopes with address markings on the front and neat slits on the side.

My fingers trembling, I pick up an envelope. Inside, I find a single piece of paper. It is mostly blank, with a date scrawled across the top and four pieces of tape forming the corners of a rectangle, as though a check might have once been affixed.

I peek at the other letters, and the contents are the same. A sheet of paper, with four squares of tape and a date, approximately one month after the previous one.

Interesting, but nothing incriminating. Nothing informative.

I flip over the envelope—and then freeze. The closet, the fresh garlands of flowers, even my dad's portrait begin to spin around me, in slow, undulating waves.

Each envelope is addressed to Sheila Ambrose. But in the upper left corner is *my* return address. Scrawled in Khun Yai's distinctive handwriting.

Chapter 42

My mind whirls. Khun Yai was clearly sending checks to Shelly's mom. Why? Did Sheila Ambrose have something over her? Or, oh god, were they . . . child support payments? They must be. I think of Khun Yai's muttering in her sleep. Of Shelly's insistence that we were sisters. It must be true. She must be . . . my father's daughter.

I pull my knees to my chest, hugging them. But how? She doesn't look Thai. Not a single bit. But I know, more than others, not to judge someone based on his or her appearance. Lots of mixed-race people don't look the way others expect. Maybe she is half-Asian. Maybe that's why she was able to fool so many people into thinking she was me.

I don't know how long I sit there, on the floor of the closet, my cheek pressed to my knees. Struggling to make sense of this knowledge that has rocked my world.

Then, I hear a car pulling into the driveway. A minute later, the front door opens, and footsteps—soft rather than brisk—tap along the floor. Shelly's back.

Wiping away my tears, I stand, shove the box back into the corner, and walk into the hallway. Shelly jerks when she sees me.

"Oh, hi. I'm sorry I took off last night," she says awkwardly. "It was just getting to be too much for me. The hospital, worrying about Khun Yai. I just needed to clear my head."

"No problem," I say, even though it's a huge problem. She can't just take my car and disappear. And yet, and yet . . . I can't bring myself to get worked up over it. She's done a lot of bad stuff—and might be guilty of even more—but she might also be my half sister. Am I supposed to feel something about our potential blood connection? And if so, what?

I have no idea. But at least she's back now. She wouldn't be hanging around if she had anything to do with Khun Yai's accident. Right? If she was guilty, she could've taken off with my car. The fact that she came back has to mean something.

I should tell her I found the envelopes. Acknowledge the truth between us. But for some reason, the words lodge in my throat and I can't pry them out.

"I'm going to take a bath," I say instead. "I'm so gross you'd think I'd been camping for ten days. But we should talk. . . ."

"Take your bath. Relax. We've got plenty of time to talk." She nods toward the room. "I'll just go close my eyes for a bit. Didn't get much sleep last night." She laughs, but it's weird and high-pitched. I don't know what to make of it.

"If you're sure . . ." I say slowly. I'm going to talk to her about the envelopes. Really. But I could also use the reprieve. A few minutes to figure out exactly what I want to say.

"Go." She waves a hand down the hall. "Oh, and Kan?" She plucks my phone out of her pocket. "This is yours. I accidentally walked off with it last night."

She sure did.

I take the phone from her and unlock the screen. No voice mail. No text messages. No word from Ethan. Of course, that doesn't mean anything. He could've texted me a thousand times, left me a million messages, and Shelly would've just deleted them.

I trudge into the bathroom. As soon as I get inside, I dial Ethan's number. Straight to voice mail again. Damn. Where is he?

I get into the bathtub and fill it with hot, hot water. And then . . . I just lie there. So much has happened in the last twenty-four hours, my brain can't handle it. Besides, I've barely slept. I need to close my eyes. Just for a few minutes . . .

The next thing I know, my chin plunges into the water, and I jerk awake. Good lord. I must've fallen asleep. My scalding bath water has turned cold. Is Shelly still here?

Climbing out of the tub, I grope for a towel and listen hard. Yep, there's the sound of thumping. She didn't leave before I could talk to her. Good.

I get dressed, suddenly realizing I haven't heard anything from the outside world in nearly a day. Even when I had my phone, the connection at the hospital was nonexistent. I pick up my cell, now that I have Wi-Fi, and scroll through my social media.

I can't believe it.
I haven't stopped crying.
Poor Ash.
How could this have happened?

My brows crease together. Huh? What happened to Ash? I keep reading my feed, looking for more information. Halfway down the page, I find a link to a news article and click on it.

Ash's body was found in a Dumpster behind the school. Her head appears to have been bashed in by a heavy object. Police are investigating.

My hand shoots to my mouth. No. NO. This has to be a joke. A bad dream. It can't be true. I just talked to her on Friday.

My heart pounds. I can't breathe. I'm so hot I might faint. But I stay glued to my phone. This isn't real. It's got to be some kind of prank for the spring carnival, a mass conspiracy. . . .

Everywhere on social media, that's all anybody's talking about. Details of the funeral and visitation. Photos of Ash. Condolences to the family. Memories of her style, her charm, her spirit.

It's not a joke. Ash is dead.

I sink to my knees, and the phone slides out of my hands. My mind still won't process—can't process—but my body reacts for me. I fling open the lid of the toilet just in time to throw up in the bowl. I retch and I retch until there's nothing left.

Minutes or hours later, I make myself get to my feet and wobble out of the bathroom. Shelly's leaning against the mantel in the living room, next to the wide mirror on the wall. It's almost like she's . . . waiting for me. Why? If she heard me throwing up, why didn't she come see if she could help?

"It must be nice having your phone back." She smiles at herself in the mirror. "Any interesting news on social media?"

The old Shelly, the one who moved into our house a few weeks ago, couldn't stand looking into mirrors. She hated seeing her scar, hated seeing who she was. This new Shelly can't seem to look at herself enough. She's more than gotten used to her new look. Hell, she might be more comfortable in my skin than I am.

For the first time today, I notice that she's wearing makeup, just like she has been at school. Mascara, foundation, even lipstick. Even though her plan was to take a nap. Who is she trying to impress? Not me, certainly not Mae. Who else is she seeing?

My mind is absolutely numb. But the words come out anyway. "Ash is . . . dead. She was murdered, and her body was disposed of like trash in a Dumpster."

"Yes." Shelly blows herself a kiss, not at all surprised. Holy crap, is that why she gave the phone back to me? So that I could see the news? "The whole town is buzzing with the drama of it. She always has to be the center of attention, even when she's dead."

My stomach rocks violently. Oh dear god. I'm not dealing with a regular girl here, with a regular way of thinking. Why couldn't I see from the beginning how twisted her perspective is?

"Why didn't you tell me earlier? Why did you want me to read . . . the gory details . . . on my phone?" My voice drops. I want there to be a simple explanation. One that will allow me to go back to my regular life, before Shelly.

Wishful thinking. Khun Yai is hurt. Ash is dead. Nothing will ever be the same again.

"You were sick with worry over Khun Yai," Shelly says. "I didn't want to burden you with this, too."

"Why hasn't Ethan called me?" I need to shut up. I need to get out of here and call the police. I don't know for sure if Shelly was involved with Ash's death, but the cops need to know everything about this strange girl. And there's a growing dread in my stomach. Two crimes in two days. Both of the victims close to me. What if there's a third victim, a third crime? What if it's Ethan? "It's been half a day since he got back from the dance competition. Shouldn't he have called—or picked up the phone—by now?"

She shakes back her hair. That long black waterfall of hair so similar to mine. "There's no telling with boys. I've told you from the beginning, Kan. They're not worth your time."

"You don't seem too broken up over Ash's death," I say, my voice cracking. "I know you didn't like her, but shouldn't you feel something?"

She doesn't answer, and I grab her arm. "Goddamn it, Shelly. Tell me! Tell me why you don't care that Ash is dead!"

"What was I supposed to do?" she says, her voice robotic. "She was going to ruin everything. I was so close to having everything I ever wanted, and she threatened to destroy it with a single word. It's just like you said. She didn't think of anybody but herself, and she deserved to be taught a lesson."

My stomach heaves. Oh dear lord. She's confessing. She's actually admitting that she killed Ash. I'm in my house with a goddamn murderer. I look wildly around, searching for a curtain rod, a ceramic tissue box, anything that could be used as a weapon. But there's nothing.

"I didn't mean it like that," I whisper. "You know I didn't."

"Well, that's not what the police are going to think. At this moment, they're analyzing the scene of the crime. They're going to find your DNA. Specks of your blood mixed in with hers. I only had a few drops, but it will be enough."

My heart stops. The blood sister ceremony. My blood, preserved on a paper plate. Was that why she wanted a "before" sample?

"Your favorite scarf is wrapped around her neck, and your fingerprints are on this heavy, rock-shaped item found next to her body. It won't take long for the police to determine that was the murder weapon."

My fingerprints? What . . . ?

And then I remember. *Go ahead,* she'd said on the morning after she arrived at my house, gesturing to her suitcase of paperweights. *Pick one up. You need to experience for yourself how heavy these are.*

Oh dear god. How long has she been planning this?

"Your mom's art," I whisper. "So that's why you lug those things around. That's why you wanted me to touch the paperweight. It wasn't in memory of your mother at all."

She ignores me. "Everyone saw you hooking up with her nemesis just the day before. Coupled with the voice file I sent to Lanie's phone, the one where you said that Ash's opinion doesn't matter, I'm afraid you've all but confessed to the crime."

"You recorded me?"

"My phone was in my pocket. It was so easy to reach inside and hit the record button. You didn't have a clue."

I'm nearly vibrating with rage now. "You set me up. From the very beginning, you set me up."

She shakes her head sadly. "I'm really sorry, Kan. I didn't want it to turn out like this. I didn't want to frame you. But you have to understand, I had to be prepared in case things didn't work out. That's what I was taught: always have a backup plan. It's not my fault that you gave me no choice." She pulls a gun out of her waistband and points it straight at me.

Rage turns to fear. Sweat pops out on my neck, and my knees begin to knock against each other. Oh, god. That's why she was so willing to confess. That's why she gave me my phone back. She wants to see my reaction. She wants me to know everything she did. She wants me to hurt the way she thinks she's been hurt.

And now, she's going to kill me.

"You murdered my best friend," I say, as much to myself as to her.

"Ex-best friend. You had a new one," she says fiercely. "But you didn't treat her right. I don't want to kill you, Kan. I hadn't even planned on killing Ash. Believe me, it was a scramble to drag her body to the Dumpster, to set everything up without anyone seeing me. I only wanted to distance you from her and that whole group of girls. I could see how terrible they were for you. They weren't real friends. But you refused to see that. That's your worst quality, you know. Your biggest failing as my friend: You don't trust me."

"I do trust you," I say. Keep her talking. Oh god, just keep her talking, so she doesn't pull the trigger. "I swear, Shelly. I've learned my lesson. I know now you're my only true friend."

She advances toward me, not caring, and I grasp wildly for another topic. "Wait, Shelly. Tell me first. Where's Ethan?"

She stops. "You mean, our boyfriend? He's under my care now."

Perspiration drips down my back, and my chest feels like it's about to explode. "What have you done with him?"

"Don't worry. I'm not going to hurt him—not permanently, anyway. I mean, he is our boyfriend. Can't have him not functioning at full strength."

"Stop saying that!" The words slip out, even as I tell myself I shouldn't be making her mad. "He's not your boyfriend. He's mine."

She brings her arm up, as if to get a better aim at me. "We're sisters. Sisters share everything."

I swallow hard. "You're right. We are sisters. That's why I'm going to help you."

"What?"

This might be the most important argument of my life. If I can't persuade her, I'll never see Ethan again. Never see Khun Yai, never see my mom. My life, everyone I know and love—gone.

"You don't know anything about Ethan," I say, choosing my words carefully. "You don't know what he likes, what he doesn't like. You've said it yourself. Boys are impossible to decipher. If we're truly sisters, you can talk things over with me. We'll figure it out together."

She lowers the gun a fraction of an inch, and I rush on. "I made a mistake, Shelly. I didn't value you the way that you deserved.

Give me another chance. We can go back to the way we used to be. When it was just the two of us against the world."

She tilts her head to the side. "Who will take the fall for Ash's death, then? My fingerprints are on that paperweight, too. I didn't have time to put on gloves like normal."

A kernel of hope sprouts in my stomach. She's considering it. She's actually considering it. "It doesn't matter. If they can't find us, they won't be able to arrest us. And we can still be together."

She steps forward, her eyes glittering. "Are you sure?"

"As sure as I've ever been."

Her arm arcs through the air, with the heavy metal gun.

Uh oh, I have time to think. *Maybe this was the wrong decision.*

And then, the gun connects with my cheek, and everything goes black.

Chapter 43

When I wake, I'm sitting in a chair—one that's heavy, wooden, and difficult to move. My hands and feet are cuffed, and a piece of duct tape is plastered over my mouth.

What the hell? I yank my hands against the cuffs. There's very little give, and the metal bites into my skin. The room is dim, but I can tell I'm in a living room inside what looks like a cabin. Bookcases line the wall, and I'm next to a threadbare sofa and an old TV. The eaves slant low, and the decor is dark and muted.

Soft music plays, and I hear the clink of silverware. Huh? Where am I?

I crane my neck, shifting my body weight to one side so that the chair tilts up on two legs. Ah, now I can see into the next room. Tall white candles. A crystal vase filled with blooming pink roses. And Shelly and Ethan sitting at the dining table, eating off beautiful gold-rimmed plates. It's the very image of a romantic dinner. Except for one thing.

One of Ethan's hands is restrained, and a metal chain leads from the handcuff to the floorboard. The chain is so long it's coiled on the floor.

Shelly is wearing one of my favorite dresses, an outfit I made for homecoming the previous fall. The skirt is short and flouncy, and white feathers cover the entire torso. Her hair is piled messily on top of her head, and she wears a pair of my chandelier earrings. She swings her head, and the earrings swish against her shoulders.

The back of Ethan's chair blocks my view of his clothes, but I catch a glimpse of his bare shoulder.

"How do you like the food?" Shelly asks, her voice soft and solicitous.

"It's fine," Ethan answers shortly.

"You're not eating much. Here, let me help you with this escargot. I know they're snails, but they're actually really delicious."

"I'm not hungry."

"Would you change your mind if you knew this was your last meal for two days?" she asks mildly. They stare at each other for a long second. And then, he picks up the fork with his free hand and shoves a bite into his mouth.

"That's better. You should be more grateful for this meal," she says. "It's not easy to find French food in Kansas, you know."

That's when I notice the rest of the food on the table. A bowl of hot onion soup, with cheese melted over the edges. A thick slice of pâté. Shredded carrot salad with crusty French bread.

My heart lurches. The tall candles, the fancy china, French food. Oh dear god. Shelly's enacting her dream date. With my boyfriend. While he's cuffed.

I lean a little too far, losing my balance. The chair tips over, and I crash to the floor. OW. Black stars dance in my vision, and when they finally clear, both Ethan and Shelly are looking at me.

"Kan! Are you okay?" A bare-chested Ethan tries to pick me up with one hand, but the chain, as long as it is, pulls taut behind him, and he can't get a good grip. No wonder Shelly restrained him this way. He has some freedom of movement, but he can't get very far. "Are you hurt?"

"*Hhhmmmmph,*" I say, through the duct tape over my mouth.

"She's fine," Shelly says. I can almost hear the roll in her eyes. She stalks over and heaves me and the chair back upright. "Now can we please get back to our date?"

"She might be hurt." He crouches in front of me, cupping my face. His eyes are deep, brilliant, and blue, a bottomless pool into which I'd like to jump and disappear. It's only been a short while since I've seen him, but it feels like an eternity.

"You're okay," he says, his voice weak with relief. "Oh, Kan, I thought I'd never see you again."

You, too. My hands are bound, my mouth is taped shut, but I tell him with my eyes how much I miss him. How very glad I am that he's still alive.

Our reunion is short-lived. Shelly steps forward, tugging his arm. "Come on, Ethan," she whines. "Our food is getting cold."

He straightens, and my eyes fasten onto the hard muscles of his chest.

He sees me looking and jerks his head in Shelly's direction. "She wouldn't let me wear a shirt."

"It's my date," she says. "I get to decide what we wear. And when we eat. Which is now. Come. On."

"No." Ethan peers at my temple, where I begin to feel a nasty throbbing. "She needs ice," he says in a strained voice. "She might have a concussion. We need to get her out of those restraints and keep an eye on her."

In response, she strides across the room and takes a black metal object from the top of the bookcase. "You don't get to call the shots, Ethan. I do. I like you, but don't make me regret giving you a little freedom."

My eyes widen. Not a gun this time. The object is blunter and more square. A Taser? Where the hell is Shelly getting all these weapons? Apparently, she has way more resources than I realized.

"I have to say, Ethan, our date's just started, and so far, it's not even close to measuring up to my dreams. You'd better try harder." She pushes the Taser into his ribs, although as far as I can tell, the weapon is still off.

"No." He sets his jaw. "Unlock Kan first. She's not comfortable like this. She needs food and water. She should sit at the table with us."

"You wish," she hisses, and the earrings bounce wildly. "This is a date, or have you forgotten?"

"I wish I could forget," he mutters.

Her mouth drops, and for an instant, I glimpse the girl I

thought I knew. The girl who's been excluded all of her life, the one who doesn't belong and maybe never will.

And then, the mask shifts back into place.

"You are my date tonight, Ethan," she bites out. "And you will treat me with courtesy and respect—"

"Not a chance," he says stubbornly, loudly. "I don't care about you. Only her. Never you."

She steps around him, and the electric hum of the Taser suddenly fills my ears. She's turned it on. Before I can comprehend what she's planning, she thrusts the weapon into my stomach. My nerves explode. They rip into a million pieces and fall onto the floor like shredded confetti. I forget my name, forget where I am, forget everything. There is only pain. Deep, overwhelming, never-ending pain.

When I come back to myself, I'm panting and drenched in sweat. Ethan cradles me with one arm. The chain to which he's attached is pulled in a rigid line. "Oh my god. I'm so sorry, Kan. So sorry. Please be okay."

"That's for disrespecting me," Shelly says, her arms crossed. "You seem to be having a hard time being nice to me, Ethan. Maybe this will motivate you. Every time you make me unhappy, I take it out on Kan. Is that clear?"

His face crumples. He squeezes me for a brief, hard moment. And then he straightens and faces her. "Very."

"Good." She approaches him slowly and splays both her hands on his chest. Fondling him.

I struggle against the restraints, so hard that the chair rocks back and forth. I want to bat her hands away. I want to scratch her eyes out. I want to do anything and everything to make us not be here, in this situation, under Shelly's control.

But I'm helpless. And so is Ethan.

He takes a deep breath and holds himself perfectly, absolutely still. "It's okay." I can't tell if he's talking to me or himself. "It's going to be okay."

"It's going to be more than okay," she purrs. "I could do this all night. And I will. I bought a bearskin rug just for this occasion, and we're going to snuggle on it, in front of the fire. We'll reenact some of our texts. But first, we're going to eat."

She loops his chain over her shoulder, and he turns his head to me. He doesn't look helpless at all. In fact, he looks . . . determined. "I love you," he mouths.

Maybe it's too much, too soon. Maybe we've only known each other for a few short weeks; maybe we've only hung out a few times. But in this moment, in this situation, nothing else feels more true.

I look into his eyes—and hope he understands that I love him, too.

Chapter 44

They last a few minutes at dinner, and then Shelly slams her fork against the table. "This is ridiculous!" she explodes.

Moments later, she's back in front of me. Huffing out a breath, she bends and unlocks the cuffs around my hands and feet.

My heart leaps. Is she letting me go?

"Don't get too excited." She pulls me up by my hair and drags me across the room, the Taser pressed against my ribs. "You're not leaving this cabin. But I can't have you in this room. You're too distracting, and I need Ethan's undivided attention."

She shoves me into a bedroom and forces me onto the mattress. I roll over and kick out with my legs, but she's too fast for me. The Taser hums alive, and the next thing I know, an electric current zips through my body, frying every cell. I swear even my hair is singed. By the time I can string two words together again, I'm cuffed to the wooden headboard. At least this time, I'm only bound by one limb instead of four.

She rips the duct tape from my mouth. OW. If I had any energy left, I might've screamed. But all I can manage is a whimper.

She'll leave me now. She'll go back to her date, and I can hunt for the pieces of my body and try to put them back together.

But she doesn't leave. Instead, she paces across the maroon rug that's covering the hardwood floor. "You have to help me, Kan." She pushes her hand into her hair, messing up the already messy bun. It goes from artfully disheveled to knocked-around disaster. "I don't know what I'm doing wrong. He's just not interested in me."

I blink. Oh god. She actually believed me. She actually thinks I'm going to help her seduce my boyfriend.

"Maybe you could try a different outfit." My voice is hoarse, either from disuse or from all the screaming I've been doing in my mind. "Or, I don't know, a different eyeliner?"

She bares her teeth. "That's the best advice you have?"

"I'll keep thinking," I say, trying my best to keep the sarcasm from leaking into my voice. "If I come up with anything, you'll be the first to know."

She looks at me for a long moment, and I wonder if she's going to grab her gun, after all. But then, she sighs and kneels in front of me. "In the bigger scheme of things, he means nothing. I would never let a boy come between us. You know that. Eventually, we'll dump him and take off to begin our new lives. Just imagine, Kan. You'll no longer be restricted by Khun Yai's expectations. By the judgments of the kids at school. You'll be able to create your own identity. Be the person you were meant to be. With me by your side. Doesn't that sound wonderful?"

She wants to rip me from my life—my family, my friends—so that I can live an existence like hers? Drifting around, stealing other people's identities? Um, no thanks. I may be caught between worlds, I may not know where I belong, but I have people who love me. Maybe they're not perfect, maybe they can never understand the two warring sides of me. But they love me.

"If Ethan doesn't matter," I say carefully, "then why do you want to seduce him?"

"Because, Kan, for just a little while, I want to know how it feels to be cherished and loved. I want, for once in my life, to have one of my dreams come true. No, not just come true. I want it to be better than anything I've ever imagined."

She sits on the floor and wraps her arms around her knees. "I had sex at the frat party—but that's not enough. That was just a throwaway physical sensation. I want passion and romance. I need to know how it feels. Don't you want that for me? You

said you wanted to make it up to me. Well, this is your chance."
She's pleading with me now, and for an instant the old protective instinct rises up inside me. The instinct that wants to pick up this girl and cradle her, to soothe away her hurts, to ease her pain. Just as quickly, the feeling evaporates, as though it never existed.

"I do want that for you, Shelly," I say quietly. "But not like this."

"This is the only way I know." She stands, her expression tight, and leaves.

Damn it. Frantically, I scan the room. My heart jitters in my chest, but my mind is focused. As determined as Ethan. If there's a way to get us out of here, I'm going to find it. I won't let these hours cuffed to this bed be the last of my life.

Unfortunately, there's remarkably little inside this room. A decrepit desk with drawers. The wooden bed to which I'm cuffed. The rug on the floor. And that's it. No picture frames, no knickknacks. No books or plants. Certainly not a rock-shaped paperweight that I can use as a weapon.

I slide off the bed and strain, and I can just reach the desk. I open the drawers, but they've been emptied, cleaned out with a chemical with a faint lemony scent. I'm about to slam the last drawer shut when something catches my eye. An inscription on the side of the drawer, scrawled in permanent marker, in childish handwriting. *Leesa was here.*

My mind whirls. Leesa. That was Riley's mother, right? This desk must've belonged to her, or at least to her family, when she was a kid. So what is it doing here? Mrs. Watson's words drift through my mind. *Sheila said they had a home base somewhere, a cabin on a nearby lake.*

So, that's where we are, then. In Riley's mother's old cabin. The question is: Where is Riley?

No freaking clue. Sighing, I close the drawer and look around. Where else can I search?

Twisting around, I lie on my stomach on the mattress, so that I can reach under the bed with my free hand.

Some old pillows. Great. Absolutely useless, unless I think I can overpower Shelly and her weapons and smother her. A bunch of dust bunnies. Ha. Maybe I can toss them in her face and make her sneeze. I'm accumulating some really powerful tools here.

I run my fingers along the underside of the bed. It feels smooth and polished, so at least I won't get splinters. But there's nothing out of the ordinary. I'm about to give up when my hand snags on a ledge. I pause, my eyes wide. This isn't a ledge. Something's carved under here.

Notches. The kind you get by pushing a fingernail into soft wood. As if someone were keeping track of the number of days they were kept in here. Someone like . . . Riley.

I begin shaking. I might be wrong. All I have to go on is a bunch of notches. But somehow, in the pit of my stomach, I know I am dead right.

Before me, Shelly locked someone else in this room. Her former best friend, Riley.

Chapter 45

My hand goes numb. My shoulder aches. No matter how I twist and turn, I can't get comfortable. I don't know how I'm going to last one day in here.

I'm just beginning to contemplate gnawing off my arm when the doorknob turns. I brace myself for another encounter with Shelly.

But it's not my "friend" who rushes into the room. It's Ethan. Dear, sweet Ethan. Still-handcuffed Ethan, who is now carrying a plank of wood and tripping over his feet as he drags a length of chain behind him.

"Ethan! How did you get free? And why are you carrying that board?"

He turns the plank over, showing me the metal loop embedded in it. The same loop to which he is attached. "We have to hurry. Shelly's in her room, getting ready for the second part of our date. We don't have much time." He drops the plank. "I'll going to break the headboard."

Taking a deep breath, he kicks the headboard as hard as he can. It doesn't move a millimeter. "We just need a loose joint," he mutters. "Something to give me leverage."

He wraps both hands around the column and pulls. He yanks, he shoves, he pounds. My wrist vibrates, and the metal clanks into my bones and shreds skin. But nothing, nothing, nothing.

After a full two minutes, Ethan places his hands on his knees, panting. Sweat drenches his hair, and the redness of his fists matches his cheeks. "Just give me a second," he gasps. "I'll try again. I'm not giving up."

I glance at the door nervously. "You're making too much noise. She's going to hear you, and then we'll really be in trouble. Forget me. You've got to get out of here."

A pulse throbs at his temple. "I'm not leaving you."

"Please, Ethan, you have to," I plead. "She's going to kill you. I don't know when. After she gets bored, I guess. She thinks you're cute, but to her, all guys are expendable. You have to get out of here before she hurts you. It's different for me. She thinks of me as her sister. She wants me alive."

His eyes flash. "You don't know that, Kan. I'm not going to risk your life on something as changeable as her state of mind."

"If you leave, you can get help and come back."

"By the time I get back, the two of you will be long gone. We may never find you again."

"At least you'll be alive," I say, my eyes filling with tears. "You have to go. Now. While you still have the chance. Before she makes you do things that will scar you forever."

He pales but lifts his chin. "You can say whatever you want, but I'm not leaving you." He attacks the headboard with renewed energy, but the result is the same. Battered fists and no movement.

"Wait, Ethan. Stop. Let's think about this. Can we overpower her? You have the board now. Maybe you can knock her out."

"It's risky." He pushes a hand through his hair. "I'm not sure I can sneak up on her with this chain. If she sees me approaching or guesses my intention, if she gets to the gun before I can knock her out . . ." He shakes his head. "I can try, if that's our best option."

"We need something more subtle." I chew on my lip. "We have to get the key to my handcuffs. Where does she keep the key?"

"Probably on her."

"You're right. She unlocked my cuffs and by the time I turned around, the key was already gone. The dress has no pockets and it's skintight. I should know; I made it," I say, thinking quickly. "What else was she wearing tonight?"

He grimaces. "I have no idea. I was trying not to look at her."

"Come on, Ethan, think! This is important. Was she carrying a purse? Did she have on any jewelry or a belt—"

"A necklace. She was wearing this jagged thing around her neck."

My heart stops. "Of course," I whisper. "The BFF necklace."

It was the strangest BFF necklace I had ever seen. The bottom of each partial heart had a weird, jagged edge that looked almost like a key. But what if it actually is a key? What if that's the reason she kept it, when she left all of her other jewelry behind?

"That's it," I say. "That jagged pendant hanging on the chain. That must be the key."

"Are you sure?"

"No. But it's the best guess I have."

A board squeaks. It could be the cabin settling—or Shelly could be coming.

"You'd better get out of here." I swallow hard, not believing what I'm about to say. "You have to romance her. The only way we'll get the key is if you can distract her. Convince her that you're truly into her. Not because of me. But because of her."

He takes a deep breath. "If it's your safety at stake, I'll do anything." He leans forward and presses his lips to mine. It is sweet and searing and perfect. If this is the last kiss I'll ever have, I'm glad it's with him.

"I want you to know, Kan, when I'm with her . . ." He trails off.

"You don't have to say it." I bring my free hand to his face, tracing the bones of his jaw. "I forgive you, in advance, for everything."

He stops. "Even if you don't know what you're forgiving me for?"

A single tear spills from my eye. "Even then."

He kisses my cheek, swallowing the tear. And then he is gone.

Chapter 46

Shelly escaped to her room. She had given Ethan her best seductive smile and purred that she needed to freshen up before they headed on to the next phase of their evening. But it had all been a lie.

She rapped her knuckles against her thighs and paced the room, from her bed to the dresser to the door. It was all going wrong. So terribly wrong, and she didn't know what to do. She didn't know how to fix it.

Oh, sure, Ethan smiled at her. He ate the food; he listened to her talk. But she could tell he was playing a role—and not doing a very good job at that. He wasn't interested in her. He just didn't want her to hurt his precious Kan. Which made her want to hurt Kan even more.

She'd spent so much time planning. She'd gone to so much trouble to set the scene of their date. And now, she didn't even want to go through with it.

It was all Kan's fault.

Shelly kicked the door inside her room. Rage built inside her, brick by brick, until it rivaled the Sears freaking Tower.

Kan could've helped her, instead of giving her useless advice. She knew exactly how to snare Ethan's attention. Hell, she'd done it herself. She could've taught Shelly. That's what a real sister would've done. But she didn't want to.

Shelly rubbed angrily at her eyes. Contrary to what Kan

might believe, she wasn't going to make Ethan have sex with her. She wasn't a damn rapist. Couldn't they understand? She wanted him to come to her willingly. To be interested in her for her own sake.

Kan had told her she didn't have to pretend to be anybody else. That she was perfectly lovable exactly how she was.

Please. That might've been the biggest lie ever told in this world.

Here Shelly was, her true, honest self. And did Ethan love her? No. Did Kan love her? Hell no. Kan was supposed to be her friend. She was supposed to put Shelly's best interests before any boy's, the way she'd promised. But the first thing she did when Shelly took something for herself was run off and investigate her.

This made the bricks of rage build even faster inside her. She couldn't afford to lose control, not again. She'd lost control with Ash. She'd lost control with Khun Yai. Both those incidents were mistakes, and she wouldn't repeat them. When she killed again, it would be with cool, levelheaded deliberation.

She sighed. Looking in the mirror, she began to finger-comb her hair, trying to get it back into some kind of style. Kan's style. She heard thumping from outside the room, and she paused.

Maybe Ethan was trying to get free. She'd attached the chain to a loose plank on purpose, so that he could feel like he was ac-complishing something. She'd learned from the past. Her vic-tims had to feel like they were moving forward. They had to have a goal. They had to maintain hope. Otherwise, they didn't make fit companions for her. They became listless and slept all day. They stared at nothing when they were awake and made her feel like she was taking care of Pet Rocks. There was noth-ing appealing about a Pet Rock.

Just look at the last person who'd lived in the room before Kan.

Thud. Crash. Clonk. It sounded like a construction site out there. Didn't matter. Even if Ethan had gotten himself free, he wouldn't go far. Every exit in the cabin was locked from the in-side, and the only key hung around Shelly's neck.

She closed her hand around the jagged BFF necklace. Like she would've given somebody half of her heart. As she had learned, and as Kan had confirmed, she couldn't trust anyone in this world. Not even her so-called sister.

She'd had high hopes for Ethan. And even higher hopes for Kan. But so far, they were disappointing her just like everyone else. She was willing to give it one more shot, but they'd better shape up, fast.

Otherwise, she'd have to kill them both.

Chapter 47

After Ethan leaves, I have an idea. I've searched the five-foot radius around the spot where my hand is cuffed to the bed. But there's one place I haven't looked: under the floor. If Ethan can pry up planks of wood, then so can I.

Hanging my torso over the side of the bed, I stick my nails into the grooves between the hardwood and pull up as hard as I can. OW. Bad move. Two of my nails break off, and I lift my fingers to my mouth, sucking off the blood. *Smooth, Kan. Next time, make sure it's loose before you pull.*

Slower this time, and more deliberately, I check all the planks. They might as well be concrete. Except one. Of course, this plank is all the way under the bed, where I can barely reach. But it's loose. I exert some pressure, and the board slides a fraction of an inch. Definitely loose.

I run my nails around the entire plank. I push and pull and prod. I break my other three nails. But after twenty minutes of achy, sweaty work—made more difficult because I can't actually see what I'm doing—I manage to get the board off.

I stick my hand inside the hole, and I brush against an object. Several objects.

My mouth falls open. This was a long shot. I didn't actually expect to find anything. But here it is, an entire treasure trove. One by one, I pull the items out. A red plastic pot. A roll of toilet paper. Twelve bottles of water. Six peanut butter chocolate chip granola bars. A toothbrush. Toothpaste.

I look at the items. And look at them again. I don't get it. What the hell are they doing under the floor? Together, they comprise a prisoner survival kit. I can pee in the chamber pot, if that's what it is. I won't starve or become dehydrated—at least not yet.

But it's more than that. These items are specific to me. Peanut butter chocolate chip is my favorite flavor of granola bar. Shelly knows that. It's like she left this kit for me to find. But why? Why not just give me these items when she locked me to the bed? Why make it so hard?

Weird. Really weird.

I look at the granola bar longingly. I'm tempted to tear into the food, but I've only been here a few hours. Who knows how much longer she'll keep me? Better to wait until I'm really desperate.

My eyes drift to the desk with its column of drawers. If these items were under the floor, maybe there are other things hidden around the drawers.

Sure enough, I find a mirror behind the bottom drawer. A small compact, wedged behind the wood and the railing. It could've fallen back there somehow—or maybe Shelly left it there for me to find.

However it got there, I'm not about to waste a potential weapon.

I glance at the closed door. I haven't heard any noise for a long time. What are they doing out there? Has Ethan gotten the necklace yet?

I breathe out slowly. My insides are all chewed up with worry, but I can't let that feeling overwhelm me. Not if I want to get us out of here.

Saying a silent prayer for Ethan's safety, I slam the compact on the ground. I hear the sound of glass breaking. *Please, oh, please, let one of those pieces be big enough for a weapon.*

I open the compact and pick among the shards. Thank goodness, there are a couple of slivers that might actually do some damage.

I put one in the pocket of my shirt, where it hopefully won't jab me, and hold the other one in my fist, trying not to grip too tightly. But it cuts me anyway, and a trickle of blood flows down my hand.

I've never been in a fight in my life, and I certainly haven't raised a hand against my elders. That's not what a good Thai girl does.

But a good Thai girl wouldn't roll over and die, either. In this situation, if her life depended on it, I think a good Thai girl would do whatever the hell it took to survive. To win. And I think Khun Yai would wholeheartedly approve.

The next time Shelly comes through that door, I'll be ready.

Chapter 48

Shelly had lingered long enough.

She'd decided Kan's advice wasn't so useless after all. She changed into the lingerie she'd bought with Ethan in mind—a black mesh and lace bustier with matching panties, a garter belt, and thigh-high stockings. She put a flimsy, sheer robe over the whole ensemble, and her BFF necklace hung down her neck, right into the cleavage that the bustier created. She looked good. Really good, especially if you didn't notice the scar on her face. But with this outfit, who would look at her face, anyway?

When she'd tried on the lingerie at the store, she'd felt like a vision. All she'd had to do was flash a bit of lace and a lot of cleavage to Walt Peterson, and he would've left his football buddies to follow her anywhere. She'd been sure a similar outfit would work on Ethan, too.

But now, as she looked at herself in the mirror, she gnawed her lip. Would Ethan laugh at her? Maybe he would smirk and turn away. Maybe he would pity her for trying too hard, or worse, feel disgusted at the sight of her body, which was too bony in some places and too fleshy in others. Some girls were born to be sexy, and some girls just . . . weren't.

She'd been a *weren't* all of her life. And she didn't want to be one anymore. It was time for her to stop feeling so scared. Time to stop being so helpless. She had to take action; she had to take a risk. Nothing would change unless she did.

Besides, if he laughed at her, she could always tase him.

The thought made Shelly feel better. It shifted the power back into her hands, and she felt in control again. She picked up the Taser, pulled back her shoulders, and glided into the den.

Ethan was already there, facing the fire.

Her heart swelled. He'd built a fire. And she hadn't even asked. Instead, he'd found the equipment she left by the hearth—the logs, the fire-starter bricks, the matches—and started an inferno of his own volition.

This was more like it. This was the guy she wanted him to be. Considerate, not because she ordered him, but because he chose to be.

The flame outlined his silhouette, and he stood on top of the bear rug. The fur was a little ratty, not as luxurious and soft as she'd imagined, but it would caress her naked skin just the same.

A plank of wood lay on the floor, next to the coiled-up chain that was still attached to his wrist. No problem. She could take his clothes off around the cuff.

Clutching the Taser, she walked further into the room. The floor squeaked, and he turned. The moment he saw her, his mouth dropped. His eyes widened, and his breathing became labored.

Oh, my. The outfit was working, after all.

Spreading her arms out, she twirled slowly in front of him, giving him an unobstructed view of her body. His eyes feasted on her. Gone were her insecurities, her qualms. She'd never felt more beautiful in her entire life.

"Well? What do you think?" God, was that her voice? Since when did she sound so husky?

"I don't know why we ate dinner," he said, his voice low, "when everything I'm hungry for is right in front of me."

She paused. She wanted to believe his words. More than anything, she wanted to look into his eyes and see that he was sincere. But he'd been more than a little reluctant at dinner. She needed more convincing.

And so, instead of falling into his arms, she arched an eyebrow. "That's not how you were acting earlier."

"You weren't wearing this outfit earlier." In three strides, he crossed the room and caught her up in his arms. Her breasts pressed against his chest, and his eyes fastened onto her cleavage.

Oh god. She was so hot—in so many ways. The sweat dripped down her neck, and she felt like candle wax in his embrace. She didn't know it could feel this good to be held. She didn't know it would feel even better to have him devour her with his eyes.

"So you're into me now?" she said demurely.

He ripped his gaze from her chest and looked straight into her eyes. "I've always been into you, Shelly. Since that amazing, unforgettable night we spent texting. I might not have known it was you at first, but now that I do, you're all I can think about." He tightened his hold around her. "But I couldn't show you my true feelings in front of Kan. Can you understand that? I had to pretend I was being forced to spend time with you. If she knew the truth, she'd be devastated. She's got so much going on right now. Ash dead. Khun Yai in the hospital. What's happened with you. I don't know if she can handle one more thing."

He lifted his hand and traced a finger down her cheek. The chain rattled beside them. "I'm not going to lie. I care about her. But you're the one who's captivated me. You waltz in here, wearing an outfit like that. And Kan's nowhere in sight. How do you expect me to react?"

Her knees, her ankles, her thighs were weak. If he weren't holding her up, she would have melted into a puddle, right there on the bear rug. She wanted to believe. He was looking into her eyes, and he was so cute, so sincere, so earnest.

Yet, she hesitated.

He leaned forward, and gently, so gently, he closed his mouth around her lower lip, tugging softly. Her eyes fluttered closed, and then his mouth eased over hers in the most wonderful kiss she'd ever known.

This. This was beyond her wildest dreams. This was what she had been searching for her entire life. To feel precious. To feel loved. To feel like she was the most important person on earth to somebody else.

How did it feel to hold this knowledge close to your heart? Not just in a transient kiss, but as a foundational truth of your life. No wonder the other girls walked through this world differently. Confidently. They knew, at the very core of their being, that somebody loved them.

Maybe things would be different for her now. Maybe this was the secret ingredient she'd been missing. Maybe this was what she needed to feel that she belonged.

And then the kiss changed, deepened. It turned from sweet to searing in a second. The flimsy wrap fell from her shoulders to the floor. His hands roamed along her sides, and she shivered, winding her arms around him, pressing the Taser she was holding into his back.

He broke away from her mouth and groaned. "Oh, Shelly, you're so hot. You're killing me."

This was it. She had to take this chance. She had to trust, for once in her life, that someone was who he professed to be. That he meant what he said. That he loved her. For herself.

She'd always thought she would find her other half in another girl, someone she could call her sister. But maybe she was wrong. Maybe she had been searching for Ethan all along. For this boy, she'd be willing to give her heart, her soul, her everything.

He just had to pass one more test.

Without warning, she shot her hand out and grabbed his crotch. She expected it to be big and bulging and straining against his pants. She'd felt it before, under the table during dinner with Khun Yai. But there was nothing. He was panting, and she was half-naked.

And there was nothing.

Rage filled her vision. The bastard. He was lying to her this entire time.

She flipped the Taser on. And jabbed him in the ribs, again and again, until he collapsed to the floor.

Chapter 49

Outside my window, the night deepens to black and then lightens with the dawn. It's not my imagination, then. Hours have passed. It's a new day, and we're still here. If I were making notches in the wood, I'd have to carve a second mark. And there's still no sign of Ethan.

Did our plan work? Are they sleeping? What did he have to do to distract her long enough to get the necklace? Was it just a kiss or, dear god, did they actually have sex?

Or maybe it all went horribly wrong. Maybe they never got that far because Ethan is now dead.

Oh, Phra Buddha Chao, I pray. *Please let Ethan be okay. Please don't let her hurt him. Please help us get out of here and forget this whole nightmare ever happened.*

I wish Shelly had given me a chain, too. I'd give anything to pace the room so that I could work off some of this nervous energy. Instead I'm just sitting here, holding onto the glass, while the anxiety builds inside me.

My palm was bloody before I figured out I should cover the glass in a granola bar wrapper. Now, my hand is shaking from the strain. I lower it to the bed to rest, only to jerk it back up at the slightest sound.

But the noises are so soft I wonder if I'm hallucinating them. Damn it. I've been sitting here forever. For all I know, neither Shelly nor Ethan is in the cabin anymore.

That's it. I have to do something. I've been trying to be patient because I didn't want to mess up Ethan's plans, but I can't wait anymore.

"Shelly!" I call as loudly as I can. My voice is hoarse, so I clear my throat and try again. "Shelly, are you here? I need to talk to you!"

I count to ten, and I'm about to scream out again when the door opens.

"Yes?" she asks, her eyebrows raised. She's wearing baggy jeans and a torn gray T-shirt. The clothes she was wearing when she arrived at my house. I haven't seen her in this outfit since that first day. Her hair is pulled into a limp ponytail, and she's not wearing a speck of makeup.

"Can you uncuff me?" I ask. "I need to use the bathroom. It would be nice to get something to eat, too."

She nods at the red chamber pot beside the bed. "You seem to be doing just fine."

"You're not surprised?" I curl my hand around the mirror shard. A little too hard, since the glass pokes through the wrapper and into my skin. "Did you leave those supplies for me?"

She shrugs. "Maybe."

"Why would you do that? You know, I broke all five of my nails and almost dislocated my shoulder prying off that plank. What if I hadn't found it? Why not just give me the supplies if you wanted me to have them?"

She looks at me listlessly. "I had to make it interesting for you, didn't I?" she says, her voice hitching. "Make you feel like you were . . . accomplishing . . . something." She buries her face in her hands, her shoulders shaking.

"Shelly," I say, shocked. "What's the matter?"

"I tried and tried," she wails. "You asked me to bring you here, and I did. But I had to lock you up until I could be sure I could trust you. I worked so hard to make this okay for you. I've learned from my past, from the last person who was kept in this room. I tried to make it amusing—like a game—to keep your spirits up. You like games, don't you? What fun would it be if I just handed you the supplies? I'm not a bad person, Kan. I'm not cruel. I only hurt people when it's necessary. I even stopped by the convenience store, with you in the trunk, and bought your favorite granola bars. Most people wouldn't do that. They wouldn't care. But I do. And you don't even appreciate it." She bursts into fresh tears.

"I do appreciate you," I say carefully.

"You don't. You didn't help me when I needed you. You didn't teach me how to make him like me. And now, look what happened."

I go still. "What happened? What did you do to Ethan?"

She takes a deep breath and dries her eyes. The question, inexplicably, seems to calm her. "Why don't you see for yourself?" She opens the door.

Through the entryway, I look into the den beyond, where Ethan lies in a heap on the bear rug.

My heart stops. "Oh my god, Shelly. Is he dead?"

"Not yet." She pulls the gun from her back pocket, tapping it against her palm as though it were a ballpoint pen. "He might have severe injuries, though. I tased him a half dozen times. I probably should've stopped after he passed out. But it doesn't matter. If he dies now, it will save me the trouble of killing him later."

"What?" I whisper, my chest tight. I must've squeezed the glass because all of a sudden a sharp pain lances across my palm. "You can't just leave him there, Shelly. You have to help him. He needs to get to a hospital."

"No," she snaps. "You lied to me. Both of you. You thought you could trick me. Pretend to be my friend. Pretend to love me. But I'm not a complete fool. I know he came in here to visit you."

She slaps her hand against the wall. "What did you say to him? Did you guys think it would be funny to have him pretend he was hot for me? To make me feel, for the first time in my life, that I was loved—only to rip it away again. Did that make you laugh, Kan? Did you enjoy humiliating me?"

I shrink into myself. "No! I swear to you, that's not what we were doing. We weren't laughing at you. We just wanted to get away."

"I don't care what your reasoning was," she says. "It was cruel. In fact, it's the meanest thing anyone's ever done to me. And you were the one who engineered it."

She advances toward me. "Put down the glass, Kan. I know you found the mirror wedged behind the drawer. Who do you think left it there for you? I wanted to give you a moment of hope, however fleeting. I can see the blood on your hand. There's no use hiding it. Just let it go."

I don't want to. It's my only weapon. If I give up the mirror, I'll have nothing.

"Now, Kan." She raises the gun and aims it at my knee. Would she actually shoot me over this? I'm not sure. Maybe this is just an idle threat. . . .

BANG.

I about fall off the bed. I don't feel any pain, though, so she must've missed. On purpose. There's a bullet hole on the bed six inches from my leg. Holy crap, this isn't a bluff.

Quickly, I open my palm and let the wrapped shard of glass tumble onto the mattress.

"Good girl," she says, reminding me ironically of Khun Yai. Keeping the gun trained on me, she walks toward me. I flinch, but she just unlocks the cuffs. The BFF necklace, however, is still hanging around her neck. So we were wrong about that, too.

"You want out of this room? Fine." She yanks me forward. The pain blurs my vision, but that's the least of my worries. She pulls me into the den and shoves me onto the floor, next to Ethan's unconscious body. "You and Ethan love each other so much, you should do everything together. Well, now you can die together. Isn't that romantic? Don't ever say I wasn't thinking about your wants, all the way to the end."

"Why are you doing this?" I whisper. "I'm your sister."

For a moment, her face crumples. "You think this is easy for me? I didn't want this. I wanted you and me together, for always. But I can't trust you. You and your lying boyfriend. So you have to die."

"I'm sorry, Shelly! I didn't know, okay? I didn't know you were my true sister. My true family."

The gun bobbles in her hand. "Khun Yai told you?"

"I found the envelopes. The ones addressed to your mom, in Khun Yai's handwriting. It looked like she was sending your mom checks on a monthly basis. It's not a huge leap to assume they were child support payments. Am I right? Did my father have an affair with your mom? Are we . . . sisters?"

"Cousins," she says, her voice shaking. "All my life, I've wanted to know my father. I thought he might give me the love that was so . . . difficult for my mom. But she refused to tell me who he was. When she died, I found the envelopes in her office, along with a letter to me. In it, she explained everything. How she fell in love with a man from Thailand. When he was here visiting his sister—your mother. How the man's mother disapproved and bribed my mom to go away. How she never saw my father again." Her face tightens. "So, yes, we are sisters, in a sense. But that doesn't change anything."

"Of course it does." So I was right and wrong. But it doesn't matter. In Thailand, we view our cousins as sisters and brothers. I try to rise, but my foot slips on the bear rug. "You could have a family, Shelly. Not just my mom and Khun Yai, but our whole family over in Thailand. So many aunts and uncles and cousins you won't know what to do with them. We could go there together. The police would never find us there. I'll introduce you to the family. I'll show you around Bangkok, I'll translate everything, teach you the language."

"They won't accept me."

"They will." I attempt to stand again, and this time I succeed. What's more, I feel something sharp against my chest. Of course. How could I forget? The second shard of mirror that I put in my pocket. I'm not without a weapon, after all. "I'll explain everything to them. They're not all as strict and traditional as Khun Yai. You know they love foreigners over there? They're obsessed with all things *farang,* and they'll see you as a movie star."

"Me?" The gun lowers. "A movie star? That's absurd."

"It's not absurd," I say. She's no longer looking at me. She's staring at the floor, thinking. I ease my hand up to my shirt pocket and dig around for the shard. My fingers brush against something sharp. Got it. "We can book a flight tomorrow. Before either of us is a suspect in any crime."

Her head snaps up suddenly. She sees me holding the mirror shard, and her eyes narrow. "Once again, you're lying to me." She raises the gun and points it at me. "Seriously, Kan? You really think a little piece of glass is a match for this gun?"

I exhale slowly until my body, my mind, my breath become perfectly still. I need more than words to convince her. I need something to show her, once and for all, that I'm on her side. That I'll do anything for her.

"You are my sister, Shelly. No matter what happens, you will always be my sister."

I raise the piece of glass, not toward her but up to my own face. "There's something you never told me. Something I never asked. Your mother. When she died, why was there a zigzag scar on her face?"

Her mouth twitches. "She didn't understand my pain. She dismissed the scar on my face, belittled the trauma I went through. So, I just wanted her to know. A few minutes before she died, I wanted her to know how it felt to be me."

So Shelly killed her mom, too, I thought dully. Did she enjoy choosing the wedding dress? Was her mother's murder another chance for her to enact one of her fantasies?

But as curious as I am about the answers, now isn't the time to ask questions. Before I can change my mind, I press the glass into my cheek. The pain is deep and immediate, but I push the mirror in further. Quickly, I zigzag the glass up my face, ripping, shredding, destroying my skin.

Her mouth drops open. "What the hell are you doing?"

Somewhere in the deep recesses of my brain, I register that the cut hurts. It hurts like hell. I should be on the floor by now, writing and screaming. But I don't feel the pain anymore. I feel like I'm hovering somewhere above, watching myself perform these actions, say these words.

"I'm making myself look like you, Shelly," I say, my voice ridiculously calm. "We're the same, you see? Not just on the outside, but on the inside, too. We've both been alone. We both felt like outsiders. We both know how it feels to stand outside a group, when everyone else is laughing and we don't even understand the jokes. We both know how it feels to be excluded. Even if it's subtle, it's no less devastating. We both know how it feels to be passed over, to have a crush on a boy who would never, ever be interested in us. I've felt all these things, Shelly. I know you have, too. You don't have to be alone anymore. That's what this scar represents. We're the same. Sisters in every sense of the word."

She blinks, tears rushing to her eyes. "You would disfigure yourself permanently, for me? You would give up your beauty for me?"

"I'd give up everything for you, Shelly." I walk closer to her and gently, ever so gently, reach out and caress her scar. She buries her face against my neck, weeping. I put my arms around her, and the gun falls limply to her side.

In one smooth motion, I grab the gun and whack her in the head. She slumps over, and I whack her again, putting everything I have into the motion. Seventeen years of keeping my mouth shut and going with the flow. Seventeen years of straddling two worlds, not knowing where I belong. But also, seventeen years of love and friendship and laughter. Seventeen years of the bright, shiny moments that make life worth living. I whack and I whack and I whack. This isn't about me being a good girl anymore. This is about me surviving.

When she is well and truly unconscious, I run for the door. There's no way I can carry Ethan. I need to get help, quickly, before she wakes up. But the door's locked from the inside. Damn it!

This. Can't. Be. Happening. Not now, not after all this. I pound my fists uselessly against the wood—and then I remember the BFF necklace. The key might not be the one for the handcuffs, but it just might fit in this lock.

Sprinting back to Shelly, I yank the necklace from her. I run back to the door, and, oh dear god, it fits. It actually fits.

I fling the door open, and the woods rush up to greet me. I want to stop and savor the blinding sun, the crisp air, the earthy scent of the soil. But I can't. Not yet. Ethan's not safe yet.

I look around wildly, but it's all the same. A dense bunch of trees and vegetation, with narrow paths in about five directions. Which way is it to civilization? Shelly had to drive here some-how. She certainly didn't carry us to the cabin. I scan the ground. There! Tire tracks. The narrow opening barely looks like it could fit a car, but this has to be it.

Throwing a prayer to the wind, I start running. I'm not a distance runner. Never have been. In fact, I'm that girl who gets winded after two laps in gym class. But being tired is not an option. I pump my arms; I leap forward with each stride. I push my way through that forest. So many times, I stumble on a branch. So many times, I want to stop, to give my fiery lungs a chance to cool down.

But I don't. Who knows how long Shelly will be out? The difference between Ethan's life and potential death could be a matter of seconds. I won't lose him because I took a break.

And then, amazingly enough, I hear it. The roar of a car engine. I put on a burst of speed and crash onto the middle of the road just as a car is approaching. The minivan slams on its brakes, and the woman in the driver's seat gapes at me.

I limp to her window and see a toddler with curly dark hair behind her in a car seat.

"You're that girl who's been missing," the woman blurts out. "The one whose fingerprints were on the paperweight. It's been all over the news. They cleared you, you know. They found another set of prints on the rock, one that was more consistent with the blows. Everyone's looking for you and that boy."

"Yes," I pant, almost weeping. "He's still back there, with the kidnapper. We have to call the police."

Without a word, she punches three numbers into her cell phone and hands it to me. Through the earpiece, I hear an operator's voice say, "Nine-one-one," and it is the single sweetest sound in the entire world.

Chapter 50

A few months later . . .

I'm in my room, packing. We leave in a couple days for a one-week vacation to Chicago. For the first time since my dad passed away, my mom's taking an entire week off. We're going to sight-see and take a tour of the Illinois Institute of Art.

After Khun Yai returned from the hospital, she had a change of heart about my future. She agreed to let me apply to the school of my choice. After I confessed that I'm already designing clothes in secret, she even helped me properly set up the studio over the garage. No more sewing machines and dressmaker's dummies shoved into the closets. Instead, all of my equipment is displayed out in the open, the way it should be. More importantly, she supports me. When my designs won first place in the county fashion show, she hugged me tightly and said, "It might be the most impractical star in the universe, but so long as you catch it, that's what counts."

I don't know if it was nearly losing her granddaughter or knowing that her rigidity could have been the cause, but she's mellowed out. A lot. Even my mom works less at the hospital. She told her colleagues she would no longer work extra shifts, and the practice ended up hiring another doctor.

Ash is still dead. I mourn her every single day, but I'm slowly trying to rediscover the joy in my life, too. Ethan's going to apply to Northwestern University, so maybe he'll be in the same city as me after graduation. He's recovered fully, and he's already being recruited for their ballroom dance team.

And the future looks promising. After what we've been through, our relationship isn't going to follow the same easy path as other high school couples. I'm not going to delude myself otherwise. But the other night, we took a trip to the park. We swung, holding hands. We didn't reach as high into the sky as we would have by ourselves, but the swings arced through the air together, in sync. I'm hoping that together, we'll be able to reach the heights, after all.

Later, we climbed to the top of the jungle gym, and he kissed me. After the hundreds of kisses Ethan's given me this summer, you would think they would start feeling the same. But this particular kiss, I've never felt before. His lips rooted me to the spot, and yet, somehow, his kiss also opened my eyes to the future. It made me hopeful. That's an emotion that's been hard to come by since Shelly.

The cut on my face has healed. It's not as deep as Shelly's, and it is not as noticeable, either. Still, when I apply foundation, I'm careful not to touch it. I have no desire to hide this scar.

And even less desire to hide who I am.

I'm trying to figure out how to cram my final pair of shoes into my suitcase when Khun Yai appears at the door.

She ambles inside. She's slower than she used to be. Frailer, too. But I also think she's more at peace.

I think the actions she took to hide my uncle's transgression have gnawed at her over the years, and she's relieved that the secret's out in the open now. This way, she can begin to make amends. She continues to send checks, but this time, the money goes to an account in jail, so that Shelly can buy slippers and gum and other sundries.

"Are you done packing?" she asks.

I look at my suitcase sprawled on the floor. "Almost. I have to find a place for these shoes, and that's it."

"I always said you're my granddaughter. Packed and ready to go days before anybody else." She smiles softly. "It was because we're so similar that I've always been so strict with you.

If I hadn't been so worried about your future, I would've given you the world. Still would if I could."

She pulls a jewelry bag out of her pocket. My breath catches. It's the one I've admired all my life—bloodred velvet, decorated with gold lettering, tied shut with a drawstring. The one that holds our family heirloom.

Opening the bag slowly, she takes out the necklace. If possible, the sapphires and rubies flash even more brilliantly than I remember. The hammered gold gleams. Old. Ornate. Thai.

"This necklace is yours," she says. "It's always belonged to you. I was simply keeping it until you were ready. You may not be eighteen, but you're ready now, Kanchana." She crosses the room, and we both turn to the mirror.

Our reflections look back at us, one old and one young. Sixty years separate us, but the similarity in our features is unmistakable. The slightly flared noses, the teardrop-shaped eyes. It's because Shelly doesn't have these same features that it took me so long to see the truth of her parentage. I thought I was good at not judging someone based on her appearance. I guess I was wrong.

I lift my hair, and Khun Yai places the necklace around my throat. I haven't worn it in four years, but not for an instant have I forgotten how it feels.

The piece of jewelry settles on my collarbone, dense and heavy. Just as before, it makes me feel special. It gives me confidence. It assures me I can do anything in this world.

"Are you sure, Khun Yai?" I lick my lips. "Am I . . . worthy of this necklace? Will I do it honor?"

Instead of ducking my head, however, I hold it high. With my recent decisions, it's more clear than ever I'm not the Thai girl she was. And yet, I'm not purely American, either.

But I'm no longer ashamed of that.

She nods. "It took me eighty years to learn this, but I now know that a person's culture does not reside in her outer trappings. It's in the heart. And in your heart, *luk lak,* you are as Thai and as good as I would ever want you to be."

Tears spring to my eyes, and I bring my hand up to stroke the sapphires and the rubies, the uneven towers of the necklace. "This makes me feel so beautiful."

"You are beautiful. Never doubt that. You may not look like or feel like other people, but that's what makes you so special, through and through. On the inside and out."

I run my fingers along the necklace one more time. And wish with everything in my little girl's heart that I can keep this heirloom I've coveted for so long.

"You know how much this necklace means to me." I swallow hard. "But as our family tradition dictates, the necklace is bequeathed from grandmother to eldest granddaughter. And there's another girl who has your bloodline. She didn't grow up with our family, and she's had a difficult life. She's made mistakes. Big ones. Maybe unforgivable ones. But I have to wonder if it's because we weren't there to support her. To love her." I unclasp the necklace and let it fall into my hand. "No matter what her sins are, Shelly is still my cousin. She's still your granddaughter. I'm not saying I want to give this necklace to her. Not yet. Maybe never. But perhaps, like you, I can just hold onto it for a little while. And then . . . we'll see."

"Yes. Perhaps you are right," Khun Yai says haltingly. "I've . . . made mistakes, too. I turned away a child when she should have been living with us, her family. That is a sin that will stay with me not just for this life, but for the next one, too. It is a blemish on my soul for which it will take much to atone." She places a hand on my shoulder. "Do what you think is best, *luk lak*. The necklace is yours now. Someday, if you ever choose to give it to Shelly, then I will fully support your decision."

I turn and hug her. I no longer need a necklace to prove her love for me. Because I now know that in my heart. "Thank you, Khun Yai. I'm so lucky to have you."

She smiles. "No, *luk lak*. I'm the lucky one."

Chapter 51

The next morning, I wake up early and drive two hours to the Prairie County Jail, where Shelly is being held before her trial. We leave for Chicago tomorrow, and there's nothing more important for me to do on my last day before vacation. I've packed a bottle of water and a granola bar for the trip. Oatmeal raisin, this time. I've somehow lost my taste for peanut butter chocolate chip.

Last night, I told Ethan my plans, and he offered to accompany me. But this is something I need to do by myself. At its core, my relationship with Shelly was always about the two of us.

I park the car and enter a large, rectangular brick building. In the waiting area, clusters of people sit in metal chairs. Lawyer types, with their briefcases and sloppy ties. A man with tattoos covering every square inch of his visible skin. A little girl eating cubes of cheese, and a young woman knitting a scarf, her needles clacking in the air.

I approach the service window. The guard gestures to a clipboard and pen, and I fill in my name and Shelly's before retreating to a metal chair.

A few minutes later, the guard calls me back to the window. She has puffy hair and wears a navy uniform. Her fleshy cheeks and firm jaw make her face both soft and hard. I hand her my driver's license.

She takes the card but doesn't look at it. "Sorry, dear, we've got a problem. There ain't no one named Shelly Ambrose here."

I pull my phone out of my purse. "I have the right place. I'm sure of it."

I tap on the phone, pulling up the proper document. "See?" I hold the screen out for her to see. "I even wrote it down."

The guard doesn't give my phone so much as a glance. "You can look at the inmate list yourself. I'm telling you, there's no Shelly Ambrose here. We're not even holding anyone named Shelly."

"Could she have registered under a different name?" I ask, gripping the counter. "Maybe Shelly's a nickname or something. She's about my height. Last time I saw her, she had hair just like mine, long and black and straight, but she might've changed it. She does that a lot. She has a scar." I stumble over the words. I hate using the scar as an identifying feature. There's more to Shelly—and to me—than the remnants of a blade on our faces. But whether or not I like it, our scars set us apart. "It goes along her cheek, kinda like mine. Except hers is much deeper."

"Oh." The guard brightens. "You must mean Jane. She's got a zigzag scar just like that. I swear, we could call her Chameleon. She changes looks and personalities by the day."

I wrinkle my forehead. "Jane?"

"Jane Doe. She came into the system without a verifiable identity. And clearly, we can't trust any of the aliases she's given us. So we just call her Jane." She types on the keyboard. "Would you like to see her?"

I blink. I'm still not convinced this Jane is my Shelly, but I have nothing to lose. My only other option is to go home. "Sure. Why not?"

Another guard shows me into a room with a table and two chairs. The floor's swept clean, but the air feels sterile, cold. As though the heat doesn't reach inside here.

I wrap my arms around myself and shiver. If this is how I feel after being in here for a few seconds, how does Shelly—or Jane—or whoever the hell I'm about to meet—feel being locked up for months?

A few minutes later, the door opens, and Shelly shuffles into the room. A jolt of electricity runs up my spine. So it is her. The same girl I knew, but with a new name.

Her ankles are shackled, and she wears an orange V-neck top and pants. The black hair dye is fading, and streaks of her natural hair color show through. Only it's not brown like it was when I first met her, but a dirty blond.

She no longer looks like me or even like a distant relative, if she ever did. It's amazing how one unique characteristic, such as hair color or fashion sense, can make two girls look so similar.

For a long moment, we don't say anything. She observes me with a completely neutral expression. Maybe this is who she is when she's not trying to be someone else. Maybe she truly is a chameleon and can take on any identity she wants. The old Jane—the one who went by the name of Shelly—always had a yearning in her eyes. She always wanted something, anything, even if it was just a pat on the head.

There is no such desire in Jane. Maybe all those wants died with her Shelly persona.

I speak first. "So your name is Jane now, huh? Where's Shelly Ambrose?"

"Shelly is dead," she says flatly. "She died months ago, on the same day that her mother committed suicide. Or at least . . . that's what I've been told."

The air jams in my chest, and I pound it, trying to get my breath dislodged. My fingers shake, and my heart mourns. Oh god. Shelly Ambrose, dead. The girl who was my cousin. The girl who was forsaken by my family. And I never knew her.

The tears build behind my eyes, piercing them as though they were a hundred sharp needles. I wish I could've taken her to Thailand. I wish I could've introduced her to her family. I never felt like I fit in over there. I was always too big, too inelegant, too outspoken. I didn't understand the Thai subtleties. I was awkward, even with my own relatives. And yet, they are my family. They love me. And I'm certain they would've loved Shelly, too, whoever she was.

But now it's too late. We will never be able to make it up to her. She was dead before I ever knew about her. Before Jane Doe ever entered my life. And that's something my mom, Khun Yai, and I will always carry on our souls.

"Did you kill her?" I ask in a low voice.

She gives me a look, as if to say she's not about to incriminate herself. "Of course not. I don't know anything about it. All I can tell you is what's in the police report. After Sheila Ambrose's body was found in the church, a policeman drove to the Ambrose residence to inform the daughter. A girl matching Shelly Ambrose's general description opened the door. She had the proper identification, and she was the only one in the house. The police didn't check her fingerprints; there was no reason to. Shelly was over eighteen and legally an adult, so that was the end of her involvement with the police."

"Until you were arrested," I prompt.

"Until I was arrested." She cocks her head. She wants to tell me more, I can see. She's dying to tell me more. She's just not sure if she should.

I wait, not saying a word. We stare at each other, and one second flows into the next.

"A few weeks after Sheila's death, a body washed up from the river," she finally says. Her voice is soft now, almost dreamy. "She was unidentified for a long time. Her fingerprints and dental images didn't match any from the missing persons file—maybe because she was never reported missing."

She's watching me carefully now. She wants my reaction. She craves it—to what end, I can't even begin to guess. "And then, I was arrested as Shelly Ambrose. Problem was, my fingerprints didn't match Shelly's. And my dental records didn't, either. Someone had the brilliant idea to compare Shelly's metrics with the unidentified body. Bingo. A perfect match. Enter my new, but surely not final, identity: Jane Doe."

I bring my hand to my mouth, horrified. "You're Riley. You killed both Sheila and Shelly Ambrose and began impersonating Shelly from that day forward. When you talked about Riley being dead, you meant her identity had died. Everything you said about Riley—it was all true, but reversed. Shelly was the one who broke your trust. And she died for it. Am I right? Is your true name Riley?"

She shrugs. "Maybe. Maybe not."

"But what about the notches under the bed?" I ask. "You said there was a person who was kept in there before me. If it wasn't Shelly . . . then who was it?"

She studies her hand, as if she's trying to map the veins underneath. "Maybe Riley had a mother who treated her like a possession. Maybe she made her daughter participate in cons, even though Riley hated it. Maybe the mother needed to be taught a lesson on how it feels to be kept. On how it grates the soul to be forced to do things against one's will."

My jaw drops. "You locked up your own mother?"

"Maybe." She glances up, and the look in her eyes sends chills up my spine. "Maybe not."

I think I'm going to be sick. My stomach churns so violently I may never keep anything down again. I lift my eyes to the ceiling and breathe deeply through my nose. I've got two options here. I can run screaming from this room. Or I can stay and get the answers I need.

"The real Shelly," I say faintly. "My cousin. What did she look like?"

"You can find out from her yearbook photo." She smirks. "Brown hair and eyes. Her skin is paler than yours. She has more Caucasian features. But the eyes are a dead giveaway. They could be yours."

"I always wondered how you could be related to me," I murmur, shaking my head. "Appearances can be deceiving, but still. You look nothing like me."

"We believe what we're told to believe," she says. "That's why I've been so successful in my impersonations. I understand that, and use it to my advantage."

"What are you saying? Are you saying you've stolen identities other than mine and Shelly's?"

A small smile plays on her lips. "Hate to say it, Kan, but

you're simply one in a long line of victims. I've been stealing identities for years. I told you I was eighteen, but can you tell, truly, how old I really am?" She thrusts her face forward, showing me the scar that draws so much attention, that hides so much. Most people are so busy looking at it that they don't notice anything else. "I could be five years older. Hell, I could be ten years older. Can you really ever know? Riley may have hated what her mom made her do, but that doesn't mean she didn't learn from her."

Acid sprints up my throat. To think I felt sorry for her. To think I considered, for even one moment, that I might someday give her my necklace. I'm surprised I'm not retching over a trash can. But I hold the nausea down, for just a little longer.

"Who are you really, Jane?" I ask. "Who is the true girl lurking beneath your surface?"

She breaks into a smile. "Do you really want to know? I have no past, and I have no future. I can be anybody I want, which means I will always fit in, but I will never belong. We're the same, Kan. That's why I was going to break the pattern for you. That's why I was going to let you live. You feel the same loneliness, and you feel the same dread. You, too, would do anything to belong." She leans back, her eyes glittering. "Face it, Kan. I am you, and you are me."

"No," I whisper. "I never would've done what you did. I never could've hurt all those people."

"But you did, Kan. You hurt Khun Yai by lying to her. You hurt Ash by not being there when she needed you. Hell, you even hurt Ethan, by judging him for something that wasn't his fault. Don't forget, Kan. I know all your secrets. I know how you think. In order to be you, I had to study you. Your every word, your every feeling. I know you better than you know yourself. And when I look at you, I feel like I'm looking in a mirror."

I've heard enough. I push my seat back and stand up. "We're nothing alike, Jane. NOTHING."

"Deny all you want." Jane laughs. She's the one sitting in jail, and she's laughing. At me. She thinks she's won, once again. She thinks she's gotten inside my head, crawled around, and made it her own.

But it's not over. She's not done.

"You and me, we're the girls who walk between lives. The girls who live between worlds. We can change our appearances, Kan. We can make different friends, adopt different personalities. But we can never change our core. We will never belong." She smiles, and her teeth flash under the fluorescent lights. "By definition, we can't. You see, that's who we are. We're the girls in between."

"You're wrong, Jane." As I stand there, looking at her, I'm more certain than ever that I'm right. "You see, I used to think just like you. I used to feel that because I was in between worlds, that I was part of neither. Now I know the truth." I reach up to my collarbone and touch the bare skin there, where I can still feel the weight of gold. I'm not wearing any jewelry today, but I don't need to. I remember how the necklace feels. I understand, at the core of my being, what it means. "Different worlds aren't mutually exclusive, and you don't have to pick one world over another. I can choose to belong to both—or neither. Or make my own world altogether."

I lift my chin. "I'm not a girl in between. I'm a girl *on the verge*. Of new adventures, of new possibilities. I can be whoever I want to be. And now, I know that I'm not alone. And maybe, just maybe, I never was."

Acknowledgments

I've wanted to be an author ever since I was six years old, but I grew up believing that if I wanted to be published, I would not be able to write about characters who looked like me. I couldn't be any happier that I was wrong.

First and foremost, I would like to thank Kensington Publishing for making my unacknowledged dream possible. My heartfelt thanks to Mercedes Fernandez, who championed this idea from the beginning, and to my editor, Alicia Condon, for her insights on this story. Thank you, as well, to my fabulous publicist, Lulu Martinez, and the rest of the team at Kensington for turning this manuscript into a book.

Huge thanks to Beth Miller, agent extraordinaire. I feel lucky every day to have you on my side.

Thank you to Meg Kassel, Abigail Hing Wen, and T.A. Maclagan for helping me make this book so much better. I am very grateful to Brenda Drake for encouraging me every day that I was writing this story. I am also indebted to Vanessa Barneveld and Denny Bryce for their constant support. Huge hugs to my writing groups for giving me a community.

The biggest thank you in the world to my family, the Hompluems, the Dunns, and the Techavacharas. You support me at every turn, but more than that, you make me feel loved. In the end, that's what is most important. Special thanks to my dad, Naronk Hompluem. I've been told I have a pretty good imagination, but I couldn't conjure up a better father.

To Aksara, Atikan, and Adisai, the breath and joys of my life. I hope you will never feel as alone as the two girls in this book. Because you're not. You will always and forever have me.

To Antoine, I've felt like a girl in between most of my life, but you put me in the center of your world, and the center of your heart, every day. Every moment.

And finally, to my lovely readers. Thank you so much for picking up my books. It means the world to me. I hope you enjoy Kan's story!

GIRL ON THE VERGE

Pintip Dunn

About This Guide

The suggested questions are included to enhance
your group's reading of Pintip Dunn's
Girl on the Verge.

Discussion Questions

1. What is a "girl in between"? How does this phrase differ from "girl on the verge"? How does Kan's understanding of herself change as the story progresses? Have you ever felt like a "person in between" or a "person on the verge"?

2. Kan and Shelly have one thing in common: They both feel like they don't belong. How does each character react to this feeling? At the end of the book, Shelly asserts that the two girls are the same. Is she right? If not, in what ways do they differ?

3. Soon enough, Shelly emerges as the villain in this story. But is she sympathetic at the same time? Why? If so, how does the reader's sympathy for Shelly complicate her role as the villain?

4. When Kan puts on the gold necklace for the first time, she feels beautiful. Similarly, when Shelly wears the blouse Kan made for her, she also feels beautiful. What does beauty mean in these two instances—as opposed to cultural and media norms of beauty? Even if the feeling is sparked from an external object, is it intertwined with something internal within each character?

5. Kan is a Thai-American girl caught between cultural worlds. Whether or not you share her background, do any of her experiences resonate with you? Why and in what ways?

6. What is a microaggression? Can you identify any microaggressions in this story? Although they may be subtle, how are microaggressions harmful?

7. Near the beginning of the story, Kan says, "I love my *Khun Yai*. I always have. . . . And yet, the gulf between us feels as wide as the ocean between Thailand and the United States." Discuss Kan's relationship with her grand-

mother. How is it possible to feel so close and yet so distant from someone? Do you think Kan and Khun Yai manage to close this gulf between them by the end of the story? Why or why not?

8. People say that imitation is the sincerest form of flattery. Is this true? Why or why not? When does someone take imitation too far, and where do you draw the line?

9. Kan says that "the surest way to offend [Khun Yai] is to refuse to eat her food." Why is this the case? How are food and culture intertwined? In what ways does food represent culture?

10. There are many portrayals of friendship in this story, such as Kan and Shelly's early relationship, Kan's long-standing friendship with Ash, and Ethan's history with Walt and the other guys. What qualities do you value most in a friendship? Is there an attribute that makes someone a candidate to be a "BFF"?

11. Kan and Ethan are immediately drawn together without knowing too much about each other. However, it is difficult to make a relationship last on initial attraction alone. What are the qualities that make them work as a couple? How does this contrast with Shelly's notions of romance?

12. What are the relative merits of secrets versus transparency within a family? What might have been different if Kan's family had acknowledged their secrets earlier?

Don't miss Pintip Dunn's *The Darkest Lie*, available now!

In Pintip Dunn's gripping and timely novel, a young woman whose life unravels in the wake of her mother's alleged suicide sets out to clear her parent's name.

"The mother I knew would never do those things. But maybe I never knew her after all."

Clothes, jokes, coded messages . . . Cecilia Brooks and her mom shared everything. At least, CeCe thought they did. Six months ago, her mom killed herself after accusations of having sex with a student, and CeCe's been the subject of whispers and taunts ever since. Now, at the start of her high school senior year, between dealing with her grieving, distracted father and the social nightmare that has become her life, CeCe just wants to fly under the radar. Instead, she's volunteering at the school's crisis hotline—the same place her mother worked.

As she counsels troubled strangers, CeCe's lingering suspicions about her mom's death resurface. With the help of Sam, a new student and newspaper intern, she starts to piece together fragmented clues that point to a twisted secret at the heart of her community. Soon, finding the truth isn't just a matter of restoring her mother's reputation, it's about saving lives—including CeCe's own. . . .

Connect with Us

Visit us online at
KensingtonBooks.com
to read more from your favorite authors, see books
by series, view reading group guides, and more.

Join us on social media

for sneak peeks, chances to win books and prize packs,
and to share your thoughts with other readers.

facebook.com/kensingtonpublishing
twitter.com/kensingtonbooks

Tell us what you think!

To share your thoughts, submit a review,
or sign up for our eNewsletters, please visit:
KensingtonBooks.com/TellUs.